MW00636378

The Dark Eagle

BOOK 1
RUIN & RESTORATION SERIES

BY

AND

SIMON DRISCOLL

JAMES T. PROUT

GRENDELMEN PUBLISHING
MESA, ARIZONA, USA

The Dark Eagle
Book 1 Ruin & Restoration Series

First edition copyright
© 2018 Grendelmen Publishing

Imprint Publisher:
Grendelmen Publishing
Mesa, AZ
http://grendelmen.com

ISBN: 978-1-948451-42-0
Version 1.07

1. Fiction 2. Mainstream 3. Conspiracy 4. World Religions

Printed in the United States of America

ACKNOWLEDGMENT

SPECIAL THANKS TO THE FOLLOWING

First, thanks be to God for the inspiration received by the authors and others in writing this book.

Christie: Your love and support make all I do possible.

The Writers' Squad of Doom: Your critiques were insightful, helpful, and thorough.

Dear Reader,

This book is dedicated to bringing people to Christ and preparing them for His Second Coming. This is a work of fiction based on prophecy and recent history. It is intended to show one way in which End Times Prophecy may be fulfilled in the near future.

As always, let the Spirit guide you in your quest for truth.
– Simon Driscoll

A Note about Endnotes:

The Endnotes found throughout this series are provided to give the interested reader a resource for learning more about the prophecies used to construct the main plot. There are many more references which I haven't included in the book. I would enjoy discussing any and all prophecies with those who want a better understanding of what is to come.

The authors can be reached in the following ways:

Simon Driscoll
Facebook: Author Simon Driscoll
email: simon@grendelmen.com
website: http://ruinandrestoration.com
Twitter: @AuthorSDriscoll

James T. Prout
Website: www.LastDaysTimeline.com
Email: author@lastdaystimeline.com

Table of Contents

The Recent Past
The Muslim Messiah

August 20th, 2017 - Damascus, Syria

Mohammad Arsalan Malik nudged the rocket launcher into place while his men checked the dials. Sweat trickled down his face as he aligned the feet of the launcher with three marked points in the middle of an empty cotton field. Every second wasted decreased the chances of success and they all needed this attack to go well. He was running out of time.

The summer heat beat down on them, making Arsalan wish they'd stuck to their original timetable of early morning. Why the market would be more crowded in the heat of the day, he couldn't understand.

Karim started to load the mortar round.

"N-no!" Arsalan shouted, the stress making his stutter worse. "Check the l-level first!"

"Sorry, Mahdi," Karim said as he pulled the ammunition back out.

Arsalan was known to his followers as Mohammad Al-Mahdi, though some were starting to doubt. While he was tall enough, fair complexioned, was the son of Abdullah and Aamina, and even stuttered, his fortieth birthday had already come and gone without an official pronouncement.[1] One of the many prophecies said the 12th Imam would be forty years old when he revealed himself to the world. If he turned forty-one before that happened, it was too late. There were too many signs[2] which hadn't been fulfilled and even Arsalan was doubting whether he could accomplish all that was required of him before his next birthday.

They got the launcher leveled and dialed in. If their practice sessions and measurements were accurate, this would land right on the doorstep of the fairgrounds. Today the government was reopening the fair as a sign that the fighting had died down. His forces may be diminished, but they weren't entirely defeated.[3]

"We are ready, Mahdi," Karim said.

Arsalan quickly checked the settings and said, "Do it," as he backed away.

Karim dropped the mortar shell into the tube and Hamoud pressed the launch button. The rocket-propelled grenade soared into the air, leaving behind an acrid smell.

Ten seconds later Arsalan's radio buzzed. "Get out of there! The military is on their way!" the spotter shouted.

No one needed to be told twice. They threw the rocket launcher into the back of the van and piled in. The driver gunned it and they were on the road in less than a minute.

"Mission accomplished," the spotter said. "Direct hit." The only round they'd been able to fire had hit the market in the fairgrounds.

It was a tight squeeze, but the driver managed to get to regularly trafficked roads before the troops arrived. Three minutes after that, they were on the 110, heading south. It wasn't much, but it just might be enough for the Shadow Council to let him live.

The Great American Eclipse

August 21st, 2017 - Sublimity, Oregon

"Rise and shine, sleepy-head," Tonya said. "We've got to get to the meadow early to pick out our spot." Her blonde hair tickled Scott's face as she leaned over and kissed him.

"Alright, I'm up," Scott said as he rolled out of bed. He stretched and tried in vain to reach the ceiling. For the first time in more than a week, he'd gotten to sleep before midnight and he almost felt fully rested. Despite being deep in the forests of Oregon, they had nearly all the comforts of home, including hot showers.

Scott and Tonya Knox were on the ninth day of their honeymoon, and the sixth day at Silver Falls Lodge. He had booked the cabin when he was eighteen and learned that The Great American Eclipse[4] would pass right over the cabins where his parents frequently went on vacation. It had been a bit of a rush getting the wedding planned in time, but when his parents learned he was taking her to the lodge for a week, they insisted it wouldn't be a problem.

He knew he'd married the right woman not only because they were the same height, but by her enthusiasm for seeing both of the twice-in-a-lifetime events. They were already planning a trip to Missouri in 2024 [5] to see the next total solar eclipse on American soil.

As they entered the dining hall half an hour later, Scott almost moaned at how crowded it already was. Most of their week here had been fairly quiet, at least in terms of seeing other people. But today there were people everywhere. Well, that was to be expected for such a spectacular event. It took twice as long as usual to get their food, and there was no way they were going to have a table to themselves this morning.

"Scott! Over here!" Kevin called. He was Scott's best friend all through high school, and easy to spot, still having the build of a linebacker.

"What is *he* doing here?" Tonya asked as she came up beside him.

"Well, right now he's got two seats for us."

Tonya scowled at him.

"Hey, at least we get to sit next to each other," Scott shrugged as he headed for Kevin's table.

"I knew I'd find you two this morning," Kevin said as the couple sat down. "I'll bet you didn't even know I've been here all weekend."

Tonya gaped as she scowled at Scott. "All weekend?"

Scott shrugged. "We originally planned this together, along with Mark and Patrick. They were all bummed when I hijacked the entire cabin for just the two of us."

"Hey," Kevin broke in, "I stayed out of your way, didn't I? You didn't even know we were here."

"We?" Tonya repeated.

As if in reply, Mark and Patrick sat down across from her.

"Morning, lovebirds," Mark said. He was the shortest one at the table by a couple of inches.

"I told you we couldn't avoid them today," Patrick said. His red hair always made him stand out. "Everyone's going to be in the same place at the same time this morning."

"Did you know about this?" Tonya asked Scott.

Scott nodded. "Of course."

"And when were you going to tell me?"

Scott just shrugged and said, "Surprise!"

"You know I hate surprises," Tonya said.

"Like I said," Kevin interjected, "we've stayed out of your way so far, and after the eclipse, we'll disappear again."

"Just like the sun," Patrick said with a grin. No one laughed.

"You don't have to sit with us in the meadow if you don't want to," Kevin offered.

Tonya sighed. "I guess it's okay. I just thought I'd have my husband to myself on my honeymoon."

"Tonya, honey," Scott pleaded, "we knew we were going to be surrounded by people this morning. I'm sorry I didn't tell you three of those people would be my best friends. We've barely seen each other since high school. All three of these knuckleheads are in college."

"So how come you didn't go with them?" Tonya's eyebrows were raised the way they always were when she asked a question he'd already answered a dozen times.

"He's still working on that charity app, right Scott?" Kevin said with a smirk. "You know, the one that will change the world."

Scott scowled. "Do you have to bring that up now?"

"Ouch!" Patrick said. "Sounds like the honeymoon is over."

Scott set down his fork, leaned over and Tonya obliged him with a passionate kiss. "Definitely not over," Scott said.

Tonya smiled back at him. "Don't you ever let it end." She paused before adding, "And no more surprises, okay?"

An hour later, Scott was sitting in a lounge chair with Tonya at his side staring at the sun through their special flimsy glasses. The moon started to move into place. There were almost a hundred people around them doing exactly the same thing.

"Looks like the show has started!" Patrick shouted.

Whoops and hollers came from the crowd. He'd heard weaker cheers on opening day of *Rouge One*.

Kevin leaned over to Scott and asked, "You're not superstitious, are you?"

"No, of course not. Why?"

"Well, they say that an eclipse is a bad omen," Kevin explained. "That it marks the beginning of difficult times for the lands touched by it."

"I don't believe any of that stuff," Scott said.

"Neither do I," Tonya added.

"Good," Kevin said as he sat back. "I'd hate to see your marriage ruined by superstition."

Tonya gasped. "What an awful thing to say! We just got married, and already you're talking about our marriage being ruined?"

"Well, no," Kevin said. "Not if you don't believe in that stuff."

"Well, I don't!" Tonya said.

"Good," Kevin shot back.

Gideon is Waiting for Something Bigger

August 21st, 2017 - Marion, Illinois

Gideon Shumway studied the star chart on his laptop in awe after reading the latest blog post about the upcoming alignment of the planets. He had skipped the first day of classes at Notre Dame and gone on a mini-vacation, staying in a tiny hotel room so he would be close enough to witness a total solar eclipse. Yet it was a blog post which now had him in total awe.

"Come on, Gid!" Duane said. "I want to get out of the city before the eclipse starts!"

Gideon was a foot taller with red hair and freckles, almost the opposite of Duane's black hair and brown eyes. They had only one class together the previous year; Introduction to Comparative Religion. Yet they had become great friends.

"I'm coming," Gideon replied. He pulled on his shoes, picked up his laptop, and followed Duane out of their hotel room. "Don't forget those silly glasses you bought."

"They're not silly!" Duane protested. He dug the glasses out of his backpack. They looked like cheap 3D glasses from ten years ago with stars and stripes on the side behind the words *American Eclipse* August 21, 2017. "These things allow us to look directly at the eclipse without burning out our eyes."

"Okay, 'Mom'," Gideon chuckled as he climbed into the passenger seat.

Duane got behind the wheel and put the glasses on the dash. "Hey, I'm not kidding. You're a football player. If you damage your eyes you could lose your scholarship."

Gideon rolled his eyes, even though he knew Duane was right. Staring at the sun, even with most of it covered by the moon, would damage his precious eyesight. How could he throw the ball down the field with pinpoint accuracy without his perfect eyesight?

"By the way, what were you reading about?" Duane asked as they pulled onto Highway 13 and headed east.

"It was a blog post about the alignment of planets and stars next month."

"Oh, yeah? 'Cause right now we're about to witness the most spectacular alignment of this planet with the moon and our favorite star. Yet you seem more engrossed by whatever you were reading."

Gideon chuckled. "That's because next month the stars could be fulfilling a prophecy straight out of the Bible."

"You don't think 'The Great American Eclipse' qualifies as that?" [6] Duane asked as he passed another car.

Despite the many signs telling them not to, some people were already pulling off to the side of the highway and setting up their observational equipment.

"Eclipses happen all the time," Gideon replied. "There's going to be another one in America in less than seven years. It's even going to hit this same town. How could we possibly identify this particular eclipse as the fulfillment of prophecy when there's nothing extraordinary about it?"

"You mean besides being the first total eclipse in centuries to only cast its shadow on American soil?"

Gideon shook his head. "That's not enough to fulfill biblical prophecy."

"But this alignment of stars next month is?"

"Revelation 12 says,"

> "1 And there appeared a great wonder in heaven; a woman clothed with the sun, and the moon under her feet, and upon her head a crown of twelve stars:
> "2 And she being with child cried, travailing in birth, and pained to be delivered." [7]

"How does a group of stars give birth?" Duane asked as he pulled off the highway onto a rural road.

"Well, according to this blog, Jupiter has been inside the 'womb' of the constellation Virgo since December of last year. It won't exit that area until September 23rd, 2017."

"That doesn't sound too unusual," Duane said. "Jupiter goes into retrograde motion about every thirteen months. I'm sure it's been in that region of the sky for nine months before."

"And how, exactly, do you know that?"

"My dad. He took me camping almost every month to show me the stars through his telescope. He taught me all about planetary motions."

"Then I guess you would know," Gideon conceded, "but according to this blog, it's never happened with the moon at the feet of Virgo and the Sun on her shoulder with three of the planets in the constellation of Leo."

"What does Leo have to do with it?"

"It's right over her head, acting as a sort of crown."

"But only three planets will be there. I thought you said there were supposed to be twelve stars in her crown."

"That's right," Gideon said. "Add the three planets to the nine stars of Leo and you get a full dozen."

Duane chuckled as they pulled onto a dirt road. "You're more excited about a sign in the future you won't even see with your eyes than you are for the eclipse which is about to blot out the sun."

"I came because you invited me," Gideon said.

"Thanks, man," Duane said. "Who would have thought a Mormon and a Muslim would become friends while studying comparative religion at a Catholic University?"

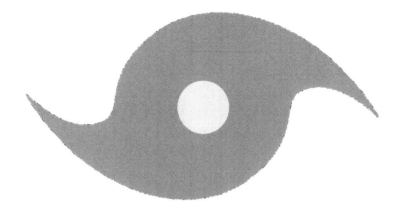

Moroni's Helping Hands

September 1st, 2017 - Houston, Texas

Moroni Whitefeather heaved the remains of the last sofa on one shoulder and headed out of another Houston home flooded by Hurricane Harvey. With the black mold growing on it, this couch, like so much else in this city, had become hazardous waste.

"Slow down, big fella," Thomas Pahona said. "Leave some work for the rest of us." They'd grown up together on the Hopi Reservation in Arizona, and he was the one who'd asked Moroni to join him on this service project.

Moroni laughed but didn't slow. He'd already taken the other three sofas out of this house by himself, and it wasn't the first house they'd emptied that day. Nor was it their first day here. He was covered in sweat from the combination of heat and physical exertion, but he didn't care. The rank smell of the area had nothing to do with body odor.

Once all the furniture was gone, he went back inside and helped tear out the lower row of drywall. This was the most costly hurricane the world had ever endured, and the costs were still adding up as the black mold spread over and through everything.

He was on vacation, volunteering his time to help during this crisis. Yet as a headhunter for Sanctuary Foods, the fastest growing all-natural food company in the world, he couldn't help but notice the kind of people he was looking for everywhere he went. He'd already found two couples who seemed perfect for leadership training and he couldn't resist offering jobs to them.

It was always sad to see people lose all their worldly possessions, and there were plenty of people here who had lost everything. He hadn't yet spotted the owners of the house he was helping to clear at the moment. They were usually easy to spot as they cried over the water damage to their family heirlooms. Even he sometimes cried at seeing pieces of history being tossed into the trash. Occasionally he spotted people digging through the hazardous waste looking for treasures they thought they could restore. Just the thought of all the irreplaceable history being ruined brought a tear to his eye.

This particular home looked like it belonged to a younger couple, which usually didn't have many heirlooms. He still expected to see someone crying over their photo albums, sofa or television.

"Excuse me."

Moroni turned to see a man in a dark blue polo with the FEMA logo on it holding a clipboard. "Can I help you?"

"Are you the homeowner?"

"No. I'm just a volunteer."

"I'm the homeowner," a woman in her early twenties said.

Moroni was surprised to hear her speak up as she'd been working alongside him during the last four homes they'd cleared.

She acted more like an out-of-state volunteer than a neighbor. Although, now that he thought about it, she did seem to know several people here.

"Your name?" the FEMA worker asked.

"Patricia Redd."

The man wrote on his clipboard. "How do you spell Red?"

"R-E-D-D."

"And who else lived here with you?"

"Just my husband."

"And, where is he?"

"Staying with his parents in Utah," Patricia said. A tear formed on her cheek, the first sign of sadness she'd shown that day. "His flight home from his business trip was canceled."

Moroni pondered this amazing woman as she gave her information to the FEMA worker. Here she was, throwing away nearly all her worldly goods, and the only thing that fazed her was thinking about being separated from her husband.

The FEMA representative handed her a yellow piece of paper with instructions for filing a claim before moving on to the next house. Moroni knew those claims would only pay enough to fix most of the damage to the home, with little, if any, left over to replace everything else.

Moroni couldn't keep his mind off her for the next several hours as they finished clearing her home of damaged items and moved on to the next house. When they took a break for dinner he finally approached her.

"I must say, I'm quite impressed," Moroni said.

"With me?" Patricia asked.

Moroni nodded.

"I can't imagine why. You're the one who picks up couches by yourself."

He chuckled. "I've always been strong, physically. But I was impressed by your spiritual strength."

"How so?"

"Most of these homeowners are devastated to lose all their worldly goods. Even I have a tough time throwing away a treasure from the Civil War or the Civil Rights Movement. Yet, you helped us clear several of your neighbors' houses before you even entered your own home."

She shook her head. "It's not my home anymore. My husband's job washed away with the flood from Hurricane Harvey. There's no way we'll be able to make the payments *and* make repairs. It was a house we lived in. We'll eventually find another."

Moroni smiled. "See? That's what I'm talking about. That kind of eternal perspective is quite impressive. I'm a representative of Sanctuary Foods, and I'd like to invite you and your husband to consider applying for our leadership training program." He held out his business card.

She looked down at the card for a moment before hesitantly taking it. "You're a Native American right?"

Moroni nodded.

"Navajo?"

"Hopi," he corrected.

"And you're working for a food company that sends you here to recruit people in a disaster zone?"

Moroni shook his head. "No. I'm on vacation and volunteering my time here. But when I see someone who feels right for our program, I can't keep my mouth shut."

"What kind of program?"

"We're expanding our leadership training, and I think you'd be a good fit. I'm hoping your husband will be as well, if he's anything like you."

15

She studied the card, then looked up at him. "How do I know this isn't a scam?"

"Does it feel like a scam?" he asked.

"No . . ."

"Well, you don't have to decide right now. Think about it, talk to your husband, and if it feels right, give me a call."

She pocketed the card while she studied his face. "I've never met a man named Moroni before."

He smiled. "It takes all kinds."

Scott Takes a Spin in Mexico City

September 19, 2017 - Mexico City, Mexico

Scott Knox kissed his wife goodbye outside the movie theater.

"Are you sure you won't join us?" Tonya pled one last time.

Scott nodded. "The movie is in Spanish, and I only know enough to read the title."

"The captions will be in English," Tonya explained. "No one else is objecting."

There were three other couples joining Tonya, all of them here on a week-long vacation to Mexico City, provided by Juuva. These were the second quarter's newly crowned double diamond earners and their spouses. Tonya was by far the youngest among them.

"Even if it was in English," Scott replied, "I don't think I'd be interested in a movie titled "*Mi Nueva Yo*. It sounds like a coming of age story." He'd spent almost every moment of the last week with her, and he needed a break.

Tonya laughed. "Most coming-of-age movies don't have a forty-year-old single mom as the main character."

Scott frowned. "Sounds like that new Romcom you wanted me to see. What was it called again?"

"*Home again*," Tonya said, nodding. "And, yes, it's the same movie. They just gave it a different title here. So instead of sitting in the theater, holding my hand, you're going to what, wander around the city?"

Scott nodded. "Don't worry. Wherever I go, you can find me with the locator app I created and installed on your phone. It's accurate within three feet."

Tonya scowled at him. "I told you not to install any of your apps on my phone without asking. The last one corrupted the system and I had to get a new phone."

Scott raised his arms in exasperation. "That wasn't my fault! It was that fake anti-virus program you installed. All the apps I design are clean and tested for compatibility."

She smirked and shook her head. "Okay, whatever you say. I gotta go before the movie starts."

They kissed one last time before she ran to catch up with the others.

Scott turned around and took a deep breath. The combined scents of bread, cheese, and tomato grabbed him and he followed his nose. Crossing the street, he found a Peter Piper Pizza. He ordered a personal pan size and looked around at the games while he waited. They were all kids' games designed to keep little children busy while the parents enjoyed a semi-delicious meal. He needed something more challenging to keep his interest. Something with a real element of risk.

As it was the first pizza Scott had eaten in a week, it tasted better than he expected, but that wasn't saying much. All too soon the meal was over, and he wandered back outside, looking for more distraction.

With his hunger partially satisfied, the noise of the casino next door drew him in. He looked for the buffet but found instead a short-order cook. He ordered a cheeseburger and fries, watching the news while he waited.

The reporter talked about the moment of silence observed that morning to remember the 5000 people who'd lost their lives in 1985 because of an 8.0 magnitude earthquake.[8] They also mentioned another, larger earthquake which hit only eleven days earlier in Southern Mexico.

He wandered around for more than an hour, eating his second meal and looking at all the games. He debated back and forth in his head whether to play or not. These were certainly more challenging than the games next door, and the rewards were much greater.

He'd never gambled in his life, as his parents had strictly forbidden it. But he wasn't a child anymore, and he could make his own decisions. They were in Mexico to celebrate Tonya's success. Certainly they could afford to gamble away a thousand pesos. That was only fifty dollars, after all.

He found his way to an electronic roulette table, watching for several minutes as others gambled. There was an actual wheel in the middle with nine electronic displays around it where the players placed their bets. The wheel spun one direction, while the ball circled in the other. There was also a small light show which highlighted the slots corresponding with the bets.

He'd always wondered what the thrill of gambling felt like. Why shouldn't he waste a little money to get a cheap thrill? He checked his phone and saw it was 12:47 p.m. He had to decide quickly and get back, before the movie ended.

Scott sat down at one of the electronic displays and put a thousand peso note into the slot. He bet it all on 12 Red, as he was born on January 12th.

A soft female voice counted down in Spanish. "Cinco, cuatro, tres, dos, uno. No más apuestas." A box popped up on the display reading, *"No more bets."*

The wheel lit up with a simulated lightning storm, striking the numbers 12, 17, 22, and 36. which remained highlighted.

The machine said in a more excited voice, "Lanzar el balón!" The display read, *"Launch the ball!"*

He swiped to the left to launch the ball.

The wheel spun counterclockwise and he felt his pulse quicken as a little ball spun clockwise, letting fate decide where it would land.

"Doce," the machine said.

Scott looked down at his display. He'd won! The credit line now read $36,000, sending his heart pounding. The rush of endorphins was intoxicating. No wonder people enjoyed gambling!

But now he had a problem. How would he explain the extra money? Tonya wouldn't be happy to hear he was gambling, even if he'd won thirty-five thousand pesos, whatever that was in American money.

"I just have to bet it again," he told himself. So once more he bet the whole amount, but this time on Black 17, as Tonya was born on November 17th.

The machine once more did its countdown in Spanish, lit up the 17, 21, 28, and 35. Then it begged Scott to launch the ball.

He hesitated. A fifty-dollar loss was easy to swallow, but he now had thirty-five times that much on the line. He tried doing the math in his head, but his mind wouldn't function. He looked for the button to cancel his bet, but it wasn't lit. His winnings were already committed to the next spin.

As he launched the ball a familiar voice said, "What do you think you're doing!"

Scott shot up from his chair and turned around. Tonya stood there with a confused look on her face. "Hi, honey! Is the movie over already?"

"It let out ten minutes ago," Tonya said.

"Diecisiete," the machine said behind him.

Scott turned around to look at the display. It said he now had a credit of $1,296,000 pesos. His mouth went dry. He'd just won over a million pesos! He quickly pressed the "COLLECT" button.

The display changed to, *"Please wait for attendant."*

He turned back to Tonya and tried to swallow. "I just won a million pesos."

"You what?"

"I won!" The thrill in his heart was barely diminished by the sour look on Tonya's face.

"You are the one placing bets here?" a big man in a gold vest and bowtie asked. Scott had never seen a Mexican that tall or broad. He was bigger than Kevin, who'd played linebacker in high school.

"Yes," Scott replied.

"Follow me."

Scott and Tonya followed him into a hallway marked *"Casino Employees Only."* It wasn't long before they were sitting in the office of the casino manager, though there was no one else there.

"Has he done something wrong?" Tonya asked the big man.

"You wait," was all he said.

Scott swallowed hard, trying to think whether he'd done anything wrong or illegal. He certainly hadn't intended to.

"What did you do?" Tonya asked.

Scott opened his mouth to protest his innocence, but the muscle said, "You wait silently."

Scott clamped his mouth shut, while his mind raced for what to say to her. Would she believe this was the only time he'd ever gambled in his life? He doubted it.

A woman walked in wearing a dress suit and sat down behind the desk. "You can go, Roberto."

The muscle left the room, closing the door behind him.

"My name is Veronica, and I'm the manager of the casino. Sorry for the delay, but I had to check the tapes before we talked. Congratulations! You've won a million pesos!"

"You mean he wasn't cheating?" Tonya asked.

"Not that I could see," Veronica said. "Why? Has he cheated other casinos before?"

Tonya shook her head. "I've never seen him enter a casino before."

"I've never gambled before," Scott said quickly.

Veronica turned to stare at him. "Never?"

Scott shook his head.

"Not once?" Tonya asked. Her face showed she didn't believe him.

"No," Scott protested.

"You're telling me that the first ever bet you placed was that roulette wheel?" Veronica asked.

Scott nodded.

Veronica smiled. "That makes you the luckiest man I've ever met. Now, let's get some information from you so we can send you your winnings."

"You mean I don't get it in cash?"

Veronica laughed. "Do you really want to walk around with a million pesos on you?"

"Yes." Scott said.

Veronica frowned. "As you wish. I'll have it brought in. Do you have a way to carry it inconspicuously?"

"Not with me," Scott said. "Do you have something for situations like this?"

"We do have a metal briefcase you can purchase for $2500 pesos."

"Yes! That's perfect!" Scott's broad smile was diminished only slightly by Tonya's scowl. He knew she was upset with his gambling but figured he could find a way to appease her with his winnings.

"Of course," Veronica said. "I'll be right back."

As she left, Scott turned to Tonya and said, "Isn't this exciting?"

Tonya just scowled deeper and said, "I don't want to talk about it."

Scott tried to wipe the smile off his face to appease her, but he couldn't. Ever since high school he'd felt like a loser. None of his apps were taking off the way he'd planned. His wife made all the money in the relationship. This was the first serious money he'd brought into the relationship, and he intended to relish every moment of it.

Veronica returned with a metal briefcase, just like he always saw in the movies.

But when she opened the case, Scott was confused. "Are you sure you counted it right?" Scott asked. "I expected a million pesos to fill the case."

Veronica gave a brief smile. "If I used $100-peso bills, it would fill the case. But these are $1000-peso bills. Do you want me to take it back and get $100-peso bills?"

Scott chuckled a bit, about to say yes, but one look at Tonya told him she didn't want to spend one more minute in this casino than she had to. "No, this is fine."

Scott closed the case and headed out the door with Tonya right behind him. She didn't say a word as they walked out of the casino. His knees buckled with excitement at the thought of carrying around a million pesos.

Somehow his excitement engulfed the world around him as everything shook.[9]

Tonya grabbed his shoulder and shouted, "Earthquake!"

The ground shook hard and continued to shake, longer than Scott had ever experienced. It felt like hours, though it was less than thirty seconds. Noises increased around them as apartment buildings fell over, or had the front sheared off by the shaking. Power poles and street signs fell as well. The theater was hit by a falling power pole, setting it on fire.

As soon as the ground stopped shaking, Tonya grabbed Scott's hand and pulled him away from the casino entrance. He was confused by this for only a few seconds as a mob of people ran outside, some of them screaming.

"Was that an 8.0?" Scott asked, thinking back to the news report of the 1985 quake.

Tonya shook her head. "I doubt it. It felt stronger than the Eureka quake of 2010, and that was a 6.5. This one might be a 7, or 7.5, but probably not an 8."

Big Government Finds Scott & Tonya

September 20th, 2017 - San Francisco, California

Scott and Tonya Knox flew home after their Mexican vacation with a level of tension between them that deserved its own seat on the flight. Scott was carrying his million pesos in a steel briefcase. Part of him regretted not having them change the $1000-peso bills for $100-peso bills so it would fill the briefcase, but at least this way there was room for the other souvenirs they'd purchased on their trip.

Five minutes after the plane took off, Tonya asked, "What are you going to do with all that money?"

Scott smiled at the question. He'd spent all the previous night and that morning pondering the best way to turn his winnings into some sort of income. "I'm not sure yet. All I know is that I want to invest it. Find some way of making money on my own."

Tonya scowled at this response and went silent again.

Scott spent the rest of the flight trying to decide why that was the wrong thing to say.

As they passed through customs, the officer opened Scott's briefcase and examined the contents. "I see you got your standard collection of knick-knacks and knock-offs," the officer said. "What isn't standard is all this money. Where did it come from?"

"I won it," Scott said.

The officer raised one eyebrow. "Where exactly did you win this money?"

"At a casino in Mexico City."

"Okay," the officer replied. "You're going to have to fill out form W-2G, and I'm going to need to see two forms of ID."

"Why?" Scott asked.

"Because you have to report your winnings to the IRS."

"But I won it in Mexico. Why does the IRS care about that?"

The officer sighed. "Look, if you have issues with the IRS, take it up with them. I'm required to collect thirty percent of your winnings for taxes and . . ."

"Thirty percent!" Scott shouted back. "That's outrageous!"

"No, Mr. Knox. It's the law."

Scott grumbled as he filled out the form and watched the customs officer confiscate $388,000 pesos of his winnings for the IRS.

Tonya insisted they go straight to the bank, and when the teller counted what was left, he barely had nine hundred thousand pesos. Still, that came out to more than fifty thousand dollars, which wasn't a bad haul from his initial fifty-dollar bet.

As they drove back to their apartment, Tonya asked, "What are we going to do with all that money?"

"I'm not sure," Scott said, not for the first time. "I've never had this much money in my life." He was still getting over the shock of having thirty percent of the money confiscated. It no longer felt like enough to launch any kind of successful business, or enough leverage to buy out someone else's. He would have to think of something less grand, and perhaps something to appease Tonya.

"Maybe we should invest it in the stock market. It's been doing really well lately."

"I'll think about it," was all Scott could manage to say. He was still upset at President Towers for taking thirty percent of his winnings, wishing now that he'd bought cryptocurrency to hide it from the government. Nothing he could do about that now, but he didn't think he could handle watching what was left of his winnings go down in value if he picked the wrong stock. Plus, he knew the IRS would take another chunk of whatever increase he was able to achieve.

The rest of the drive was in silence, which had become the norm since they left the casino the day before. As Scott carried their suitcases up the stairs to their third-story apartment, a new idea came to mind. He hauled the suitcases into their studio apartment and flopped down on the couch, panting from the effort.

He flicked on the TV for distraction while he caught his breath. When he could finally breathe normally, he said, "Why don't we use it for a down payment on a house?"

Tonya turned to him. "Really? Are you sure?"

Scott nodded. "You make plenty of money now. We should be able to get something nice. Fifty thousand must be enough for a down payment. Even in California."

Tonya climbed onto his lap, facing him and gave him a long kiss. "I thought you were going to buy some ridiculously expensive truck or a boat or something. But buying us a home . . . That almost makes up for placing the bet in the first place."

"What else would it take?" Scott asked.

"I can think of a few things." Tonya laughed and kissed him again. They kissed for a long time as all the tension between them finally melted away.

An hour later they were watching the news together, discussing each story that came up. A report came on about the ten wildfires currently raging across Northern California, and the two-dozen others that had already been contained in the last three months alone.

"Maybe we should move to Southern California," Scott suggested.

"You may have a point," Tonya conceded.

The Revelation 12 Sign

September 23rd, 2017 - Mt. Hamilton, California

Scott and Tonya Knox spent the night at the Lick Observatory, as part of an exclusive private tour, provided by Tonya's college roommate, who now ran one of the telescopes perched along the ridge of the mountain.

They'd finished submitting all their paperwork on Thursday to get preapproved for a mortgage. At the same time, they found a real estate agent in Oxnard who was searching for just the right home.

It felt strange to take a long weekend the same week as returning from their vacation in Mexico. But this had been planned for months, and the planetary alignment couldn't be postponed.

Besides, Tonya was making well over ten thousand per month at Juuva, and she never worked on Fridays. Scott also worked from home, developing apps for the Android market. Between her income and the nature of their careers, he was starting to realize they would be taking a lot of long weekend adventures.

Scott was glad they'd arrived in the afternoon when there was plenty of light as the winding roads leading to the observatory would be downright frightening in the dark.

They watched Jupiter descend below the horizon the night before, and now the three of them were up at 4 a.m. on Saturday, watching Venus rise while sipping hot cocoa.

The view was stunning, both in the skies above and in the valleys below. It was easy to see why Brenda had chosen the isolation of a telescope operator after her husband left her for another woman after less than a year of marriage.

"Do you think this is the sign of the end of the world?" Scott asked. "Or perhaps the rapture?"

Tonya had told him all about Brenda's obsession with the end of time during their college years. Tonya and Brenda were roommates in the dorms because they'd both skipped two grades.

Brenda shook her head. "I gave up on predicting the end of the world a long time ago. These days I think in terms of billions of years, not one or two decades." She had brown hair and was several inches shorter than Tonya. They both majored in Astronomy, and Brenda had told them last night she had just started her graduate studies.

"Besides," Tonya chimed in, "even Revelation 12 doesn't say this is the end of the world." [7]

Scott tried to sip his cocoa, but it was still too hot. "Well, that's what they're saying on the news. People are claiming this is the sign of the end of the world."

Brenda laughed. "How many times do we have to hear that prediction before people give up on it? The world was supposed to end in 2012 when the Mayan calendar ended. [10] Grigori Rasputin said the Earth was going to burn in 2013. [11] Then there were the

30

blood moon tetrads.[12] What was it that was supposed to destroy the Earth today?"

"Planet X?" Scott said, more as a question.

"That's right!" Brenda blurted out. "The mysterious Nibiru is supposed to suddenly appear and trigger the end of the world." [13] She laughed again.

Scott sipped his cocoa as he waited for her laughter to abate.

Tonya jumped in first. "Well, the Bible says this is the sign of the birth of the Kingdom of God on the Earth."

"Really?" Brenda said. "So where is it?"

"How many people knew about the birth of Jesus Christ?" Tonya asked. "How many people saw the sign of his birth?"

"Well, there were the three wise men, of course," Scott said.

"And the shepherds," Brenda added.

"And the Native Americans," Tonya said.

"The what now?" Brenda asked.

"The Book of Mormon talks about the people on this continent seeing the star, and knowing that it signaled the birth of Jesus Christ," [14] Tonya said.

"Really? I've never heard that," Brenda said. "I guess they would have seen that conjunction, the same as the people in Jerusalem."

"What conjunction?" Scott asked.

Brenda smiled and set down her cocoa. "Well, many astronomers believe the sign of the birth was the conjunction of the planets Jupiter and Venus near the star, Regulus." [15]

"That star right there?" Scott asked. "Right above Venus?"

Brenda nodded. "I didn't think you were paying attention."

"Oh, I listen," Scott said. "I always listen."

"Anyway, those two planets lining up would have been bright enough to see in the daytime and cast a shadow that you could see at night."

"I've always wondered what the sign of the birth was," Tonya said. "That whole notion of a supernova never made sense to me. How could the death of a star signify the birth of the King of Kings?"

Brenda shook her head. "Nope. It was probably the planetary alignment of Jupiter and Venus. There is beauty in the symbolism. Jupiter was the father of the gods, and Venus is the only female planet. They met together in the constellation of Leo, which symbolizes both royalty and the Tribe of Judah."

"Well, we might be watching the sign of another birth, right now," Scott said. "And it just happens to involve Jupiter, Venus, and Regulus."

"Not to mention the other stars in the constellation of Leo," Brenda added, "the planets Mercury and Mars, as well as the Moon, the Sun, and the constellation of Virgo."

"So, do you think it will be another thirty years before we see this mysterious Kingdom of God?" Tonya asked.

"Why thirty years?" Scott asked.

"Well, that's how long it was between Jesus' birth and the start of his public ministry." [16]

"Perhaps," Brenda said. "Perhaps." They all drank deeply of their now perfect temperature hot cocoa and watched Mars rise.

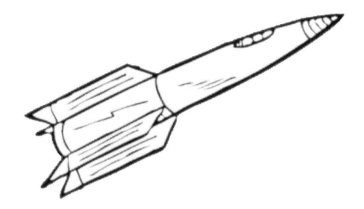

The City of Leon Cologne

September 23rd, 2017 - Hawthorne, California

"Sir, we've found the perfect site for the new city," Frank Brazzo said as he came into Leon's spacious office. His enthusiasm was obvious.

"Lay it out for me," Leon Cologne said calmly. Excitement was a fine thing, but multi-billion-dollar investment plans required cool heads. He pressed a few buttons and the stars which almost always adorned the walls and ceiling of his office disappeared as the lights came on.

Leon was one of the richest men in the world, and one of the few people who could build an entire city incorporating all the latest technology. He was also frequently featured as California's most eligible bachelor, despite being thirty-two years old and having two children from a failed marriage.

"The land is a blank slate of twenty-five thousand acres between Phoenix, Arizona, and Las Vegas," Frank explained. "And when they finish the freeway between them, it will go right through this land."

"There are no structures of any kind?" Leon asked, his excitement rising.

"None."

Leon pondered this a moment. It sounded perfect. Undeveloped land along a future highway, making it a relatively short drive to two major metro areas. "How much do they want for it?"

"The land is worth $150 million, but we can get a controlling interest for about half that."

"They're willing to stay invested in the project?" Leon had planned to buy the land outright, but if he only had to invest half the money upfront and could still keep most of the profits, it was almost too good to be true.

"Yes. They are projecting around eighty thousand homes will go in, and they expect to make even more profit as the homes are individually sold."

"What's the name of this place?" Leon asked, finally letting his excitement show.

"Belmont." [17]

"Let's do it. I want you to handle this project personally."

Frank nodded before turning to go.

Leon lowered the lights again and stared at the stars for a few minutes. Belmont would serve its purpose as a testing ground for a large city, like the one they would eventually establish on Mars, but it wasn't the only testing ground he was currently running. He also had to focus on being self-reliant, especially for the first twenty years or so.

He turned back to his computer screen with the latest specification for the Big Falcon Rocket he was helping to design. He made a quick note to fire his personal assistant, his third that year. This was the fourth interruption in the last hour, despite marking this time as Do Not Disturb. He would have to find someone more qualified.

David's Sanctuary City

September 23rd, 2017 - Near Panguitch, Utah

David Andrews stopped his car as he crested the hill, giving him a perfect view of the green valley below. There was a farmhouse and a barn, and miles of land in every direction. He'd spent the last ten years preparing for this day, and it was finally here. Today was the start of something big.

"What is it?" his wife Abigail asked as she climbed out of the passenger seat. Her black hair framed her toned face beautifully, contrasting with David's red hair and ruddy complexion.

"I just wanted to take it all in."

"It's just another farm. We've done this half a dozen times."

"No," David corrected. "This isn't just another farm, this is where I'm going to build my prototype Sanctuary City." [18]

"This old song again?" Abigail said. "You're never going to get the funding to build housing for seventy-five thousand people out in the middle of nowhere."

"I'm the owner of Sanctuary Foods. I'm going to use corporate profits to build the city here."

"What will you tell the board?"

"As far as the rest of the company is concerned, this farm won't be much different than the others. It will produce delicious all-natural foods which we will ship around the world to give people proper nutrition."

Abigail huffed. "What about the millions of extra dollars in construction that will happen here?"

"That goes under company research."

"Research? You're going to spend the last five years' worth of profits on research? The stock will plummet!"

David laughed. "Honey, you know we're not publicly owned. That means we don't trade in stock. Besides, I'm getting a boost from a friend of mine to test out their theories."

"Theories? What kind of theories?"

"My city will incorporate some future tech in everything from solar power generation to aeroponic food production. They are paying me to build the prototypes of their designs. No one's ever tried it on such a massive scale before, so the research alone is invaluable. The entire city will be self-sustaining. This could be the prototype city for building a colony on the Moon, or Mars."

"What friends are you talking about? Who do you know that has that kind of money?"

David swallowed hard. The name of his backer was the reason he hadn't told her before now. "Leon Cologne."

"You took money from Cologne? When were you going to tell me?" Abigail asked.

David gave a sheepish smile and said, "Right now."

Abigail groaned. "At least we don't have to deal with a mob of reporters," she replied. "How did you get Cologne to avoid a press release on this? With him involved I would expect at least a dozen reporters."

He smiled. "For some reason, Leon doesn't want anyone else to know about this project. He's investing his personal wealth, using a proxy company."

"How could you take money from a man like Cologne?" Abigail demanded. "One false step and he'll destroy everything we've built."

"No, no," David said, shaking his head for emphasis. "I worked it all out. He doesn't own any piece of this, or of Sanctuary Foods."

"How did you manage that?"

David sighed heavily. She was taking this better than he thought. "This farm is a joint venture between Sanctuary Foods and the new research company we're founding today, officially called Andrews Research. Cologne's proxy company is contracting with us to build a few prototypes."

"Officially? Are you saying it has an unofficial name?"

David nodded, unable to keep the smile off his face. "To me, it will always be known as The Kingdom."

California Dreamin'

September 30th, 2017 - Ventura, California

Scott and Tonya Knox stood in the back yard of the sixth house they'd looked at that day. They'd started in Oxnard, where the homes were decently sized, but the crime rate was too high. Now they were in Riverpark.

"The house is nice," Tonya said, "but the yard is too small."

"You said the same thing about the last two," Jeremiah said. He came highly recommended as a real estate agent, yet he didn't seem to understand what they were looking for. "This is what's available for under $650,000." He sighed. "Let me show you one more home."

Scott followed Jeremiah's car as he drove them across the riverbed and up the hill. They parked next to Jeremiah in the driveway of a large home in an upscale neighborhood.

"Now this I like," Scott said.

"It is really nice," Tonya said. "These homes must be worth a million dollars. That's outside our price range."

"Let's just look anyway," Scott said.

"Sure," Tonya said as they got out of the car. "Let's dream big for once, even if we can't afford it yet."

Jeremiah punched in the code that released the key to the front door. He led them inside and through the house as he talked. "Now this property definitely has enough home and land for a young couple, such as yourselves," he said. "It's got four bedrooms, three bathrooms, 1,975 square feet of living space, and one more thing."

They went straight through the home and out the back door. The back porch had a stunning view looking out over the Santa Clara River, and on to the ocean.

Scott whistled. He tried to speak, but the words failed him.

Tonya took his hand and squeezed it. "This home really is a dream. Look at this view!"

"I'm looking," Scott said, without taking his eyes off the valley. "Believe me, I'm looking."

Jeremiah cleared his throat, causing both Scott and Tonya to look over at him.

"This home is amazing!" Tonya said. "Show us the rooms before you tell us the price. Let us dream a little longer."

Jeremiah scowled slightly but quickly smiled again. "Of course."

The tour of the home lasted half an hour as they examined everything from the oversized shower and built-in spa in the master bath to the extra tall cupboards and large walk-in pantry off the kitchen. They finally returned to the foyer, thrilled to even look at such a home. Everything in it was perfect.

"Okay," Tonya said at last. "We've dreamed long enough. How much does this home cost?"

"That's why I didn't bring you here first," Jeremiah said. "You told me you could only afford $650,000. They are asking $750,000 for this home, and I know they'll get it."

Tonya's jaw dropped.

"That all?" Scott asked. "Only $750,000? We can afford that!" He turned to stare into Tonya's big blue eyes. "What do you think, honey? Should we put an offer on this home?"

She just nodded as a tear rolled down her cheek. She gave him a quick kiss and said. "Yes. It's perfect. Let's do it."

The Prince and the Gunman

October 1st, 2017 - Las Vegas, Nevada

Davoud Khanum stood ten feet from the stage on the third night of the Route 91 Harvest country music festival in Las Vegas[19] wishing he could ditch his security guards. It wasn't that he hated them, but that he always felt so conspicuous, even when they were blending into the crowd. Being the grandson of the deposed leader of Iran[20] had its perks, like front row tickets everywhere he went, and backstage passes to boot. But it also had its downside, like living his life with a target on his back.

This wasn't the first concert he'd been to, but it was the first time he'd been in Vegas since he turned eighteen. There were a few things which were now legal for him which his bodyguards had specific instructions to prevent. Still, the music was good, and he was having a good time, despite his father's restrictions.

Unexpectedly, a strange staccato rhythm mixed in with the music and Davoud was suddenly crushed by one of his bodyguards. "What are you doing?"

"Saving your life," the guard said.

As the music stopped, more rapid-fire shots rang out.

"Get me out of here!" Davoud tried to figure out where the shots were coming from, but the chaos around him made it impossible. His heart was pounding, and he felt like he might throw up. His mind was racing, trying to determine if they were after him specifically, or if he'd just stumbled into a terrorist attack by chance.

"Just stay down until the other guards get here," the mountain of muscle on top of him said.

"We have to move now!" Davoud was convinced they must be after him, and any minute now his guard would be hit, and he would be kidnapped. That was always his father's greatest fear.

The rapid gunfire continued. Some people were screaming, while others were trying to figure out what was going on.

Three of his security guards surrounded them and they finally let Davoud up off the ground. He heard one of them say into his earpiece, "Bring the car to location Tango."

Davoud was close enough to hear the response of the confused driver. "Now? The concert isn't . . ."

More shots rang out.

"On my way."

The guards surrounded him with a human shield as they led him away from the concert and back to the stretch Hummer Limousine. Two more guards showed up as they entered the parking lot.

By now, people were running in every direction as the rapid-fire shots continued. Some were screaming, while others were saving their breath for running.

Davoud's heart pumped fast as he scanned the parking lot for the car. He heard at least fifty more shots fired before the stretch Hummer pulled up in front of him. A guard opened the front passenger door to make sure it was the right driver before nodding to the others who practically threw Davoud inside. He didn't care. Now he was safe.

As the doors closed and cut off the screams and gunfire, Davoud said, "I'm so glad I got the bullet-proof upgrade. They'll never get me in here." He paused a moment as the gunfire continued. "Why isn't it stopping?"

The car pulled forward slowly as people streamed around it.

"I don't think you were the target," one guard said. "It appears to be a terrorist attack."

Davoud looked out at the frightened crowd of people still running for cover. He thought the danger would end as soon as he was safe. But the longer it continued, it felt more and more likely that this was just some nut with a gun. "How could anyone have such reckless hate?"

The White Ash of the California Forest Fires

December 14th, 2017 - Ventura, California

Scott and Tonya Knox drove his new truck back toward their home after spending two solid weeks with Tonya's mom. They'd gone up to see her for an extended weekend, only to watch in horror the night before they planned to return as the Thomas fire ripped through the mountain which was practically their backyard. It was joined by two other fires in the Los Angeles area, stretching the abilities of the firefighters to contain the blaze.

They'd only been in their home for one month before the order came to evacuate and they didn't have an opportunity to go back and collect anything. They hadn't even made the first payment on their mortgage yet.

Smoke hung in the air and the Thomas Fire still raged on. Scott turned onto Victoria Avenue, and as he passed Telegraph Road, less than a mile from their home, they came up to a roadblock.

Scott rolled down his window as they pulled up to the National Guard soldier standing in front of the barrier. "How far has the fire reached?"[21]

"I'm not an information booth," the soldier said. "This road is closed. Only emergency vehicles can come through here."

"What did he say?" Tonya asked.

Scott ignored her as he focused on the soldier. "We just got back from vacation, and we live a few blocks from here. We need to know if our home is still standing."

"I see. Give me a few minutes, and I'll get someone to escort you. Do you have your ID's?"

Scott pulled out his wallet and handed over his driver's license.

"Is he going to let us through?" Tonya asked.

"Yes. I'm handling it," Scott replied softly. He knew Tonya was stressing out over the fire. He was trying to retain some shred of hope, but even that was vanishing quickly.

The soldier studied the ID for a moment before pulling out his radio. "I need an escort for a homeowner to 740 Via Cielito."

There was a short pause before someone replied, "I'm on my way. You can tell them to prepare for the worst."

Scott's heart sank as he heard those words.

"What did they say?" Tonya asked again.

"Someone is coming to escort us to our home," Scott said, "or at least what's left of it."

"Did he say whether our home is still standing?"

Scott shook his head. "All he said was to prepare for the worst."

Tonya squeezed his hand hard. There was a look of pain in her eyes he'd never seen before. No, it was more than pain. It was fear. She was having a harder time dealing with this than he was, and he didn't know what to say to her. He studied her face and shifted his nearly bruised hand to put it over her shoulder.

Just as he thought of something to say, a red truck pulled up with a fire department logo on the door. He noted it was an older Dodge Ram 3500. A decent vehicle, and basically an older version of his brand-new Sierra 3500 Denali HD. Tonya let him buy it after she'd won a car for being the top seller in the third quarter.

"I'll take them from here. Follow me, folks."

The soldier moved the barrier, and they followed the red truck. It wasn't long before the homes vanished, replaced by piles of ash. Burnt out cars dotted the street, either in front of the homes, or in the driveways. There weren't as many as he expected, but Scott reminded himself that most of the people on this street had time to evacuate.

As they pulled onto Via Cielito, Tonya said, "This can't be our street. You turned too early."

Scott didn't know how to answer her. Every home was gone. He had to look at the addresses painted on the sidewalk to know where he was. As they pulled up to 740, it was as bad as the rest of them. The red truck stopped next to the property, and Scott pulled into their driveway.

"This can't be our house," Tonya said. "Check the GPS."

Unable to speak without breaking down in sobs, Scott just turned off his truck. He got out with Tonya right behind him, once more placing a death-grip on his hand. They walked over the remains of their house.

Somehow their front and back lawns had survived, and two of the three trees in their yard looked completely untouched. The third tree lost a few branches that had been close to the house.

"A forest fire did this?" Scott asked aloud. "How is that possible, if all that's left is the forest?"

"The trees in the subdivision were well-watered, compared with the forest," their firefighter escort said. "As for the homes, I can't really say. I've never seen this much destruction before."

It was hard for Scott to convince himself this was their home. The stepping stones in the backyard were still there, where he'd placed them two weeks earlier. He walked out to the third stone, the one with their handprints on it.

He picked the stone up, wiping the white ash off it. Sure enough, his handprint was there, right next to Tonya's, with their names etched below.

"Our stone!" Tonya exclaimed. She buried her face in Scott's shoulder and cried.

Scott stood there, choking back his own tears as he took in the devastation around him. They'd put thirty-five thousand down and spent another twenty thousand dollars on closing costs. Now everything they owned was a pile of white ash.

Where their garage once stood, the remains of the Mercedes Tonya won two months ago was barely recognizable. The paint was gone, as were the tires, leaving only a gray metal frame, which was twisted in places from the heat.

As they stood there, they saw a line of fire trucks and police cars preceding a hearse, followed by at least a dozen more fire trucks, plenty more police cars, and more people.[22]

"Looks like a funeral procession," Tonya said.

"Yeah, but who died?" Scott asked.

"Isn't it obvious?" The firefighter said. "All those fire trucks are here to salute one of our own. He died trying to protect your neighborhood."

Scott's gut wrenched at hearing this. All week he'd been worried about their home and all their valuables. When he heard the fire had hit their neighborhood, he held out hope that the flames would be stopped in time. Even after he knew the fire had torn through his street, he still hoped something of value had survived. All his hopes had been dashed. He never once stopped to consider that the firefighters might die while battling the blaze.

At that moment, the wind shifted, and a white powder began to fall.

"It looks like snow." Tonya said, "but it can't be. This is Ventura." [23] It wasn't her usual tone of voice. This sounded more child-like.

"That's not snow," Scott said. "That's the ashes of our home."

Tonya walked over to what used to be the front porch. Her foot banged against something amid the ash. She bent over and lifted a twisted piece of metal out of the ashes.

Scott swallowed hard as he realized it was the Kitchen-Aid mixer they'd ordered. It must have been delivered sometime between Friday morning and Monday afternoon. There wasn't much left of it.

"Our home," Tonya said softly as more tears poured down her face.

Scott put the stone in the back of his truck before he walked over to Tonya and pulled her into a tight hug as his own tears poured out.

Shortly to Come
The Lost Denali

September 20th - San Mateo, California

Scott Knox made the final cuts to the lumber he was working and loaded the last pieces onto the pallet. He didn't understand why people ordered pre-cut custom patio kits, but he was grateful for the work.

After the loss of their home in Ventura, their life took more turns for the worse. They first moved into a rental in Montecito while they waited for the insurance company to process their claim. They'd opted for a furnished home, as they'd just lost what little furniture they'd managed to collect.

Less than a month after they moved in, a mudslide filled their backyard and kitchen, forcing them to move yet again. Fed up with Southern California, Tonya insisted they move in with her mother until their property in Ventura sold.

They got four hundred thousand from their homeowners' insurance policy, but it took six months to sell the land, which sold for another four hundred thousand.

Scott wrapped the pallet in plastic and marked the order number on it before signaling that it was ready for shipping. He didn't know whether the patio would be built in San Mateo, or even in California. All he knew was the measurements the computer spat out, telling him where to make the cuts. It was a job, and it paid the bills.

Those six months of living with Tonya's mother drove a wedge between Scott and Tonya that they both acknowledged was there, but didn't know how to remove. Tonya's mother was devoutly religious, something Scott never really took to heart. He'd gone through all the motions, done everything expected of him, and was a member in good standing, but he had doubts and questions which had never been answered. Tonya had her faith rekindled during that time, while Scott's doubts only grew deeper.

When their property was finally sold, and their mortgage on it paid off, they took the eighty thousand they had left and used it as a down payment. They bought a home in San Mateo, about an hour away from Tonya's mother. It wasn't long before Scott wished they'd moved farther away.

Less than a month after they bought their new home, someone in Tonya's downline who'd been with her for almost three years, defected from Juuva. She took most of those below her in Tonya's network to Herbalife. As a result, Tonya's paycheck was cut in half.

At the same time, they found evidence of termites and had to pay for the treatment. They had sworn statements from the previous homeowner that the home had been treated only two months earlier, yet there was no denying the termites were there.

Between their new mortgage payment, Scott's truck, and Tonya's car, they barely had enough left to buy groceries. Yet there were still bills to pay, so Scott had reluctantly agreed to get a job. Any job.

No one was hiring app developers, so he'd found a job in unskilled labor through the Ward Unemployment Specialist. He'd been cutting lumber for the last three months, growing ever more unhappy with his life. He had two dozen apps available for both Android and Apple products, but no one was downloading the free versions, let alone buying the upgrades he'd put so much time into.

Scott clocked out and headed to the parking lot. As he walked to the far end where he always parked, he saw a Prius instead of his truck. A quick scan of the lot didn't help. *Where did I park?* He clicked the lock button on his remote twice, but nothing happened.

He clicked the panic button. Again, nothing. He pulled out his phone and opened the *Locate My Car* app he'd created. It worked off his truck's Bluetooth. If it was anywhere within a hundred meters, he'd know which direction to head based on signal strength.

It took a moment to load. When it did, the screen read, *No signal found.* His truck was gone.

He was so stunned he dropped his phone. Thankfully, it wasn't damaged by the fall, and he dialed 9-1-1.

"9-1-1. What is the nature of your emergency?" a male voice asked.

"I think my truck's been stolen."

"Are you at home?"

"No, I'm at work."

"Have you checked the whole parking lot?"

"I always park in the same spot," Scott said as he spun around anyway. "Plus, I already tried to locate it via Bluetooth, and it's not in range."

"Are you in immediate danger?"

"No." The question threw him for a loop. Why would it matter if he wasn't in immediate danger? Wasn't this enough of an emergency?

"I'm transferring you to the non-emergency line of the police. Please hold."

There were several clicks before a deep female voice said, "Officer Haskins speaking. Do you want to report a crime?"

"Yes," Scott said. "My truck's been stolen."

The woman sighed heavily. "Do you have the VIN or license plate number?"

"The license plate is 7ZFD346." He heard a keyboard clacking, then a short pause. Every second felt like an eternity with the blood pounding in his ears.

"2018 GMC Sierra Denali?"

"Yes."

"Well, I have good news and bad news," Officer Haskins said.

"What's the good news?"

"Your vehicle wasn't stolen."

"How can that be the good news? My truck isn't here."

"Well, that's the bad news. Your car's been repossessed."

"What! Ugh! I was about to send in the payment. I'm only three months behind."

"Look, I'm sorry about your car, but unless you have another emergency to report, I need to take the next call. I've been getting these calls all day, and no one likes to wait to speak to the police."

"No, this is the only emergency."

"If you want to dispute the repossession or make full payment on your car, you'll have to contact the lender. Have a nice day." She hung up before he could reply.

Scott let out a long sigh. His truck was in decent shape, and the eight hundred dollars a month he paid had been fine for the first six months. Now, though, the eight hundred felt like a weight around his neck. Still, he needed a way to get home. "Now what?" he asked himself.

He didn't have cash for the bus, and he didn't want to pay for a cab. The solution seemed obvious, but it took him a few minutes to find and install the app and create an account. He'd heard about Google's car service giving cheap rides during their testing phase. Seven minutes later, a minivan pulled up.

He double-checked the app, and sure enough, this was the car they'd sent. But when he opened the door, there was no driver. It looked like an ordinary minivan with a large omega symbol on top, which he assumed was where the sensors and cameras were housed.

"Welcome to the Waymo Self-Driving car service,"[24] a female voice said. "Please confirm your identity by placing your thumb or phone on the scanner."

He climbed in, sat down, and placed his phone on the scanner.

"Thank you, Scott Knox. Please close the door."

He looked over at the door and realized he hadn't shut it when he got in. He was too blown away by the self-driving car. He kept expecting them to have robots or no steering wheel. It felt strange by looking ordinary.

"Please close the door," the female voice said again.

Scott finally complied.

"Please buckle your seatbelt."

He did as he was told.

The car started moving, navigating the parking lot perfectly. "Your estimated travel time is thirty-seven minutes."

At least the journey wasn't any longer than usual. Scott lifted his phone off the scanner and dialed home, still unsure how to tell his wife their truck had been repossessed.

She didn't have much to say over the phone but kept insisting they'd discuss it when he got home, no matter how many times he tried to explain.

When he did finally get home, his nose was overwhelmed by the mingled smells of hamburger, tomato, and garlic. Tonya sat at the kitchen table in front of a steaming bowl of spaghetti with a plate of toasted garlic bread next to it. She patted his chair, and he dutifully sat.

They said grace and dished up. He was half finished with his plate before Tonya said, "Car repos made the news today."

He nearly choked on the bread in his mouth. He gulped down half a glass of water to clear his throat before he replied, "Somehow, I don't think my truck was important enough to make the five o'clock news."

"No, not your truck," Tonya replied with a smile. That look told him she'd timed her news for maximum effect and was pleased with the results. "Lenders got much more aggressive today in repossessing vehicles where the payments are more than sixty days past due."

"Why? I thought they wouldn't do anything until we hit at least 120 days late."

"There was an announcement by the federal reserve. They are raising interest rates again, starting October 1st."

"Why would that make a difference?"

"They raised mortgage rates to eight percent. This is the tenth interest rate hike in the last year and the first time in almost a decade when rates have been this high. The stock market took a hit for the first two hours, but it's already recovered and climbing again."

"What did President Money say about that?"

"I wish you wouldn't call him that," Tonya said. "It's demeaning."

"Hey, I didn't invent the nickname, and I didn't vote for the guy. Besides, what else are they going to come up with for a billionaire named Daniel Mahoney Towers?" He twirled up more spaghetti and started eating again. She'd already dropped her bombshell, so it was probably safe.

"No. You, the dyed-in-the-wool Republican, threw away your vote on some no-chance-to-win third-party candidate."

"Third parties are gaining in support. I wouldn't be surprised to see an independent party candidate win in the next election."

"You think someone could beat President Towers?"

Scott shook his head. "I mean after his second term, or if he gets impeached or something. Heck, he might run on a third-party ticket if the Republican Party ousts him in the Primaries."

She ate quietly for a few minutes as she finished off her plate. "I could see that happening. He hasn't posted anything about the latest rate hike yet. His advisors have been pretty good about keeping him off Twitter lately."

The conversation was just starting to sink in, and Scott realized he'd skipped over a couple of important points. "Why does a hike in mortgage rates cause a rise in auto loan repos?"

"Auto loan rates have risen as well. They're at ten percent, and they don't like the interest free loans they handed out last year," Tonya said as she took another scoop of spaghetti. "Plus, now they'll have a large stock of used cars to sell to people, at a higher interest rate."

"They're expecting to make new loans?"

Tonya nodded as she finished chewing. She swallowed and said, "With interest rates on the rise, they are relaxing the lending requirements a bit."

"What are we supposed to do?" Scott asked. "Our credit rating is going to take a big hit after that repossession, and we can't afford to pay cash for another truck."

Tonya just shrugged her shoulders as she took another bite.

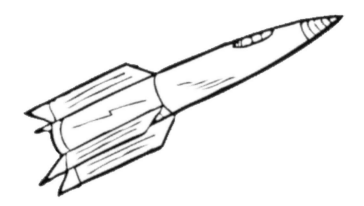

Leon Cologne's Weight in Gold

September 20th - Hawthorne, California

Liz Smith walked toward her boss' office, trying not to reveal her nervousness. She'd been working as the personal assistant for Leon Cologne for three months now, and the needs of the eccentric billionaire always grew stranger as the day went on. It was almost 6:30 p.m., well after the day-shift went home. Yet he'd had her hopping for the last four hours running memos, grabbing his coffee, relaying messages, and even picking up his dry cleaning.

Why she needed a college degree for this was beyond her. Sometimes she thought Leon hired her because he liked her long blonde hair. He certainly gave her enough compliments on it. At least it paid well.

The lights in his office were off, but the glass wall was still transparent, meaning he hadn't left for the day. A series of bangs and clicks grew louder as she approached. It took her a minute to realize it was African drums and chanting. She let out a long sigh and walked in.

Leon was lying on the floor, staring up at a projection of stars as they moved across the ceiling. "Oh good, you're still here," he said, smiling as he looked over at her. Whenever he wasn't behind his massive desk, it meant he wasn't focused on a specific task. No, this was far more serious. He was thinking.

"Of course," Liz replied. "What can I do for you?"

"Have a seat. I need a sounding board." He clicked a remote, and the drums shut off.

She nervously sat in a large lounge chair near him, setting aside the tablet that ruled her life and kept his on track. "What's on your mind?"

"Space." This was a common response for Leon, but that shouldn't be surprising as he ran the largest private space enterprise in the world. The recent success of the largest rocket launch ever attempted caused their stock to soar along with Leon's mood. Now they were building an even larger rocket. Something called the Big Falcon Rocket. Once it was ready, they'd be launching actual cargo to Mars instead of just test loads.

Liz waited, but he was still staring at the fake stars on the ceiling, playing out some sort of drama only he could understand, no doubt. She finally jumped in with, "That's a very large subject."

He sat up and turned to look her in the eyes. His smile hadn't diminished, and there was a twinkle in his eye. With most men, she would have thought that kind of twinkle was meant for her. But she'd learned it was Leon's standard reaction whenever the subject of space came up, which was often.

"Yes, I suppose it is," he said. "I think it's time for me to see it for myself."

A chill ran through her from head to toe. Definitely not the answer she'd been expecting. "That's a very bold move."

"But a necessary one." He stood and started pacing. "Our goal is to put a colony on Mars in the next ten years. I plan to go there myself. Perhaps not on the first trip, but certainly within the first ten. The world still perceives space travel as dangerous, difficult, and risky. I have to dispel that idea."

"I thought you had."

He shook his head. "The human memory is very long, and the difficulties with Apollo 13 still haunt anyone planning a trip to the stars."

"We got them back safely, as I recall."

Leon nodded and sat back down, facing her once more. "But it was a close call, and the Space Shuttles Discovery and Challenger both ended in disaster. No matter how many rockets I launch with bigger and bigger payloads, people still fear space travel. I need to inspire the best minds of this generation and the next one to join me on Mars. How can I do that if most of them still fear the journey?"

Liz didn't know what to say. She always wanted to take a trip into space, but when she found out NASA only accepted people with multiple advanced degrees, she changed the course of her life. Watching the disintegration of Columbia on reentry had diminished her desire a little, but she still held out hope. "You've got a good point there. But taking the journey alone isn't going to inspire a generation to believe in the safety of strapping into a rocket."

He smiled at her, the twinkle in his eyes growing larger. "I don't pay you enough, you know that?"

She smiled too but bit her lip. She was being paid twice what she expected for her first job out of college.

"You're right. I can't do this alone." He stood and paced once more. "I need to take a group of brave citizens with me. Not astronauts trained for years to overcome their fear. I need to sell seats on a week-long trip in space."

"You can't have billionaires orbit the Earth for a week in a capsule," Liz shot back. This line of thinking was becoming dangerous in its ability to distract him. "There wouldn't be enough room for their egos." She gave a smile to let him know it was a joke.

He smiled back before his eyes shifted to the stars. "You're right again. We need something bigger. Some place for them to visit, like the International Space Station."

"Won't that require approval from all the countries involved?"

He nodded without looking at her. "Yes, definitely. I wonder how much money they'll need to take on tourists for a few days, maybe a week tops."

"Not to mention the cost of the launch."

"Of course," Leon said.

"By the time we add up all the expenses," Liz said, doing some quick math in her head, "it could easily cost your weight in gold for a one-week trip."

Leon stopped pacing and started laughing. "That's exactly how I'm going to sell it. I'll charge them their weight in gold."

"Are you going to ask them to pay in gold, or accept a check?" Liz asked with a wry smile. At times like this she wasn't sure how seriously to take him.

Leon's laugh grew louder. "That would be quite the media event, wouldn't it? To have a dozen people bring their weight in gold to purchase passage to the International Space Station! That's exactly what we're going to do! Great work, Liz. Let's go get dinner to celebrate! Someplace nice."

She grabbed her tablet and used it to reserve a table at Ruth's Chris Steak House, one of the dozen restaurants on his approved list.

Liz let out a small sigh. As crazy as it sounded, it was just the kind of thing Leon would pull off. Sure, there were plenty of factors to consider, and it would take months of planning, mostly involving late nights for both of them. Still, if anyone could convince an international group of bureaucrats to let a dozen billionaires turn the International Space Station into the most expensive resort in the solar system, it was Leon.

The Former Mahdi

September 21st - London, England

Mohammed Arsalan Malik walked into The Shard, right past the front desk and into the first elevator he could find. Two other people followed him in before he could push a button.

"Which floor?" a young woman asked him.

"S-seventy-t-two," he said. "I w-want to see the r-roof." He was so nervous about this meeting that his stuttering was worse than ever.

Up until three months ago, he went by Mohammed Al-Mahdi. Then he turned forty-one, and everything he'd trained for since the age of eight was gone, just like that. His rocket attack in Damascus over a year ago wasn't the last one he'd planned, but it was certainly the beginning of the end. He'd only been able to launch one rocket, and it hadn't changed anything. That's when his followers started to doubt. Perhaps that was because he'd already started to doubt himself.

Now he was meeting with a representative of the Shadow Council to discuss whether he still had a future and what it would be.

Thoughts of everything he'd lost flooded his mind as the elevator rose ten floors before the first person got out. It was another fifteen floors before the second person got out. As the doors closed, finally leaving him alone in the elevator, he opened the panel beneath the buttons and typed in his code.

The elevator came to a halt somewhere around the twenty-eighth floor and started descending. It was somewhat poetic that the elevator never reached its intended height before descending below the ground, just like his life. It went down longer than it had gone up, though Arsalan had no real way to know how far underground he was going.

He exited the elevator into a large plush hallway. So many of these hidden underground levels looked the same. The ornate carvings and masterful artwork always felt so garish for someone who'd spent most of his life moving from camp to camp around the world. Yet this hidden enclave was where he first came when he was eight years old. The building above had changed, but the chambers below London looked the same.

He allowed the guards to pass their wands near him to search for weapons. Of course, they found none. He knew better than to come armed without permission. He entered the empty conference room and took a seat. There was only one thing he truly hoped for from this meeting, and he knew it would be difficult to convince the council to let him finally marry the woman he loved.

As he was starting to get lost in his thoughts, the doors opened, and a familiar face walked into the room. "Ah, good, you are on-time," the man said. Arsalan had no idea what the man's name was, only that he was known as Thirteen. The first time they met, Thirteen was dressed as a holy man, leader of a Mosque in

London. Back then he was known as Eleven until his superior was disgraced and Thirteen shared in the shame.

"I ap-preciate you m-meeting me yourself, Thirt-teen," Arsalan said as he rose. "I thought p-perhaps I would be addressing the full council, but p-perhaps it is best to handle things this w-way."

"You seem nervous," Thirteen said. "Sit down. Relax. If we didn't have a future in mind for you, you wouldn't have made it through the doors."

Arsalan considered this. He hadn't really thought through how the council would act if they believed he no longer had value. He sat back down and tried to relax. "So w-what do you have in m-mind for my future?"

Thirteen smiled. "That's better. Now, we don't have an assignment for you right away, but in time, I'm hoping you'll help train the true Mohammed Al-Mahdi."

"I a-am the true M-Mahdi," Arsalan said.

Thirteen shook his head. "No, I'm afraid that's impossible. You didn't fulfill all the prophecies before your forty-first birthday. Your age disqualifies you."

"M-my age?" Arsalan asked. "How o-often do you f-find someone who f-fits the right des-scription, has a m-mother named Aamina and a f-father named Abdullah?"

Thirteen smiled. "You might be surprised. You know there are thousands of people right now who claim to be the Mahdi. Very few of them meet the prophesied physical description, and of those who do, it is rare to find one with a stutter. Oh, some fake their stutter, others attempt to change their appearance. Even those who have the right look and the stutter are usually not born to the right parents, though some try to fake their parentage as well. Most, however, simply ignore the prophecies they don't like."

"Such as the a-age requirement?" Arsalan suggested.

Thirteen shook his head. "The Shadow Council does not ignore facts or prophecies. Either you are the true Mahdi, or you are not. You are one of the rare few who has the look, the stutter, and the right parents. But make no mistake, you are not unique in these qualifications. We are working with a young man in his early thirties who already shows great promise."

"What exactly d-do you want from m-me?"

"Right now, I want you to live your life and think about why you failed. In four or five years, if this young man lives up to his potential, we think you could provide him with valuable insight."

"Four or f-five years? M-might I m-make a r-request?"

"What do you want?"

"S-Sariah Khanum."

Thirteen shook his head. "I'm afraid that's absolutely out of the question. You see, you need to disappear for a few years. I don't want to hear from you, see you, or find out you're responsible for something that makes the news. Don't contact your parents, don't look in on old friends. Vanish."

Arsalan swallowed hard. This was only one step below being killed. As far as everyone else knew, he would be dead.

Thirteen nodded as if reading his thoughts. "I think you're getting the picture."

His heart sank as he left the room, the building, and his entire life. He vanished into the crowd, just like his hopes of marrying Sariah.

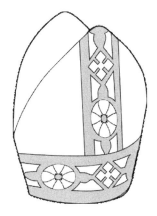

500 Years of Hate: A Future of Love

September 23rd - Vatican City

Pope Ferdinand stood before a packed crowd in St. Peter's Square. They were all eager to hear what he had to say, though he was worried they wouldn't easily accept his message. He walked to the podium and noticed the ever-present smell of tobacco smoke. Even the Cardinals of the Church hadn't all kicked the habit yet.

He'd chosen his regnal name carefully, publicly declaring it was in honor of Saint Ferdinand III, the patron saint of engineers. He was, after all, trying to engineer a better tomorrow.[25]

Very few knew it was also in honor of Ferdinand II, the Holy Roman Emperor from 1619-1637.[26] Yes, his plans stretched beyond building a better tomorrow, but to do that, he couldn't reveal his ambitions. At least not yet.

As he waited for his speech to appear on the teleprompter, he noticed the pigeons waiting above to feast on what the crowds always left behind.

"Good Sabbath to you all, wherever you may be," he said. He spoke in Italian, though he knew interpreters would be translating his message into at least a dozen languages. "This morning, my comments will be brief. It has been more than five hundred years since the great protest against the Catholic Church caused a rift among the followers of Christ.[27] The last fifty years[28] has seen much of that schism removed.

"We, as true followers of our Lord and Savior, Jesus Christ, cannot afford to let another five hundred years go by with hatred separating us from our brethren. Indeed, we should not even allow another fifty years to pass without reconciling our differences and putting past mistakes behind us. All the followers of Jesus are, after all, one in the body of Christ. We can at least agree on love.[29]

"To this end, and after much prayer, it has been decided that the best method for removing the hatred caused by this great schism is to extend the hand of fellowship to any and all who truly believe in Christ's message of love. In the coming weeks, months, or even years, I will personally be extending this hand of fellowship to our fellow Christians.

"This is not, as some will claim, an effort to reunify the Catholic Church and bring all our Protestant brethren back into the true fold of God. Instead, we must heal wounds caused by the words and actions of the various sects over the last five hundred years. I will not ask anyone to abandon their faith or their Church. If belonging to a particular sect helps them come closer to Christ, it is enough for me.

"It is only to the rest of the world that we must be united. We must show those who do not believe in Christ that the message of Jesus was one of love. We must show that love to more than our fellow Catholics. We must show it to all who profess to follow Jesus Christ, be they Methodist, Baptist, or Amish.

"I ask that all who hear my voice follow my example. Reach out to your fellow Christians, your neighbors and brothers and sisters in Christ. Show them that we are united in our love of Christ Jesus. Do not go with the hope to bring them into the Catholic Church, or prove their cherished beliefs to be wrong. Go only with the hope that we can find mutual love and understanding, being united in our love of God and of all men.

"It has been the fervent prayer of every Pope for the last fifty years, and it continues to be my prayer, that the body of Christ be united in love, that the truth of His message of love may be clear to all the world. Thank you."

Limitless Ambition Knows No Bounds

September 30th - Washington, D.C.

Frank Baldwin paced in his office as the butterflies in his stomach churned to a boil. He grabbed the bottle of Tums and ground his teeth on a couple of them while he gazed up at the clock. Sanders was ten minutes late, and that didn't bode well for his request.

"Mr. Baldwin, I have a Mr. Sanders here to see you," Betty said through the intercom.

Frank pushed the button and said, "Thank you, Betty. Show him in."

The man who entered a moment later was clearly not Gary Sanders. He was at least six inches shorter than the tall Texan, and his brownish skin tone suggested a heritage from south of the border.

As soon as the door shut behind the stranger, Frank flipped a switch which activated a cell-phone jammer, closed the blinds, and turned on a pink-noise generator, all to prevent any chance of eavesdropping. The soft whooshing of the pink-noise generator was the most reassuring of all. It generated frequencies designed to garble any attempt to record the conversation, but not so much that it prevented those in the room from hearing each other. "You're not Sanders. Who are you?"

The man shook his head. "Call me Edwin. I'm here to speak on Sanders' behalf."

"Why?"

"Come now, Mr. Baldwin, you can't be seen meeting with a media mogul like Sanders less than two months from the election. People would call it a conspiracy. Anything you planned to say to Sanders you can say to me."

"Prove it," Frank said.

Edwin reached out his hand and gave the secret handshake. They exchanged the sacred script known only to their brotherhood, and Edwin did everything required.

Frank took a deep breath and let it out slowly. Edwin had passed the ritual of identification. One mistake, and he would have been required to report this meeting to Sanders and ensure the imposter was killed.

"You have my trust," Frank said. "Okay, Edwin, I've called you here to formally request your help with getting me elected as Speaker of the House."

Edwin smiled in a way that unsettled Frank. "You make quite a presumption, Mr. Baldwin. Being Speaker right now could be risky."

"It could also offer great rewards." [30]

Edwin's laugh was less reassuring than his smile. "You think if we unseat President Towers and his V.P., Spencer Michaels, that you could take his place."

"The thought had crossed my mind," Frank admitted. "Even if you don't, being Speaker is quite an honor and a position of power. It could easily lead to me winning a presidential election. If not the next one, then the one after that. I'm willing to be patient, but my ambition is clear."

Edwin looked Frank up and down as if eyeing a juicy piece of meat. "You're tall, blond, and look almost physically fit. I'd say you've got the presidential look, but do you understand what comes with the office of President?"

Frank swallowed hard, unsure how far to reach right now. "I think I have an idea, and I'm willing to learn."

"We don't need someone who is willing to learn. We need someone who knows how to obey."

Frank scowled at him. "I've already proven myself to the council, or you wouldn't even be here. They know my loyalty; don't you dare question it."

Edwin's unsettling smile returned. "Good. Because if we do grant your request to become Speaker, your responsibilities will be quite high. I think you know the cost of failing to achieve."

He did know. He'd always known. Yet the thought of it still made him shiver. They kept their members in check by ensuring they could take everything from them. Power, wealth, even family, all with a single phone call. "I won't fail. I know what it takes to get things done in Washington."

"Getting things done is easy. But sometimes the Speaker must appear to be getting things done while at the same time blocking unfriendly legislation."

It was Frank's turn for a wry smile. "I have experience with that, too."

How Not to Make Money in the Stock Market

October 1st - San Mateo, California

Scott Knox took Waymo to and from work every day for more than a week. He hated the idea at first and argued with Tonya daily about how to get his truck back or get a new one. But the bank wouldn't give him a new loan and wanted him to pay the truck in full or refinance. Because of Tonya's loss of income, and his reduced credit score, no one would lend him money.

By the next Monday, however, he was wondering why he would ever need another truck. Between no longer paying for auto insurance and not needing to buy gas, he was saving several hundred dollars a month, even after paying for the self-driving car service.

As he checked the news during his ride to work, the top story was a drastic drop in the stock market.

Stocks dropped today amid rising fears that the higher interest rates which took effect this morning will only lead to more adjustable-rate mortgages going into default. The drastic rise in auto loan defaults is particularly troubling to investors. The DJIA dropped an additional ten percent over the weekend, bringing them below 21,000 and marking the official start of a bear market.

The drop wiped out twelve months' worth of growth in a single day, leaving investors pessimistic about the future. Not everyone sees the interest rate hike as a bad thing, however.

"We're confident that consumers will take advantage of the new lending programs," Frank Zazz, CEO of Ford said in a press release on Friday . . .

Scott checked his IRA. His jaw dropped as he saw it was almost five hundred dollars lower than the last time he'd looked. He'd put several thousand dollars into his retirement account before all the misfortunes began. Now a good portion of it was wiped out in a single day, bringing up fears that the misfortunes were starting again. He switched over to Facebook and posted a quick blurb about how much money he'd lost.

By the time he got to work he had fifteen likes, twenty-three sad reactions, and half a dozen comments ranging from *"That sucks,"* to *"I wish I had enough to lose $500!"*

Elder Shumway's Missionary Miracle

October 5th - New Delhi, India

Benjamin Shumway Jr. cleared out his fourth house of the day after another devastating earthquake. He heard it measured 9.3 on the Richter scale, and the number of dead was already in the thousands after only twenty-four hours. The President of the India New Delhi Mission for the Church of Jesus Christ of Latter-day Saints had called and told every missionary to cancel all teaching appointments and help with search and rescue and clearing of debris.

There were lots of people helping, and every American stood out, though the American Indian named Moroni Whitefeather stood out less than most. He'd been working alongside Elder Shumway and Elder Bhatia all day. His bright green Sanctuary Foods shirt was barely visible under the yellow Mormon Helping Hands t-shirt.

Ben wondered briefly if his brother Gideon would lead the Fighting Irish to another football victory that weekend, or if he'd even hear about the earthquake on the news.

The house they were currently working on had been particularly hard hit, and the second floor was now the ground floor. At least what was left of it. It was hard to imagine anyone surviving such an event.

As he was leaving the home, certain there was no one trapped beneath the rubble, the Spirit whispered to him to stay where he was. He stopped dead in his tracks and strained to hear, either for a sign of life, or a further prompting from the Holy Ghost.

"Elder Shumway, come on," Elder Bhatia said. "This house has already been cleared." He was native to India and joined the Church only two years earlier. At age twenty-four he was easily the oldest missionary.

"Just give me a minute of silence," Ben said.

"Sure thing," Moroni said, jumping into the conversation. "Hey, everyone! We need a minute of silence!"

Ben almost laughed at that, but it was the standard procedure. Not only did everyone in the house stop moving or talking, everyone within earshot did as well.

Thirty seconds later, Ben was about to give up when he heard a faint rhythmic tapping.

"I hear something!" he shouted.

"Where is it coming from?" Elder Bhatia asked.

Ben said a prayer in his heart while everything fell silent once more. This time it was only a few seconds before he heard the tapping again.

"The pipes. Someone is tapping on the pipes. Follow me." He led the small team of four into what used to be the second-story bathroom. The rubble was piled higher here than in most of the home. Ben grabbed hold of the pipe beneath the sink and felt the tapping. "We've definitely got a live one, somewhere along this pipe."

"We've got a live one!" Moroni called out. "Get an excavation team in here!"

"Are you sure?" a man asked as he stuck his head into the home.

"No, but can you take that chance?" Moroni asked.

"I'm sure," Ben said.

"Good enough for me," the man said as he left. He came back quickly with half a dozen men with shovels, pick-axes, and buckets.

Ben grabbed a pick-ax and started hacking away at the floor beneath him. He felt an urgency that he hadn't felt all day. Despite the hours of hard labor he'd already endured, he attacked the pile with a strength he didn't know he possessed. He almost kept up with Moroni's seemingly inexhaustible strength.

It took five minutes to cut a four-foot hole through the floor and when they did, Ben's pick-ax clanged against an overturned porcelain tub.

Someone inside banged back.

"He's in this tub!" Ben shouted.

Everyone focused their efforts on expanding Ben's hole to expose the tub. The first thing they saw were two small feet sticking out of the side of the tub. This fueled the weary muscles of the group, and soon they had the tub dug out and lifted off the infant. His mother was crouched over him, crying.

The woman didn't say anything, she just stared at her infant son. The baby's legs were covered in bruises from the knee down. Ben's heart sank as he realized both the infant's legs were badly broken and would likely need to be amputated.

"I thank you for saving my life," the woman sobbed, "but my son is as good as dead."

"What do you mean?" Ben asked.

Elder Bhatia put his hand on Ben's shoulder. "He'll be crippled for life. Among the poorer classes that is almost always a death sentence."

A combination of the woman's grief and Ben's exhaustion caused him to sink to his knees. *I can't endure this!* he cried silently to the heavens. *There must be more I can do.* His lips moved, but no sound came out.

"What is he doing?" the mother asked.

"Praying," Elder Bhatia said.

"You are men of God?"

Elder Bhatia nodded.

She placed her child in his arms. "If he stays with me, he will surely die. You must take him."

"No, I can't," Elder Bhatia protested, trying to hand the child back.

Ben stood up and looked at the child again. He thought it strange that the boy wasn't crying, despite the extensive bruising. Then he realized the infant must have already cried himself to sleep.

Give him a priesthood blessing of healing.

Ben heard the words and knew immediately what must be done. He'd given many blessings of comfort and a few blessings of healing while on his mission, using the power and authority of God through the priesthood he held. The blessing consisted of several parts. The sick or afflicted had to be anointed with sacred oil, addressed by name, and the authority of those giving the blessing stated. Using these blessings, he'd healed fevers and colds but never mended broken bones. Still, he was not one to ignore a prompting of the Spirit. "What is the child's name?"

"Arjin Bhola."

Elder Bhatia stared at Ben for a moment. "We can't take care of this child. We're here to preach the gospel."

"Just get out your oil," Ben said.

Elder Bhatia nodded and did as he was told. He anointed the little boy with oil and said the short prayer which was required by the ordinance. Then they both held him as Elder Shumway blessed him in English using the authority of the Melchizedek Priesthood and commanded Arjin's body to be made whole. He closed in the name of Jesus Christ.

Ben handed the child back to his mother, and the baby began to cry and kick his legs.

"The bruises are gone! Yah ek chamatkaar hai!" the woman exclaimed. "Chamatkaar!" she shouted again and again.

"What did she just say?" Ben asked. His Hindi wasn't bad, but she was speaking so fast and shouting so loudly that he couldn't understand her.

"She said, 'It's a miracle,'" Elder Bhatia said.

"It sure is," Moroni said. "That was quite impressive."

"It wasn't really me. It was the power of God," Ben said.

The man nodded. "Of course it was. Still, I'd like to meet the parents who raised their boy to have enough faith to heal broken bones."

"They live in Utah," Ben replied.

"Which town?"

"It's a small town called Nephi. He was a …"

Moroni laughed. "I know who Nephi was. My name is Moroni, after all. I'm originally from Arizona, but I've been up and down Utah many times, and I've even been to Nephi. Now I have a reason to go back."

The Dark Eagle's Shadow

October 5th - New York City

Peyman Ahmadi pressed his pass key to the card reader in the elevator of the United Nations Secretariat Building. The doors closed, and the elevator descended at least a dozen stories before opening into a well-lit corridor. Today was the quarterly meeting of the Shadow Council, and they always met as close to the action as possible. Right now, that meant New York City.

He followed the corridor and turned right into the third hallway. He submitted to the security guards who waved their wands to search for weapons. Finding none, they permitted him to enter the large conference room.

He took his place at the foot of the table, in the chair designated for the thirteenth member of the council. Numbers were everything here. They told everyone his level of importance and power among the group. To the rest of the world, he was a religious leader, a Muslim Imam with a thriving congregation in London.

Here he was the subordinate of Seven, a Russian Orthodox priest, and as such was designated Thirteen. Together they oversaw the religious affairs of the world. Five years ago, he'd been designated Eleven. That was before his immediate superior was demoted from Five to Seven when he failed to get the right person elected as Pope. Peyman had automatically fallen in importance as well.

He'd gone against the council's instructions by not having Arsalan killed. It was a risk he took, which he hoped would offer great rewards later on. After all, as the lowest member of the council, he had to take risks to progress. If Arsalan obeyed his instructions, no one would ever know what Peyman had done.

The council members filed in over the next half hour, with One arriving last. His dark hair had receded into a pronounced widow's peak. He took his place at the head of the table, ordered the doors sealed, and then said, "This meeting of the Shadow Council will now come to order. As always, the penalty for disclosing anything we discuss here, without permission, is death. Three, I believe you have something to report."

Three nodded and stood before saying, "We've successfully raised the mortgage rate in the United States to eight percent. It has already had the desired effect of causing the stock market to dip."[31]

He spoke with a thick southern drawl, leading Peyman to guess he was from Georgia or Mississippi, or one of the other rebel states from the American Civil War. The council had nearly ended America with that war.

"How is that the desired effect?" Two's accent betrayed his Swiss upbringing.

Peyman had studied these people for years, secretly trying to learn their true names. After all, knowledge was power.

"We must do all we can to make Towers look bad in the upcoming election," Three explained. "When they see that his fiscal policy is costing the average person thousands of dollars lost in their retirement accounts, they will turn away from him and the candidates he supports. Thus, the establishment candidates we control will stay in power."

"What about the sharp rise in the price of Bitcoin and other cryptocurrencies?" One asked.

"That's a temporary glitch," Three said, waving it away.

"You said the same thing last year," One replied. "You told me they would never recover, yet they are higher than ever."

Three took a deep breath and said in a slow-measured speech, "Whenever the stock market dips, people move what's left of their money to wherever they think it will be safe. As soon as the stock market correction is over, they will dump cryptocurrencies and put it back into the market, causing more instability in crypto-currencies, and hence more people dumping them in favor of stock. It won't be long before even Bitcoin loses its popularity and collapses in on itself. I project that within ten years, we will achieve our goal of one global digital currency, and it won't be encrypted."

"Ten years is too long," One shot back. "The rise of the Dark Eagle has been slowed, but we still plan to establish it in less than a decade."

Peyman allowed a long pause in the conversation before asking, "Is that because Dan Towers is trying to undo our work?"

One glared at him for a moment before his expression softened. "Yes, Thirteen. You perceive well. Towers has indeed upset our plans and threatens everything we've been working toward for the past century. The only reason he still lives is that he would be more of a problem dead than alive. Four, you are responsible for what goes on in Washington. Please, enlighten Thirteen about how we are progressing."

"Very well," Four said as he stood up. "President Towers . . ."

"Dan," One interrupted.

Peyman had Four pegged as a Texan. He always wore his three-piece suit, stood over six feet tall, and his voice filled the room.

Four nodded to One's authority and restarted. "Dan has politically attacked several of the congressmen who are with us, and we are in danger of losing a critical majority in both the House and Senate next month. As such, we have increased our campaign efforts to ensure our operatives retain their seats, focused mainly on the Senate, where the risk is greater.

"We have a promising candidate for Speaker of the House, and while I'm expecting a bit of a fight, I'm sure we have the votes needed to put him in place. I am confident we will retain enough control to prevent any adverse legislation from ever making it to the P . . . to Dan's desk." His pause was caused by a stern look from One.

"Thank you, Four," One said. "As you know, if things don't go well, you will be demoted." He paused before adding, "Or possibly beheaded."

Four glared only briefly at One before turning his baleful stare to Peyman. He then turned back to One and said, "I'm confident that won't happen. We have everything we need to ensure Dan won't have the support he needs to cause us any further disruption."

*   *   *

Gary Sanders left the United Nations building with a storm cloud over his head. He wanted to pound Thirteen's smug face into the pavement for making such a comment. Didn't he know his place? He wasn't supposed to speak unless spoken to. Yet One had let it slide, even seemed to appreciate the little brown bug's impudence. Gary knew that if he wanted to rise from Four to Two, and someday take over the council, he would have to ensure this election went badly for President Towers.

He climbed into the waiting limousine, pulled out his laptop, and immediately began drafting instructions to his media outlets to increase the political attacks on President Towers. Gary was personally responsible for the nickname President Money, based on Dan's middle name, Mahoney, and his status as a billionaire. Sure, it seemed obvious, but Gary was the one who gave the order to plaster the internet with the nickname, and it quickly stuck.

Now he needed to use those same channels to destroy Dan's character and increase the level of anger on both sides of the political aisle. He closed the memo with, *"Start a war if you have to, but do not let Towers gain any political advantage."*[32]

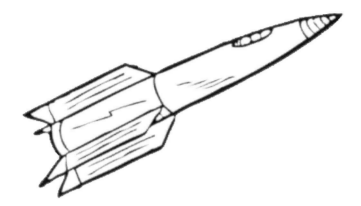

Astrotourism – The Future of SpaceX

October 5th - Hawthorne, California

Liz Smith rushed around the conference room one final time, making sure everything was in place. Leon Cologne had spoken of little else the last two weeks besides his upcoming vacation to the ISS. He'd surprised her by insisting she accompany him to the Steakhouse. She would have thought it was a date if he had stopped talking about the ISS for more than two minutes.

They'd gone to a different fancy restaurant almost every night over the past six weeks so that Leon could spend an hour talking with her about the upcoming visit to the ISS. She was actually grateful because it meant he spent the rest of his day focused on all the other projects he was already pursuing.

The whole plan hinged on this meeting today between all five space agencies responsible for the ISS. NASA, ESA, CSA, Roscosmos, and JAXA were each sending three representatives, which meant they were all willing to at least consider the plan.

A knock at the door made her turn around.

"Miss Smith?" a Japanese woman asked, flanked by two Japanese men.

"You must be Sadako Shirasu. Come in!" she said sweetly. They were half an hour early, but she was ready for them anyway. "I've got your seats set up right over here."

Sadako nodded to her and walked to their seats.

"The meeting isn't scheduled to start for another thirty minutes. Is there anything I can get you while you wait?"

"Information," Sadako said.

"Everything will be explained in the presentation and the question and answer session afterward," Liz said.

"Everything about the proposal, yes," Sadako said quietly. "What I want to know is whether Leon lives up to his reputation."

Liz shook her head slightly. "Not all of it, no. There are many wild stories about him which aren't true." This was a more common question than she'd ever admit. Her answer was quite practiced, even if she wasn't sure she believed it. Her job depended on denying those rumors, even if they were true.

"No," Sadako said. "I don't care who he sleeps with or where he spends his vacations. I want to know if he is taking this effort seriously."

Liz paused a moment to compose herself properly for the answer. "He is very serious about this proposal. It is essential to his life's goal."

"And what goal is that?"

"To put a self-sustaining colony on Mars."

"Why does he need to use our space station as a tourist attraction to accomplish that?"

Liz smiled broadly. "Mr. Cologne will be addressing that himself. I think it's best to leave the explanation to him."

Sadako nodded. "I admire your loyalty. I can see why he likes you."

Liz was about to ask her what she meant by that, but she was called away by the arrival of the Roscosmos representatives. As soon as she'd shown them their seats, the Canadians arrived, followed by the Europeans. No one else had time to corner her to ask similar questions, for which she was grateful.

As she waited for the last group to arrive, she kept one ear on the conference room, even though there were security guards and assistants galore to meet the needs of these international guests.

Three minutes after the scheduled start of the meeting, Liz reached for her tablet to check on the location of her boss. She had an app that tracked the movements of every employee on the campus using their security badges. As she clicked to update his location, the elevator door opened with Leon and the three tardy NASA representatives. He must have ambushed them in the lobby because they were all laughing as they walked down the hall.

Liz knew better than to interfere when Leon was schmoozing, so she just smiled and stepped out of the way as Leon led them into the conference room like old friends. Perhaps they were.

Just before he stepped inside, Leon leaned back and said, "Liz, why don't you join us. I mean this was your idea, after all." He winked at her.

Her eyes went wide. He knew very well it wasn't her idea, but she obediently walked into the conference room which had been set for seventeen, as instructed. She suddenly realized the last seat had been intended for her all along, right next to Leon.

As soon as everyone had taken their seats, the guards closed the doors and Leon dimmed the lights. "I want to thank you all for coming." A video of the ISS exterior popped up on the screen. Liz couldn't tell whether it was CGI or actual video, but it slowly circled the entire station. "By all accounts, the International Space

Station has been a great success story in microgravity research and space exploration advances over the last two decades, with another five to ten years of life still left in her."

All fifteen representatives were nodding at this compliment.

"Now is the time to look forward to the next station, and the other goals of space exploration," Leon continued.

"We all know you want to create a colony on Mars," Sadako said sharply. "What we don't know is why you need our station to do that."

Leon smiled down at her. "Is that how you all feel?" he asked the whole room.

Nearly everyone nodded while a few expressed verbal agreements.

"Well, I think my assistant Liz can answer that."

He turned to her, and she froze, unsure what he wanted her to say. The twinkle in his eyes helped calm her.

"Why don't you tell them what you told me six weeks ago."

"About the station?"

"Before that," Leon said. "I told you I wanted to take a trip into space to prove it was safe. I was picturing a trip like Yuri Gagarin, just go up, look around, orbit the Earth, and come back down. But you told me that wouldn't be enough."

Liz shook her head. "No. That's been done. One billionaire going into space won't prove anything to the average person. I told you you'd have to take more people with you."

"Exactly," Leon said. "Untrained people, "astrotourists," if you will, going into space to prove it's safe."

One of the Europeans gasped. "You want to send tourists to the International Space Station?" he shouted. "That's preposterous."

Leon smiled back at him. "Are you saying it isn't safe?"

"Of course not!" the European man shot back, "but to take untrained personnel on the station! It's not worth the risk."

"Tell me something," Leon said. "How many people can the station accommodate?"

"We've never had more than ten people on board," Sadako said.

"And it takes three to run the station, yes?" Leon said.

Many heads nodded.

"What I'm proposing is to bring six tourists aboard the station for one week, along with a chaperone, to keep them out of trouble. They would have to agree to any stipulations you created."

"It would cost millions to get them there, and a million more just to feed and house them," one of the NASA reps shot back.

"I think I can find a few people willing to pay that for a week in space," Leon said with a smile.

Several people laughed, and soon, everyone was laughing.

"I don't think it matters what the price tag is," one of the Canadians shot back. "People will pay millions for a trip like that. The real issue is whether it is safe for them as well as the scientists running the station. Don't think you're the first person to propose using the ISS as a tourist attraction."

Leon shook his head. "This isn't just about earning a few extra dollars for the next station. This is about international relations and the future of space exploration. Many objected when President Obama proposed the privatization of space launches. Yet we've far exceeded every expectation they've thrown at us. We've brought interest back to space that hasn't been seen in fifty years."

"You mean *you've* drawn their interest," Sadako said.

"And now I'm trying to do that again," Leon agreed.

"Why?" Sadako shot back. "What do you get out of it, and why should we care?"

"Why should you care?" Leon repeated. "Why should you care? Where does your funding come from?"

"Our respective governments," a NASA woman said. "You know that."

"And what will happen if the people of the world lose interest in space?" Leon shot back.

"We'll lose funding," a Canadian said.

"Exactly. You need this to keep the money flowing. Not just the few million you'll get from the visitors, but from the confidence of the people of the world. That's why you need to open the station up to a few tourists a year."

"They'd have to endure at least forty hours of training, just to meet minimum safety protocols," Sadako said.

Leon nodded. "Granted. That seems reasonable. Some sort of minimal training program. What else?"

Liz watched as the meeting moved from whether they were willing to agree to what conditions must be placed on the astrotourists. Leon's ability to control a room was truly amazing. She knew they'd all agree to this harebrained scheme, it was only a matter of setting forth the right protocols and deciding on the price tag.

Gideon's Apocryphal Assignment

October 15th - Notre Dame, Indiana

Gideon Shumway studied the assignment sheet while he waited for the class to start. Only one month into the semester, and the professor was already assigning a term paper. He thought a course on prophecy would be an easy A. After all, he just had to come up with some mumbo jumbo and claim it was the way he interpreted the prophecy, right? No one really knew what these ancient prophets meant, did they?

How many people claimed the Great American Eclipse signaled the doom of America? Yet here they were, more than a year later. Sure, there had been natural disasters, and more than once President Towers had almost started World War III, but they got through it.

"I'm glad to see you all picked up the instruction sheet for your term papers," Professor Jenkins said. "I want to call your attention to a few items on the sheet, so there will be no misunderstanding."

Gideon set the paper down and yanked out his notebook and pen. The rest of the class was pulling out their laptops, but he found he remembered the information better if he hand-wrote it instead of typing it.

"I see I got your attention," Jenkins said. "Good. First of all, this paper will constitute half of your final grade in this course."

"Half?" someone shouted out.

"Yes, half," Jenkins confirmed. "That is why it must be at least ten thousand words long, which is about twenty pages. Secondly, I'm banning you from using anything in the books of Daniel, Revelation, or Ezekiel. Analysis of those books is too readily available online. They've been studied by better minds than yours, and I don't want to be reading someone else's work on the subject. I want original thoughts, not regurgitated drivel."

He paused and looked around the classroom as if expecting an objection. When none came, he continued. "If you dare to use the book of Isaiah, remember that he speaks in poetic form, so you'll have to back up your conclusions with an explanation of the context in Hebrew literature. For those of you who are less adventurous, I've included a list of acceptable prophecies to study on the back of the sheet."

Gideon flipped it over at the same time as the rest of the class. He gasped. There were over two hundred scripture references on the back, some with names he didn't recognize like Esdras.

"I'm sure a few of you are noticing references to books you've never studied before," Professor Jenkins continued. "Rest assured I have studied them all. The goal here isn't to figure out the right interpretation, but to analyze the prophecies themselves, giving interpretations only when you can find solid historical evidence of their fulfillment. You'll be graded based on your understanding of the person who wrote it, how the book has transformed through history, and what it means to you today. I expect a lot of cross-referencing, which is why I'm giving you this assignment today."

Gideon wasn't sure what to make of the assignment, except that it would take him months to decide which prophecy he wanted to stake half his grade on.

"One last thing before we move into the lesson," Professor Jenkins said. "To avoid duplication, only one person will be allowed to tackle each of the prophecies listed on the sheet. I expect you to submit your top three choices within one week, and my TA's will let you know which one you get, based on a first-come-first-served."

Gideon gasped, along with several other students. He quickly pulled out his phone and composed an email to the class TA's, indicating his top three choices as Matthew 24, 2 Esdras 11-12, or 2 Esdras 13-14. He knew Matthew 24 really well, but he'd never heard of the other two. He'd just thrown them in there so he had three on his list, hoping he'd be the first to claim his favorite.

When he rechecked his phone at the end of the class, he found a reply waiting for him.

"Matthew 24 is taken. Good luck with 2 Esdras 11-12!"

He groaned and stuffed his scriptures and notebook back in his bag along with his laptop. How was he supposed to write twenty pages on two chapters which might not even be from a true prophet? Perhaps he could take the angle of discrediting the text.

As he left the room, Professor Jenkins stopped him. "Gideon, I noticed you signed up for 2 Esdras 11 12."

"Yes, sir," Gideon said, trying to keep the disappointment off his face.

93

"You need to know that's a particular favorite of mine from the Apocrypha.[33] Don't waste your time trying to tell me it talks about ancient Rome, okay?" [34]

Gideon just nodded his head slightly and said, "Sure. Thanks."

Jenkins smiled and winked at him. "I'll bet you've never read it before, have you?"

Gideon shook his head.

"Well, no matter. I'm sure you'll do fine."

Scott's Obsession

October 18th - San Mateo, California

Four weeks of taking the Waymo self-driving car service gave Scott Knox more time in his day to peruse the news and Facebook. Work was still a drudge and a disappointment, but he knew that until Tonya's network grew back to its former glory, he had to help make ends meet.

He'd become a devoted follower of Mark Folger, a right-wing blogger who focused on the dangers of the Towers administration, with the occasional conspiracy theory about how the Democratic Party was destroying America. His best friend Kevin had suggested the site and was a frequent commenter. Sure, Towers was technically a Republican, but he hadn't really earned his place like all those in Congress.

To make matters worse, Folger wrote, *he's recruiting others who think like him. People who've never run for public office before suddenly have a shot at being a Senator or a Congressman if they think like Towers. The chaos of the last eighteen months will be nothing compared with what Towers will do if his brand of Republicanism gains enough strength.*

"I'm just one man," Scott said to himself. "What can any of us do?"

He carried his dark mood inside with him where Tonya waited with a frown on her face. "Why are you always in such a grumpy mood when you get home?" she asked.

"I'm sorry, honey, but the world is going crazy." He shut the door and sat down on the couch, looking for the remote.

"Have things at work been slow?"

"Not really. Wally quit yesterday, so now I have more work than I can handle." He found the remote in the couch caddy he'd gotten for his birthday. "They're going to have to hire someone else, or we're going to fall behind on the orders." He turned the TV on and dialed in Fox News where they were talking about the various candidates on the ballot.

Tonya stood in front of the TV. "You still have some explaining to do."

Scott let out a huge sigh and looked up at his wife. "What is it?"

"I want to know why you're so grumpy every day. Do you miss your truck that much?"

Scott tried to listen to the news and only half caught what she said. "What? My truck? No, I don't really miss that eight hundred dollar a month expense. It's the blog posts I read on the way home. They get me so angry."

She bit her lower lip for a moment, which Scott quickly learned to interpret as her feeling something deeply, usually anxiety. "This is just how it started, you know."

He cocked his head to the side for a second. "How what started? The Civil War?"

"No!" she shouted, making him look up at her. "My parents' divorce," she said softly. "Dad came back from work angry every day for months, and then one day he didn't come home."

Scott sat there for a minute, confused at how the conversation had taken such a left turn. She never talked about her father, even when Scott asked. It was a taboo topic. "I love you. You have to know that. I'm not going to leave you. But I do have to stay informed, and that blog is the fastest way to do that. It's not Folger's fault he has nothing but bad news to share."

She scowled down at him. "You're letting someone's rant on the internet ruin your evenings? How is that fair to me?"

"What are you saying? You want me to just ignore what's going on?"

She rolled her eyes. "I want you to tell me how reading all that stuff helps you. What good does it do you?"

"It keeps me informed of what's going on."

"Alright. Tell me, what's going on."

Scott turned the TV off and stood up. "The Democrats are tearing apart the Constitution with their socialist agenda, and the Towers administration is destroying what's left with his chaotic actions and destructive policies. What's worse, there's a decent chance he's going to get enough people just like him into the House and the Senate to push through anything he wants."

"That's what Folger talks about?" Tonya asked as her eyebrows furrowed. "Nothing specific about what to do or who to vote for?"

Scott shook his head. "It's a national blog. He can't list every candidate he supports."

"Well, I'm heading out with the girls in a few minutes, and you're on your own for dinner."

"What? Is that tonight?"

"Yes. It's the third Thursday, just like every month. While I'm gone, I want you to seriously think about finding a better way to use your time than reading useless, angry blog posts." She shook one finger at him as if scolding a child.

"What? You want me to stop being informed?" Scott waved his arms as if to encompass the world.

"Not everything you read on the internet is true, you know." She grabbed her keys off the hook.

"Folger's been spot on." He tapped one finger into the palm of his other hand for emphasis. "Most of what he talks about ends up on the mainstream news the next day."

"I don't care!" She flapped her arms in frustration, and the keys went flying. They almost hit Scott. Tonya let out a long sigh as she walked over and picked them up. When she stood back up, she got right in his face. "Look, you need to do some serious soul-searching. I expect you to be happy and friendly when you're here." She backed off and opened the door. "If you can read that blog and still give me an affectionate hug and kiss when you get home, then you go ahead and read it. But otherwise, you need to decide what's most important."

She slammed the door behind her, knocking their wedding picture askew.

Scott stood there for a minute, staring at the door. He thought they'd fought before, but it was nothing compared to this. She was usually so quick to back off until cooler heads prevailed. That was usually his sign to approach the situation differently and consider that he might be wrong.

This was nothing like that. She didn't back down, she didn't get quiet, and she certainly didn't leave calmly. Of all the issues to pick a real fight over, he didn't understand how she could just bury her head in the sand about all this. One thing was for sure. He needed to make a few changes in his life.

Scott's Great Idea

November 2nd - San Mateo, California

Scott Knox was on his way to work on a Friday morning a couple of weeks later. Mornings were now his blog reading time, and the ride home was reserved for catching up with friends. That way, he was usually in a good mood when he got home. It also meant there were dozens of comments on Folger's blog on Friday morning, instead of only a few.

Last night's blog, as expected, focused on the election, which was only a few days away. The latest polls showed Towers' selected politicians all had sizeable leads. There were enough of them to give the Republicans an even bigger lead, and possibly give Towers control of the entire party.

As he switched over to his email, he saw Kevin was reaching out again with a subject line of *"Get paid for political action!"* He opened the email.

Hey, Scott. I heard you still don't have another truck. What a bummer. If you need some extra cash, this might help. I've been using it to make some side money for a while now. Berkeley isn't a cheap school to attend.

It was followed by a link to a news article, and a caption that read, *"Is Towers' Money Buying America?"*

He clicked on the link and read a news article listing all the donations Towers had made to the various campaigns, as well as the uber-rich supporters who had supposedly paid for Towers' campaign. He was a billionaire in his own right, but the list of supporters each had ten or twenty times Towers' net worth. They could afford to do almost anything they set their mind to, and from the information in the news article, they had set out to take over America, backed by the big-business lobbies.

It went on to say one unnamed billionaire was willing to fight back. He was using his money to fund right-wing protesters who otherwise couldn't afford airfare or time off work to march on the streets of Washington, D.C. or even their local capitol building. There was even a link to sign up as a protestor. He clicked on the link and entered his contact information. Then he saw there were several protests scheduled in California on Tuesday, and he signed up to join.

He'd finally found a way to contribute, a way to fight back. He was going to do his part to show the world what he really believed. Maybe Tonya would join him.

That thought made him practically float through his day with a skip in his step he hadn't felt in years. Even the ride home through heavy traffic didn't bother him as he imagined Tonya's reaction.

He entered their home with a smile on his face and grabbed Tonya in a big bear hug as he gave her a kiss.

"Well, you're in a good mood," she said when she could breathe again. "What's gotten you all excited?"

"I found a way to take action instead of just talking about it. I'm going to do my part to show the country that we don't agree with the new political agenda of President Money."

She pulled herself away from him until they were at arm's length. "Please don't tell me you're going to join one of those awful, violent protests."

Scott frowned. "Well, I was hoping *we* would do it together."

She closed her eyes and shook her head before taking a couple of breaths. This was a sure sign she was about to launch into a very loud explanation of his faults.

"I thought you'd be happy about this," he said, hoping to forestall the storm.

Her eyes flew open, filled with fire. "How could you possibly think I would approve of you taking the day off work, so you can march around shouting stupid slogans? How could you think I would want to join you in a pointless effort that is likely to end in violence? Do you know how many times people get hurt at those rallies? My brother Victor was in the hospital for a week after going to one of those things.

"It's like someone is actually paying the idiots to cause trouble. Half of those people don't have jobs, or perhaps protesting *is* their job. I mean, does anyone actually think throwing a stink bomb or a flaming bottle of gasoline is going to convince the other side to see their point of view? No. It's just going to encourage more people to vote for whatever the violent protesters are against. No husband of mine is going to join in such mindless mobocracy."

Scott tried to get a word in, but she spoke so fast, there was barely enough time to hear what she said. He'd also learned quickly not to try and speak over her. That only made things worse. He stood there, listening to her rant, confused by her angry reaction to what he'd hoped would be happy news.

She finally took a breath and said, "Don't you have anything to say for yourself?"

He shook his head. "I think you've covered everything I was going to say and more." He turned and walked away, into the den, slamming the door behind him. He hated when she tried to control him and tell him what to do. He refused to be her puppet or give up on his passions just because someone else she knew had been hurt in the past.

They were struggling financially and needed the extra income. This was a way he could kill two birds with one stone. He opened his laptop, signed into his VPN, and within a few minutes, his name was on the list for two more protests.

Frank Baldwin's First Allegiance

November 6th - Washington, D.C.

Frank Baldwin shook Gary Sanders' hand as he entered the private room of B Too, three hours before they were scheduled to open.

"Thank you for agreeing to meet with me," Frank said.

"That's not the right handshake," Sanders said.

"But, Gary, you know me," Frank said.

"Our meeting today is too important not to follow protocol. Even with a trusted friend."

He nodded and submitted to the ritual handshake, giving the proper responses and gestures. "I suppose there is a reason you wanted to meet today?" Frank asked as he sat.

Sanders scowled at him as he sat. "You should already know you meet on *our* timetable, not the other way around."

"Of course," Frank said, swallowing hard. He wasn't making a good impression. "I was more concerned with the possibility of someone reporting the two of us meeting on election day."

Sanders cracked a smile. "I haven't worried about the media for a long time now, and if I like what you have to say, neither will you."

Frank cleared his throat as he gathered his wits. He knew Sanders was the man behind the media. He had more control over the headlines than anyone. "Then why don't we get right down to it. I'm assuming your friend has already filled you in on my request, or else you wouldn't be here."

"He has," Sanders said. "It's quite a bold request, and I have to wonder about the timing."

"Nothing to wonder about," Frank said. "I can see the way the tide is flowing. I know what we're trying to do, and I'm asking to be the guy to step in when the time is right."

Sanders smiled. "Very well said. However, before I grant your request, I need to know that you can do what needs to be done to help us get there."

"I'm entirely committed," Frank said. "How could you even question my loyalty?"

Sanders frowned. "I've had a dozen people ask for my help to make them President, and I haven't agreed to a single one. What makes you different?"

Frank gasped at the thought. He knew at least three of the last five Presidents were helped by Sanders, and he'd assumed they were the ones to make the request. At the same time, he wondered whose Presidential hopes had been dashed. His mind raced as to what they might have lacked, which he possessed. Finally, he spat out, "Of course I want power. We all do. I've dedicated my life to be the first head of the Dark Eagle. But I know that if I get what I want, I still have others to answer to, same as always. Being called the most powerful man in the world doesn't really make it so."

Frank paused, gauging Sanders' reaction. His frown didn't vanish, but he didn't say anything. Frank's mind raced for something more he could add, but nothing came to mind.

"What is your proficiency level?" Sanders asked.

"Fifty-four," Frank said automatically. He'd worked hard to get there, knowing that many in his position let their proficiencies slide when they had the kind of power they wanted. Very few who followed the Shadow Council ever rose above fifty, and sixty-two was the minimum to get on the council itself.

"Fifty-four," Sanders repeated. "You know if you're lying ..."

"I know the consequences for boasting," Frank cut him off. "I reached level fifty-four six months ago."

"You've been a Congressman for how long now?"

"Sixteen years."

"Yet you're still advancing in your proficiencies?"

Frank nodded, trying to decide if Sanders approved of or despised his continued progress.

Finally, Sanders laughed, breaking the tension. "I like you, Frank. I think we can work together."

Protesting Political Polls

November 6th - Sacramento, California

Scott Knox marched up and down the sidewalk in front of the California State Capitol holding a sign that read, *"Down with Towers"* and shouting "Tell Towers no! Tracy must go!" along with hundreds of others in two camps. Everyone on his side wore red hats, while the others wore blue. For once, the two parties had something they could agree on. Towers had to be stopped.

"Hey, Scott! You made it!" Kevin said as he walked up.

"You bet I did. I've been here all day."

"Really? I thought you still had a J-O-B."

Scott laughed. "I took the day off, voted as soon as the polls opened, then took a Waymo all the way here. That site you sent me pays by the hour."

"Yeah, I knew that, but the pay isn't that great."

"Are you kidding me? I used a small portion of the Litecoin I received for signing up for the rally to cover the fare here. They gave me half up front, and I get the other half tomorrow after the protest. All I had to do was check in with the rally manager."

"I know how the system works," Kevin said, "but how can you afford to take the entire day off for this?"

"I'm getting paid three times what I would have earned at work today, even after I pay for the long cab rides."

"Really? I didn't realize your job sucked that badly."

"$150 a day isn't a bad wage."

"Maybe if you're straight out of high school," Kevin said with a nasty smile. "When I graduate college, I'm hoping to make at least twice that from day one."

Scott scowled back and shouted with the group, "Tell Towers no! Tracy must go!"

"So, what did Tonya say when you told her you were taking the day off work to march around holding a sign?"

"I didn't tell her. She doesn't need to know."

"How do you figure that one?" Kevin asked. "You take a day off work, and you don't think your wife will find out?"

"Why should she?"

"I don't know. I just thought married couples always knew those things."

Scott set down his sign for a second to look Kevin straight in the eyes. "If you tell her, I will kill you."

Kevin threw up his gloved hands. "Don't look at me! I don't talk to her. I meant she might notice when your paycheck is a little light."

"She won't care when I supplement it with what I made here today."

"That reminds me, did you get a new truck?"

Scott shook his head as he hoisted up the sign and shouted with the group, "Tell Towers no! Tracy must go!"

"Then how did you get here?"

"I told you, I took a Waymo. Their self-driving cars are nice. I spent the whole ride up here catching up on the latest polls and predictions. Over the weekend several more Republicans and Independents have pledged their loyalty to President Towers' agenda, hoping to get a boost in the polls."

"Yeah, I read that too. It seems to be working for some of them, but if Towers' doesn't believe them, he sends out a nasty tweet, and they drop at least a few points in the polls."

Scott shook his head. "One sentence tweeted by the wrong man has the power to destroy the dreams of some of these politicians. No man should have that much power, not even the President of the United States."

"I hear you on that."

"Tell Towers no! Tracy must go!" they both chanted with the group.

"There's a lot more Democrats here than Republicans," Scott said.

"Yeah. California's always been a pretty blue state."

"Then why does Tracy even have a shot?"

"He switched to the Independent ticket when he lost the primary," Kevin said.

"You're telling me that a no-name like Shawn Tracy can rival a twenty-six-year veteran of the Senate like Finkelstein, just because he runs as an independent?"

"That's the world we live in. The Democrats are having troubles of their own."

Scott shook his head. "Tracy wouldn't have a prayer without Towers' money. He's outspent Greer, who's backed by the GOP."

"There's no proof his campaign is backed by Towers' money," Kevin said.

"Well, obviously not Towers directly, but certainly one of the big business people who do what he says."

"I'm still not convinced."

Scott scowled. "That's what's so sinister about a conspiracy. There's never enough proof to convince people. Otherwise, it would be called a crime. Similar stories are playing out across the country today. Half of Towers' new lackeys lost their primary, only to pop up on the Independent ticket, or some other third-party. The man is almost unstoppable."

"Tell Towers no! Tracy must go!" They both chanted with the group.

"Say, that's a nice sign. Did you make it?"

"No," Scott said. "The organizer gave it to me. They've got plenty more."

"I'd better go get one."

Gideon's Girl Next Door

November 6th - Notre Dame, Indiana

Gideon Shumway made it to the polling place and cast his vote before his first class. He didn't pay much attention as Professor Jenkins went over Joseph's prophecy of seven years of plenty followed by seven years of famine. Instead, Gideon was focused on a girl in the front row. He'd been trying to decide how to ask her out for the past two weeks. If he didn't do it today, he never would.

As soon as the lecture ended, he walked quickly down the stairs, arriving in front of her desk just as she was standing up. "Karen?" Gideon asked sheepishly.

"Yes." She looked up at him, her beautiful blue eyes were perfectly framed by her blonde hair.

"Would you, that is, I'd like to, I mean . . ." The words just wouldn't come.

"You're really sweet," Karen said, "but I don't think it's going to happen."

Gideon's mouth hung open as she walked off. He heard laughter behind him and turned around.

Professor Jenkins put one hand on his shoulder as he said, "At least you had the guts to try. I hope you're more articulate in your essay on Ezra's Eagle." [35]

"Me too," Gideon said. If he hadn't read the two chapters in the Second Book of Esdras, he might have been confused by the name. Instead, it was only the prophecy that confused him. "Though I don't know how I'm going to sort out the wings and the feathers. They seem to be interchangeable in the prophecy."

"Hmm," Jenkins said. "How many different translations of it have you read?"

"You mean there's more than one?"

Jenkins shook his head. "You're Mormon, right?"

Gideon nodded.

"You've probably stuck with the King James Version your whole life. It's about time you learned that the rest of the Christian world has several other translations to choose from. The same is true for the Apocrypha. Try reading more than one version before you jump to conclusions." He picked up his briefcase and left.

Gideon hung his head as he headed to his next class.

Scott's Sacramento Skirmish

November 17th - Sacramento, California

Scott Knox marched around the state capitol building with the rest of the protestors, carrying his sign reading, *"Tracy Tricked Us!"* Shawn Tracy had beat Finklestein to become the junior senator from California with only thirty-nine percent of the popular vote. Tempers were high for both groups of protestors as they marched in opposite directions, keeping ten feet between the groups.

The groups swelled as the morning went on, and the distance between them shrank. Scott began to worry that the two groups would soon be too large to share the same space and considered heading home early. He had to leave by three to get home in time for a special dinner out to celebrate Tonya's birthday. He decided to leave by two, giving himself an extra hour in case of traffic.

Half the fun of these protests was supposed to be his time spent with Kevin, who promised he'd be there by eleven. Noon came and went, but there was no sign of his friend. As noon stretched into the afternoon, Scott's arms grew tired from holding the sign, yet he persevered. This was a cause worth fighting for.

Kevin finally arrived at two, along with a busload of red-clad protestors. For the first time all day, there were more Republicans than Democrats, and the blue-clad mob definitely took notice. Scott was ready to head home, but decided to stay for another fifteen minutes, just so he could talk with Kevin.

As the two groups passed each other again, less than three feet separated them. Someone in blue shouted, "Go home, you bums! Tracy stole the seat from us, not you!"

"Greer would have become Senator without Tracy!" Scott shouted back as the two groups separated. Greer got twenty-nine percent of the vote and Finklestein thirty-two. Scott had spent hours analyzing the election results and was convinced the vast majority of votes for Tracy would have gone for Greer without Towers' interference.

The groups separated again on their march around the building. By the time the two groups met on the other side of the capitol, the Democrats were chanting, "Finkelstein forever!"

Scott paused a moment, feeling a little tired from carrying the sign all day. He soon fell to the back of the group. Kevin fell back with him.

As Scott passed the middle of the group of Democrats, one person stopped and glared at Scott. He was a dozen yards or so ahead of Scott, just standing there with his fists clenched. As they got closer, Scott realized it was the man who'd shouted earlier. He just stood there, staring at Scott as the rest of the blue-clad army marched on.

As Scott passed the man's position, the blue soldier marched over the Scott and punched him in the face.

Scott fell backward, hitting his head on the sidewalk and dropping his sign.

Kevin was right there, shoving the blue-clad bully back. The two of them exchanged a couple of blows before the rest of the Republicans turned around and grabbed the attacker. His screams of fright brought the rest of the Democrats into the fray, and the protest devolved into chaos.

"We've got to get out of here!" Kevin said as he helped Scott to his feet.

A loud ringing in Scott's ears almost drowned out Kevin's words. The ground wouldn't stay still, swaying back and forth beneath him. Kevin had to support him all the way to the car.

The shouts and screams of the protesters increased as the police ran forward with fire hoses.

"Good timing! I'm glad we got out of there when we did," Scott said.

"Dude! You're bleeding all over my seat."

Scott reached around to touch the back of his head and instantly wished he hadn't. A wave of pain and nausea accompanied the lightest touch. He looked around. *I'm in a car*, he thought. *Where do I find a towel?*

"Are you okay, man?" Kevin pressed.

"Where do I find a towel?" Scott asked.

"Here, take some napkins!" Kevin handed him a thick stack of napkins from a dozen different fast-food places.

"I think I'll be okay. I'm just kind of tired." Scott looked down at the napkins in his hand. It took him a moment to remember they were for the bleeding gash on the back of his head. Pain laced through him again as he pressed the pile of napkins to the wound, but he held them there, despite the pain. His eyelids felt heavy, and they started to close.

"Don't you dare pass out on me!" Kevin shouted as he sped past a truck on the highway.

Scott watched as they weaved through and passed up cars and trucks alike. Either traffic was going really slow, or Kevin was going really fast. "Slow down. We don't want to end up in the hospital."

"That's exactly where I'm taking you. You need to get that head wound checked. I think you might have a concussion."

"No. No hospitals. Tonya can't know where I was." There was something else really important, but Scott couldn't remember it clearly. He just knew there was some other reason he couldn't go to the hospital.

"What did you tell her? Where does she think you are?"

"Fishin'."

"Oh, that's just great. Now my parents' boat is part of this conspiracy."

"Every time," Scott confirmed. "Always fishin'."

"I'll make you a deal. You don't pass out, and I won't take you to the hospital. Okay?"

Scott tried to nod but decided against it. "Deal."

They kept up a running dialog for the next hour, ranging over every subject from the success of the rally to the right kind of bait to use in cold weather. As they were crossing the George Miller Jr. bridge, Kevin asked, "Any big plans tonight?"

"Yes," Scott said. Exhaustion filled his toes and started creeping upward.

"Oh? Going out with Tonya?"

"Uh-huh." Scott couldn't remember why, only that it was very important.

Kevin paused before asking, "Where are you going?"

"The Chess Facty." The words refused to come out right.

"Um … What's the Chess Factory? Is that a play?"

Scott shook his head. The exhaustion reached his eyes, and he couldn't keep them open any longer.

"Scott? Scott!"

Tonya's Birthday Pain

November 17th - San Mateo, California

Tonya Knox sipped her third glass of Dr. Pepper, wishing for the first time in her life that it was wine, or possibly something stronger. The waiter at the Cheesecake Factory was eager to take her order, as she'd been there for an hour, and he'd stopped by every five minutes for the last thirty minutes. Still no sign of Scott.

Brenda waved from across the restaurant and quickly made her way to Scott's vacant seat. "I got your text and came as soon as I could. He totally bailed on you tonight?"

Tonya nodded. "He's been acting strange lately, too. I made it clear he needed to be here tonight, that this was very important. Yet he's not answering his phone."

"Do you think it's another woman?" Brenda asked.

"Another woman? No. I don't think so. Just because Bruno left you for another woman doesn't mean every guy is a cheater."

"No, of course not," Brenda replied. It was hard for Tonya to tell when she was being sarcastic.

Yet the thought wouldn't leave Tonya's mind, despite her quick objection. She ruminated over it while the waiter took their orders.

"Is he ever gone overnight?" Brenda asked. "That's always a dead giveaway."

"No. Well, except for his fishing trips with Kevin. They've gone twice in the last month."

"Fishing? In November?"

"Yes. Kevin has a boat, and they go out on the ocean for a couple of days at a time."

"And does he come back with fish?"

"No. Are you kidding me? I 'm not going to cook those things. Kevin always keeps what they catch."

The waiter brought out their order of hot spinach and cheese dip.

Brenda scooped up the dip onto a chip and ate it slowly before asking, "Does he even smell like the ocean?"

Tonya let the flavors of her own chip and dip play across her tongue as she thought back on the last few fishing trips. "No. He showers as soon as he gets in. Two men alone on a boat for a couple days? I don't want to smell that."

Brenda nodded knowingly as she grabbed another chip. She didn't say anything, just gave Tonya a knowing look as she enjoyed the appetizer.

Tonya scowled back. "Okay, I get your point. I still don't think it's another woman."

"But he's up to *some*thing."

"Definitely. And whatever it is, it's more important than my birthday. I can't take much more of this, Brenda. I really can't."

The waiter brought their main course, and they fell quiet for a while. Her phone buzzed, but she didn't recognize the number, so she ignored it.

When Brenda's plate was half-emptied she said, "Have you talked to a divorce attorney yet?"

Tonya almost choked on the pasta in her mouth. After a hard swallow and a long drink of soda, she finally said, "What? I'm not going to divorce him!"

"No, of course not. He's been acting strange, going on mysterious fishing trips with his old friends, but bringing home no evidence that he's gone fishing, and now he's missed your birthday dinner without explanation. Why would you possibly consider divorce?"

Tonya didn't know what to say. She didn't feel like she'd reached the point of considering divorce, but Brenda laid out a pretty good case. She had to know what Scott was up to. If he was doing drugs or sleeping with someone else, she'd have to protect herself. "There's more," she said softly.

Brenda put her silverware down with an uneaten bite on her fork. "You've been holding out on me?"

"I didn't think it was related," Tonya explained, "but it could be part of the pattern."

"Don't leave me in suspense! What else has he done?"

Tonya paused, trying to decide how to bring it up. She almost didn't want to admit it to herself. Her phone rang again. She looked down at it and saw it was the same number. Annoyed, she marked the caller as spam and shoved her phone deep into her purse.

Looking back up at Brenda, she blurted out, "He knows I've been working hard to rebuild my network. Six months from now, he should be able to quit his job and go back to playing with his apps or whatever. Right now, we need his income just to make ends meet. Yet his paychecks have been smaller lately. I called his boss and found out he's been skipping work at least once a week. One time there was a mysterious deposit into our account, and he just said it was a bonus."

"I thought you said he worked a blue-collar job."

Tonya nodded. "He dreams about inventing some revolutionary new app, but the best he's come up with is a secure texting service that will read the message out loud. It's been downloaded like twenty times. That's why he has that job cutting lumber."

"What kind of lumber mill gives bonuses to the wood-cutters?"

Tonya shook her head. "Especially to someone who cancels a shift almost every week."

"Every week? Bruno did the same thing. He skipped work every Tuesday to be with *her*."

"But Scott hates his job, and we both know it. I wouldn't be surprised if he told me he's been skipping work to go to job interviews."

Brenda raised her eyebrows. "Job interviews? Is that what you're telling yourself now?"

Tonya dropped her head into her hands, overwhelmed by how silly it sounded out loud. "Ugh. How could I be so stupid?"

"Oh, Tonya, I'm so sorry. What are you going to do?"

"I don't know." She took a few more bites, chewing on the conversation as much as the food. Then she made the hardest decision of her life. "Just in case it is another woman, what was the name of your divorce lawyer?"

The background music stopped for a moment, replaced by a female voice saying, "Tonya Knox, please come see the hostess."

Brenda raised her eyebrows. "Do you think he's here?"

Tonya shrugged. "I don't know, but he'd better have a good explanation." She walked slowly up to the front of the restaurant, expecting to see Scott standing there with some kind of apology on his lips. *He'd better have flowers.*

But Scott wasn't there. She looked around before turning to the hostess. "I'm Tonya Knox."

"Great. I have a call for you."

"Don't tell me my husband phoned in his apology."

The hostess shook her head. "There is a call for you, but not from Mr. Knox. It's not even a guy, I think."

Tonya scowled as she took the phone from the hostess. "This is Tonya Knox."

"Oh, thank goodness," a deep female voice said. "I've been trying to reach you for ten minutes."

"Who is this?"

"My name is Toni Jones. I'm a nurse at Alta Bates Summit Medical Center. You're listed as the emergency contact for Scott Knox."

"Yes. Scott is my husband."

"Mr. Knox was admitted to the hospital an hour ago. It looks like he has a concussion."

"What! What happened?"

"I don't really know. I've spent the last forty-five minutes trying to figure out how to reach you."

"What's your address? I'll head right over."

Scott Lies in Bed

November 17th - Oakland, California

Brenda drove Tonya Knox to the hospital and helped escort her to the third floor. Tonya scowled at Kevin as she passed him in the lobby by the elevators. She didn't know what had happened, but she was sure it was Kevin's fault.

Her anger melted away as she came to Scott's bed. He was unconscious with the monitors hooked up. Tears poured out as she held his hand. This was a legitimate excuse for missing her birthday dinner. She almost didn't believe it until now, but holding his hand made it real. He lay so motionless she might have thought he was dead if it wasn't for the monitors confirming his heart was still beating.

She sat there for an hour, sorting through her emotions. Anger at all the time he'd spent away from her and his job, relief that he was still alive, frustration that she couldn't yell at him, ask him questions, or even tell him how much she loved him.

This was just like when her brother Victor had been hurt in one of those violent protests. It took him three days to wake up. She'd blamed him for that, for willingly going to that rally.

But this didn't happen at a political rally. It happened fishing.

The thought took some time to sink in, but when it did, she realized she was transferring her anger toward Victor onto Scott, and that wasn't fair. Scott didn't intentionally put his life in danger. He'd been fishing plenty of times before and never come back injured. It was just a freak accident.

"Oh, Scott. I'm sorry," she whispered.

"Sorry?" Scott said weakly. "Why? What happened?" His eyes fluttered open briefly before he shut them again.

"Scott!" Tonya grabbed the call button and pressed it a dozen times until a man in light purple scrubs came in the room.

"Can I help you?" The nurse gave her a smile as he deactivated the call signal.

"He spoke. He's awake."

The nurse came over to the bed. "Are you sure?"

Just as he asked, Scott rolled his head, his eyes coming open. "Why are you sorry?"

The nurse gave Tonya a smile and said, "Because I didn't believe her." Turning back to Scott, he said, "Mr. Knox, do you know where you are?"

Scott's eyes roamed around, and he tried to sit up.

"Just sit back and relax, Mr. Knox. Do you know where you are?"

"Looks like a hospital. I don't want to be in a hospital. I have to get to the Cheesecake Factory."

Tonya laughed and cried at the same time. If he was already cracking jokes, he was going to be fine.

"Do you know your name?"

"Scott," he said slowly.

"Do you know who the President is?"

"That lousy good for nothing Towers, last time I checked."

"What is the last thing you remember?"

"Kevin and I were . . . " He paused. "Where is Kevin?"

"He's in the lobby. Only family members are allowed until you say otherwise."

"Fishing," Scott said. "We were fishing. I don't remember anything else."

"That's normal with this kind of head injury, Mr. Knox. I'll go let the doctor know you're awake."

Scott nodded, then winced.

"Just lie back and relax. That was a nasty bump you took. You're lucky your friend was able to get you here so quickly."

With the nurse gone, Tonya was alone with Scott once more. "Oh, Scott. I'm sorry. I've spent the last hour blaming you for what happened. It wasn't your fault. Will you forgive me?"

Scott gave a slight nod and said, "Of course. I guess I missed your birthday dinner?"

Tonya smiled and shook her head. "It's okay. You're okay. That's what matters."

Explaining Ezra's Eagle

Thanksgiving Day - Notre Dame, Indiana

"I smell boiling potatoes!" Duane shouted as he came into the apartment.

Gideon Shumway glanced up at him before returning his attention to the laptop where he was furiously typing. "Yeah. They should be ready to mash up. Do you mind doing it? I've got this term paper to finish before I fly out to California tomorrow."

"A term paper? Aren't they due at the end of the term?"

Gideon nodded without looking up. "Yeah, but I can't get this topic out of my head. I'm already ten pages over the assigned length, and I keep finding more connections between this old prophecy and our world today. Besides, the professor said it's a subject he is passionate about, so it has to be good if I want to pass this course."

"You aren't superman," Duane said. "And neither am I. I need your help in the kitchen if we're going to be ready in time.

Besides, don't you think your professor will give you some slack after you win the game against USC?"

"We always crush USC," Gideon shot back. Frustrated at having to take a break, he saved the file and closed the laptop while he asked, "What about you? Why aren't you with your family?"

"They don't celebrate Thanksgiving."

"Is that a Muslim thing?" Gideon stood to look Duane in the eyes.

Duane shook his head. "No. My parents grew up in Syria. They came to the States when I was young, but they never adopted American traditions like Thanksgiving."

"That makes sense."

"Which paper are you working on?"

Gideon walked into the kitchen. The smell of cooked potatoes filled the room, just the first part of their Thanksgiving dinner. He scanned a scrap of paper with the meal plan hanging above the stove to remind himself what he'd agreed to make. This was going to be a pretty big effort for them, so he turned on two more burners before heading to the fridge. "It's an analysis of Ezra's Eagle for my Prophecy class." [36]

Duane followed him into the kitchen. He checked the list, then pulled out a frying pan and filled a pot with water before turning on the oven. They'd worked out a system when they became roommates, and both helped prepare the dinners. Tonight, they were 'feasting' on what they called 'Bachelors' Thanksgiving.' It was less than half what Gideon normally expected for this holiday, but like Duane said, they weren't superheroes.

"What's Ezra's Eagle?" Duane asked.

"It's a prophecy of the Old Testament prophet Ezra about a kingdom in the last days that rules the whole Earth with an eagle as the symbol." [37] Gideon pulled the green beans out of the fridge, followed by two ears of corn.

"Like America?" Duane grabbed a couple of knives and cutting boards, handing one of each to Gideon.

Gideon nodded as he handed the green beans to Duane. "Exactly. My analysis is based on interpreting the twenty feathers or wings as Presidents." [38] He started shucking the corn.

"But there have been more than twice that many." Duane was almost as fast as Gideon in the kitchen when it came to chopping things, and he made short work of the green beans.

"I know. But America didn't rule the world when it was first formed. We can't make that claim until at least after World War I."

"So, it's all the Presidents since Woodrow Wilson?" Duane asked as he poured the beans into one of the pans. Then he grabbed a serving dish and two bags of stuffing mix.

Gideon shook his head again. "No, he comes before the prophecy." He cleaned the two cobs and dumped them in the pot of water which was already getting hot.

"How do you know?" Duane grabbed an onion and started hacking away at it.

"It says the second feather ruled twice as long as any of the others in the prophecy." [39] Gideon grabbed the frozen rolls out of the freezer and put four of them on a baking sheet which he popped in the oven.

"FDR."

"Exactly," Gideon confirmed.

"But why wouldn't it start with Wilson if he could be said to rule the world?" [40] Duane dumped the onion in with the green beans. He added some butter and several herbs and started stirring.

"Well, the best interpretation I've found for the prophecy says that twelve of the first fourteen Presidents on the list are either part of a great conspiracy, or at least didn't fight against it. And I don't think Calvin Coolidge would have gone along with any such nonsense."

"We need more corn and rolls than that," Duane said.

"Why?"

Duane smiled. "I invited a few girls to join us for dinner."

"You did what!"

"I invited Nancy, Teresa, and Karen over for a Thanksgiving feast. They'll be bringing the pies, yams, salad, Jell-O, and turkey. I hope that's okay."

"Karen Emmett?" Gideon asked as he pulled out four more ears of corn and half a dozen rolls. He added the rolls to the oven right away. Duane tried to look surprised, but Gideon saw right through his bad acting and gave him a scathing look.

"Okay, I heard you were interested in her, and I suggested to Nancy she might bring Karen along."

Gideon shucked the extra corn in record time. "She already rejected me, Duane! Does she even know whose house she's coming to?"

Duane nodded. "I made it very clear my roommate was the quarterback for the football team."

Gideon drained the potatoes and started mashing them with more force than necessary. "I can't believe you would do something like this without telling me."

"I only made the arrangements an hour ago," Duane said. "You'll be fine. Maybe don't think of it as a date. Now tell me more about this term paper you're working on."

"Don't try to distract me," Gideon said as he added milk, butter, and spices before mashing them some more. "I need to know what Karen is expecting."

Duane shook his head. "Just be yourself, and everything will be fine."

Gideon scowled at him but didn't press further. There was no way he was going to cancel on Karen. "Well, can you at least tell me when they'll be arriving, so I have enough time to make myself decent?"

"Fifteen minutes. What about the other two?"

"Fifteen minutes? How am I supposed to get ready in time?"

"Once you're done with those potatoes I can handle the rest while you shower," Duane offered. "Now tell me about the other two."

"Other two?"

"You said twelve of the first fourteen Presidents were part of this big conspiracy. What about the other two?" Duane pressed.

"The other two are listed as short feathers, who don't complete their terms as President, around halfway through the list of fourteen."

"Are you talking about Kennedy and Nixon?" [41] Duane asked as he put another pot of water on to boil for the stuffing mix.

Gideon salted the potatoes and stirred them again. "That's right. But I don't see any evidence that JFK or Nixon fought against any great conspiracy."

Duane laughed long and loud. Gideon didn't get the joke and just stared at him. When Duane stopped laughing, he finally matched Gideon's serious look and said, "You really don't know?"

"History was my favorite subject, but I have no idea what you are talking about." Gideon grabbed the cheese he'd shredded earlier out of the fridge and added it to the potatoes. As he did so, he noticed the precooked slices of turkey breast in the fridge, which it looked like they wouldn't need.

"They didn't teach this stuff in history. At least not in my high school."

"Come on, out with it."

Duane swallowed hard. "Kennedy gave a speech about a great conspiracy which some say was trying to control him." [42]

"He what!" The wooden spoon in Gideon's hands broke in half. It wasn't the first time he'd broken a kitchen utensil. He'd have to find sturdier kitchenware.

Duane shook his head. "It's a historical fact that he was set to give another speech the day he died. Some claim he was going to completely expose the conspiracy that day."

"How have I never heard about this before?" Gideon pulled the broken half of the spoon out of the potatoes, making sure there were no splinters left behind. It looked like a pretty clean break.

"I can show you the links if you like, but it's all conspiracy theory stuff."

"So is my paper," Gideon said as he tasted the potatoes. They were just right. Thank goodness he wouldn't have to risk breaking something else to finish them. "I should at least read it before I decide whether I want to use it."

Duane nodded. "Yeah. But not tonight. Go hit the shower while I finish up. That way, you'll be nice and fresh when Karen gets here."

Gideon nodded as he headed to his room. His thoughts shifted from prophecies of doom upon the country to how doomed this date would be. Did she really not know he was the quarterback when she blew him off?

Maria vs. Molotov

Christmas Eve - Washington, D.C.

Maria Croix stared out at the north White House lawn, trying to get a feel for the crowd of protestors gathered on the other side of the fence. She didn't care what they were protesting and ignored their silly chants, other than to acknowledge the bums had a deep-seated personal hatred for the current President of the United States. Hundreds had gathered tonight when they should be finishing up their shopping or spending time with their families.

She'd worked hard to become Assistant Special Agent in Charge (ASAIC) and thanks to this useless protest, she'd had to draft three dozen extra Secret Service agents into cutting their vacations short or delaying them. None of her men were happy at getting the call. Not that any one of them would dare complain to her directly. She kept her earpiece rotating through their coms, hearing what they heard, waiting for something to happen.

She'd noticed an increase in the number of protestors claiming to be Republicans, wearing red hats, scarves, or other items of red, versus the blue hats, scarves, etcetera, worn by the supposed Democrats. Her men kept the two groups far enough apart to prevent any brawls between them, but if violence started, she didn't have enough men to stop it before someone got hurt.

Her earpiece switched to the next agent just in time for her to faintly hear, "I'm telling you, no one will know we were here. We just throw the bottle, and we'll get paid."

"You can't just throw a Molotov cocktail on the White House lawn and expect to get away with it," another voice said.

She checked the frequency and said, "Bronson, you've got a situation brewing. Look for two men with a bottle."

There was a short pause before Agent Bronson replied, "There are a dozen people here with bottles. Can you be more specific?"

"Look for the one with a rag hanging out of the top."

"Crap," Bronson said.

Maria didn't have to ask why as a bottle flew over the fence with a flaming rag trailing behind. It shattered on the grass, and the flames spread.

"Activate sprinklers in zone four," Maria said.

"What, now? It's freezing outside," someone said.

"Just do it."

"Alright, alright." A moment later, the lawn sprinklers came on, which slowly put the flames out.

As soon as the Secret Service started slapping the cuffs on, the crowd scattered. She only hoped they could detain enough people to prove who threw it, so she could ask who was sponsoring domestic terrorism.

Can't Buy Me Love

Christmas Day - San Mateo, California

Scott Knox woke to the vibrations of his phone under his pillow. He looked at it and wondered for a moment why it was going off at four in the morning. Then he remembered his big surprise and quietly crawled out of bed. The Christmas tree lights were blinking on and off, silently keeping rhythm with one of the five Carols programmed into them. He didn't bother trying to figure out which one.

Instead, he went to his den and pulled a dozen wrapped packages out of the closet. He'd skipped at least one day of work every week for the last two months, so he could march around and protest the results of the election. He even got a bonus for the day he got injured. How or why he didn't care. It was enough to pay for most of the extra presents.

So far, he'd managed to keep all that from Tonya, and today was the day he was going to tell her. Today he was going to prove it was worth his time to yell silly slogans while hefting a sign, by showering her with the best Christmas ever.

He'd bought her diamond earrings and a matching necklace, the finest chocolates, and everything on her wish list. All told he'd spent several thousand dollars out of his Litecoin account, yet he'd only spent half of his extra earnings. That was the point, after all, to show her they could return to their former lifestyle while doing something political.

Scott placed each of the packages strategically, so that none of them were immediately noticeable, yet they filled out the space under the tree, taking it from a less than stellar pile to the kind of Christmas every child wants to wake up to. When he was done, he filled their stockings and was just heading back to bed when he saw Tonya standing in the hallway.

"What are you doing up so early?" she asked with a yawn. Her red and white striped pajamas made her look like a giant candy cane.

He smiled sheepishly. "Just filling the stockings. Let's go back to bed."

She looked around the room a moment, wiping the sleep from her eyes as she did so. "I don't remember there being this many presents."

"Yeah. I guess Santa found us this year." Last year they'd lost everything in the Thomas Fire right before Christmas, leaving no money for any presents under the tree.

"Scott, please don't tell me you drained our savings account to buy me more presents."

"No, I didn't. Can't we talk about this at a more decent hour? I want to snuggle."

She frowned at him. "I think you'd better tell me what's going on."

He frowned back. "You really want to have this conversation at five a.m.?"

"You're the one who snuck out of bed so early. I need you to tell me why."

"I told you, so I could fill the stockings."

"And bring out a secret trove of presents," she added. "That's the part I need to know about. Are you having an affair?"

"No, of course not."

She studied him as if trying to decide whether he was telling the truth. Then her stance shifted, and she asked, "How much did you spend?"

This wasn't going the way he'd planned at all. "I didn't take anything out of the checking or savings accounts. I promise."

"Scott," she said slowly. "How much did you spend?"

"Does that really matter?" he shot back. He needed to find a way to derail this fight before it ruined their Christmas.

She shook her head. "I suppose not."

He breathed a sigh of relief.

"What matters is where you got the money. I've been working myself to the bone rebuilding my network while you skip work and bring home smaller paychecks. I wasn't sure we'd be able to keep the lights on this year. Yet you found enough funds to shower me with gifts. So, I need to know where all this came from."

Scott swallowed hard. She wasn't going to let this one go. "I've been working on a side business, and as you can see, it's paid off well."

She walked over and grabbed the first of the extra packages and tore it open.

He cringed as he realized that was the most expensive one.

"You bought me a Kitchen-Aid Series Nine?"

He nodded. "To replace the one we lost in the fire."

"This costs over a thousand dollars. There's no way your apps paid for this. What kind of side business were you doing? Selling drugs?"

Scott rolled his eyes. "Of course not. I would never do that. I just found a way to get paid for doing something I'm passionate about."

Tonya dropped the mixer, missing her foot by inches. "You've been going to those violent protests?"

He nodded again.

"And someone is paying you to take the day off and hold a stupid sign?"

He swallowed hard, knowing she was about to blow. "Yes," he said, barely above a whisper.

"You haven't been fishing, have you?"

He shook his head.

"My birthday dinner too? The injury? It was all from those awful protests?"

He slowly nodded his head, remembering briefly how painful it had been to nod that day.

The fire in her eyes ignited, but instead of yelling at him and letting it out, she stood there while the fire spread. She clenched her hands into fists, and the tension rippled up her arms. When it finally got to her head, she said softly, "I need to leave."

"What! You're leaving on Christmas morning because I bought you everything you asked for?"

"No," she shot back quietly. "I'm leaving because you've clearly lost all sense of priorities. You have no idea what kind of world you've gotten yourself into, and I won't be dragged into it with you. I warned you about those protests, but you wouldn't listen. I know where this is going, and I'm not going to stand around and be your punching bag when things go wrong."

As she spoke she grabbed her purse and her coat and put one hand on the door. "I'm going to my mother's. If you decide to stop risking your life for someone else's agenda, maybe we can figure out how to fix this. If not, you'll be hearing from my divorce lawyer."

"What am I supposed to do without you?" he asked as she opened the door.

"I don't care," she shot back. "I just can't handle seeing you right now. You're disgusting and vile." She slammed the door, and this time their wedding photo fell off its hook onto the floor, shattering the glass in the frame.

Grandma's Cookies and Grandpa's Love

Christmas Day - Nephi, Utah

Gideon Shumway followed his brother Jon and their parents into his grandparents' home a few miles from where he grew up. The wave of heat was welcome as he came in from the cold, and he quickly shut the door behind him. He was grateful to be spending Christmas with family after staying at college over Thanksgiving weekend. At least he'd gotten a girlfriend out of that holiday.

"It's so good to see you," Ruth Shumway called out as her mother embraced her in a hug.

James Tulley grabbed Benjamin Shumway Sr.'s hand for a shake, then pulled him into a quick hug. When Ben Sr. stepped back, James stumbled a bit before grabbing the wall to steady himself.

"You okay, Dad?" Ben Sr. asked.

James waved him off. "I'll be fine. Just got a bit dizzy there. It's not the first time, and it won't be the last. Been tired all morning, too. Guess I didn't sleep well last night."

Gideon and Jon both shucked off their coats while their parents were busy with the grandparents.

"It's so nice of you all to come over," Mabel Tulley said to Ruth. As the hug ended, she looked around and said, "There's one missing. Where is Ben Jr.?"

"Still on his mission in India," Ruth said. "He'll be home in six months."

Mabel nodded then turned to the boys and said, "I just pulled a fresh batch of cookies out, if anyone wants one."

Gideon always felt like a child around Grandma Mabel, and he realized for the first time, it was partly because that's how she treated them.

"What kind?" Jon asked. He was two and a half years older than Gideon, but there'd never been much sibling rivalry between them. Jon was currently working on his Master of Science in Aerospace Engineering at Cal Tech, a far cry from Gideon's Comparative Religion undergraduate studies at Notre Dame.

Mabel smiled back. "Your favorite, of course."

"Oatmeal chocolate chip raisin!" Jon said with enthusiasm as he rushed into the kitchen.

Gideon took time to hug Grandma and Grandpa Tulley before following Jon. The promised cookies were all at least six inches across and nearly an inch thick. A single cookie was enough for a filling breakfast, and Jon used to eat two or three before school as if he was a linebacker. Yet, Jon was the only boy in the family that didn't play football. Gideon carefully cut one in half and started nibbling on it, trying not to burn his mouth. Once they cooled, they would be perfect for dipping in cold milk. He intended to save the other half of his cookie for dipping.

Jon finished off his first cookie and grabbed a second before heading to the living room to join the conversation. Gideon once more followed, still working on his first half cookie.

"Well, I don't see why you'd want to celebrate it," Grandpa Tulley said to Ben Sr. "I didn't want to retire in the first place."

"You retired?" Gideon asked. "When did that happen?"

"Back in February," Grandpa said. "Management said it was either a voluntary retirement or a severance package. Everyone eligible for Social Security got the same speech."

"It's been nice having him around this past year," Grandma said. "I just wish he would pick up after himself more now that he's got the time."

"Grandma, why didn't you ever teach Mom to make these cookies?" Jon asked. "They're fantastic."

"How else was I supposed to get you to come over?" Grandma shot back.

Jon blushed.

Grandpa gave her a wry smile and shook his head. "You can't expect an old dog to learn new tricks that quickly." He turned to Gideon and said, "I caught your last game, Gid. You really tore up those Trojans."

"Thanks, Grandpa. They were pushovers this year. I only got tackled once in the whole game."

They sat in the corner going over the best plays of that game, followed by the rest of the season, while the others chatted away about other things. Grandpa Tulley had an excellent memory when it came to football, and he'd always admired Gideon's performance on the field.

Any time Ben Sr. was too busy coaching to watch his games, Grandpa Tulley was there instead, watching Gideon grow into the man he was now. In some ways, Gideon thought of him as a second father, more than a grandfather.

"With the performance you had this year," Grandpa concluded, "I wouldn't be surprised if a few NFL recruiters join the fans of Notre Dame next season."

Gideon smiled at this. He didn't think it was true, but it was always encouraging to hear. "Thanks. It's also helped win over this girl I was interested in. Sometimes I think she's only dating me because I'm the captain of the football team."

Grandpa opened his mouth to reply, then winced and flexed his right arm.

"Are you okay?" Gideon asked.

"Yeah, I'm just stiff today," Grandpa replied. "And I've got heartburn like you wouldn't believe. Some of the joys of getting old. I just need to stretch my legs."

Gideon frowned. Something about Grandpa's symptoms sounded familiar, and a voice in the back of his head was telling him it was more than heartburn, but he couldn't quite place it.

Grandpa started to stand as he grabbed his chest and cried out. His legs gave way, and he fell to the floor.

"Grandpa!" Gideon shouted.

All conversation ceased as the rest of the room turned to look at them.

"James!" Grandma shouted.

"Dad!" Ruth exclaimed.

Ben Sr. rushed over and rolled Grandpa on his back and checked for a pulse at his neck. "Call 911!" He started CPR and didn't stop until the paramedics arrived and took over.

Ten minutes later, they pronounced his death at 1:45 p.m.

No Answers for Maria

January 2nd - Washington, D.C.

Maria Croix stared at the blank faces of the investigative team with a tight hold on the fury inside her. "How can you tell me that a week after someone threw a Molotov cocktail on the White House lawn that you have no leads?"

There was a brief silence punctuated by a few people swallowing hard. As the Assistant Special Agent in Charge, all these men reported to her. They were dependent on her approval to continue protecting the President. She glared at each one, daring them to give her some sort of excuse for their failure.

Finally, Jenkins said, "Several people were wearing ski masks that day. It was bitter cold."

"Facial recognition software no longer cares about ski masks!" She slammed her fist on the thin report of what they'd learned so far. As far as she was concerned, this was professional incompetence.

"The video can't tell who threw the bottle," Talvert offered. "The view was blocked by the crowd."

Maria sighed heavily, bowing her head in frustration. "We detained a dozen people. You're telling me none of them saw anything suspicious?" Another brief pause was all the answer she needed. "Fine. What about the audio of them discussing being paid to do it?"

"I've gone over that audio with every filter I can think of," Harrison said. "I can't isolate their voices enough to get a voiceprint match. I can't even be sure of what they said."

Maria walked over and stared down at him. In his seat, he was almost as tall as her. She was famous for her intimidation, and size had nothing to do with it. "Are you questioning my statement?"

"No, ma'am," Harrison said right away. "I don't doubt you heard what you say. What I'm saying is I can't isolate the voices who said it. Which means I can't search the voice recognition database or even the regional dialect directory."

"So, what you're telling me is that we have no idea whatsoever as to who burned a full square yard of the lawn on live television?" Another silent pause was all the answer she got. "Did you at least look into who paid him to do it?"

"None of the other agencies replied to your memo," Jenkins said. "They said there was absolutely no chatter on any known channels about payment for the protest on Christmas Eve or any other protest."

"And you just accepted that?" Maria shot back.

"We don't have the resources to . . ." Jenkins began.

"We're talking about the security of the President of the United States!" Her eyes flashed with fire. "Don't tell me we don't have the resources to chase this down! We have to find this person, or it'll happen every week."

"I hate to ask," Talvert said softly, "but did you get approval for the overtime required to keep us on this task?"

Maria's jaw clenched as she said, "No. You'll all have to return to your regular duties tomorrow. But mark my words, this investigation will be reopened when it happens again!"

Scott's Disgust at the Real Free Market President

January 2nd - Berkeley, California

Scott Knox and Kevin Smith sat in their now shared apartment, prepared to watch a special address from the Oval Office. Patty Parker of Fox News was detailing the triumphs and failures of the past two years under President Towers.

"I could just kill that guy," Scott said. "Everything wrong in my life is because of him."

"That's a pretty dark thought there."

"Well, it's true! I lost my job because I've been attending so many rallies and protests. I'm pretty much a professional protestor at this point. My wife left me because she said I'm never happy anymore. How can I be happy with such a chaotic idiot for President? I heard she filed divorce papers a few days ago, so I expect to get served with those pretty soon."

"You can't really blame the President for a failing marriage," Kevin protested.

"Of course I can! Everything we fight about is caused by Towers."

"Such as?"

Scott let out a long sigh. He was conflicted between getting it off his chest or not thinking about it. Still, Kevin was usually a sympathetic ear. Perhaps it was best to vent. "I worked hard and sacrificed to put away a few thousand dollars a couple years ago in my retirement account. Half of that is gone now, and I'll bet Tonya wants to take half of what's left."

"But the stock market soared when Towers was elected. Even before he took office, the market jumped in anticipation of his coming policies."

"I didn't have anything in the market back then. I missed the ride up. Now that he's failed to accomplish what he promised, I had to ride the market back down."

"I thought Tonya was the big earner in the family."

Scott nodded. "She is. That's why she'll claim that money was hers to begin with.

"So, the failing market is because Towers didn't do what he promised?"

Scott nodded.

"What else do you fight about?"

"After Christmas, I thought she just needed a cooling-off period. But I lost my job a few days ago, and that was the final straw for her," Scott said. His anger was starting to abate and move into sadness. He really did miss her.

"We argued many times over Towers' policies and how passionate I am. She told me I shouldn't waste my time reading that stuff if I wasn't willing to do something about it. Then, when I actually did something, she had a problem with that and kicked me out on Christmas morning. I just don't know how to make her happy."

"Sounds like you've had a rough year."

"Yeah," Scott said. "The only positive thing to come out of the last year was my cryptocurrency wallet. The value doubles every six months, sometimes faster. Thank goodness my wife doesn't know about it. Let her take the house and the mortgage that goes with it. Let her take the retirement account, all $2754 of it. As long as she doesn't touch my Litecoin, I'll be set for life."

Kevin stared at him for a moment before saying, "Do you feel better?"

"A little."

"Good, because Towers is walking in right now." Kevin turned up the volume and focused on the TV.

Scott did the same.

"First of all, I want you all to know how devastated I am by what's been happening over the last couple of years," President Towers began. *"We had a good start, with growth of the economy that hasn't been seen in decades. I brought down the unemployment numbers and got America back to work by reforming taxes. But all that is threatened now.*

"There are so many good people, good men and women, who work very hard to make ends meet. They pour their sweat and their tears into their jobs, trusting us in Washington to make things a little easier. Instead, they watch their hard-earned savings dwindle every month in the worst sustained stock market decline of all time. They trusted the Federal Reserve to know when to raise or lower interest rates to prevent something like this from happening."

"Losing half my IRA wasn't the Fed's fault," Scott shouted at the TV. "It's yours!"

Kevin just sighed heavily.

Towers gripped the podium as he paused and stared directly into the camera. *"Well, I say, No more!"* He slammed his fist down on the podium, causing Scott and Kevin to jump out of their seats. *"Tomorrow begins the new chapter of the Towers Presidency. Tomorrow the new members of Congress will be sworn in. I promised you I would get the job done, and the old swamp-dwelling politicians wouldn't let me do it. Well, I've got news for you! The swamp is drained!"* He paused as the audience thundered their applause.

"Swamp-dwelling politicians?" Scott shouted. "You're the swamp-dweller."

Kevin scowled at Scott.

Towers started speaking again before all the applause had died down. *"We've got new blood in Washington, people who think like you and me."* There was more applause.

"Not like me! You don't speak for me!" Scott shouted. He didn't understand why everyone was cheering so loudly. How could anyone still follow this chaotic man?

"That's right!" Kevin joined in.

"People who have the best interests of the American people at heart." Towers' pauses got shorter with each sentence. *"People who will put American interests first! We are going to take back America and accomplish this year everything I've been trying to do for the last six years. And we're going to start by turning interest rates back over to the free market."* He paused, but this time, there was no applause.

"What?" Scott asked. "What does he mean?"

"I have no idea," Kevin said.

"Tomorrow we're introducing a bill to dismantle the Federal Reserve!" Cheers and boos could both be heard from the audience, though the cheering was slightly louder.

"It'll never pass if I have anything to say about it!" Scott shouted.

Kevin jumped out of his seat and walked over to the computer.

"What are you doing?" Scott asked as he got up and looked over Kevin's shoulder.

It took them only a minute to sign in to the Virtual Private Network and log in to the rally site. "Just what I thought. Rallies are popping up all over the country. I just wish there was a way I could do more."

"What do you mean?" Scott asked. "What more can we do?"

"I don't know but chanting silly rhymes just doesn't seem to be enough anymore."

While they were scrolling through the list and comparing how much each of them paid, a new email alert popped up with the subject line, *Want to do more and get paid more?* from the main event organizer.

Kevin opened it and followed the attached link to a new list. It was the same protests they'd just been looking at, but the payouts were much higher. He clicked on one and read the caption out loud, "Throw a Molotov cocktail during the protest: ten Litecoin."

"Are you kidding me?" Scott asked. "It's not worth getting arrested."

"They've already thought of that," Kevin said. "It says at the top of the page, if arrested, an additional 2 Litecoin per week will be paid during your incarceration, up to one year."

"Don't tell me you're seriously considering this!"

"I think I am."

"What if you get five years in prison?" Scott asked. "They're only going to pay you one hundred Litecoin."

"Imagine how much one hundred Litecoin will be worth in five years."

"Good point. One Litecoin is worth more than $400."

"And five years from now," Kevin added, "one hundred Litecoin could easily be worth millions."

Scott considered it. The money really was tempting, but it meant crossing a line which he wasn't sure he was ready to cross.

"There are dozens of offers like it," Kevin went on. "They're calling them 'bounties.' Burn down a Starbucks, twenty-five

Litecoin. Punch a cop on camera, five Litecoin. The list goes on and on.

Scott scanned through the list. "The more illegal something is, the more they'll pay. How do they know we're the ones that actually do this?"

"It says here we just have to agree in advance and submit video evidence of it happening."

"We have to commit a crime and then upload video evidence of us doing it?" Scott asked. "Sounds like a trap."

"If we do it right, we don't have to show our faces."

"What do you mean?"

"If we're wearing a body camera, it won't show our faces," Kevin said, "but it will show us throw something or punch someone, or whatever."

"I don't know . . ."

"It's not like we're going to upload the footage to YouTube and take credit for it."

Scott started pacing, his heart racing. Was he getting in too deep? Was this a trap? His gaze wandered to the TV again, where Patty Parker of Fox News was commenting on the speech. He turned up the volume in time to hear her say, "*Violent protests are expected again tomorrow, as President Towers' fiery rhetoric is bound to bring people out into the streets to express their concerns.*"

He thought about the last several years of violent protests around the country. How many of those were funded by this organization? Or by a billionaire from the other side? How much of this was really theater, and how much of it was genuine outrage? Hadn't he already gotten a bonus payment when he'd been injured?

A clip from the Christmas Eve rally at the White House came on the screen. A Molotov cocktail was thrown over the fence of the White House lawn. "*No arrests have yet been made as a result of this fiery demonstration,"* Patty Parker said, *"though police continue to assure us they are following up on every possible lead."*

"More than a week without an arrest?" Kevin asked. "Those people threw a flaming bottle of gasoline onto the White House lawn. If they can get away with it, surely we can."

Scott didn't say anything, but suddenly tossing a fireball in front of the California Capitol Building didn't sound so crazy.

Gideon Sees America's Future

January 2nd - Nephi, Utah

Gideon Shumway sat staring at the floor during President Tower's special address. The words bounced off him without sinking in. Jon drove back to California immediately after the funeral, but Gideon had a little more time before classes resumed, and he desperately needed help understanding Grandpa Tulley's death.

This was the kind of thing he could always talk to Ben Jr. about. Unfortunately, his little brother was still on his mission in India. Conversations with his father were always good, but he just didn't know how to start the conversation.

"I read your report on Ezra's Eagle," [43] Benjamin Sr. said when the President's speech ended. "It was very interesting. I've never even heard of the Second Book of Esdras before."

"Neither had I, before the assignment," Gideon said. He glanced at his father's eyes, trying to find a way to steer the conversation around to death or the meaning of life.

"Do you really think this Towers guy is the first of the short, contrary feathers?" [44]

"I don't know, Dad. It was just an assignment."

Ben Sr. gave a short laugh. "You can't get away with that. There was real thought and insight in that paper. Professor Jenkins noted you'd taught him something on the subject. No wonder he gave you an A."

Gideon heaved a sigh and decided maybe it would be good to talk about something else, to get his mind off the crushing weight he'd felt since Christmas. "Well, I found a lot of the material online. There are a couple of authors who've written extensively about it in recent years. After they pointed me in the right direction, it was easy to match up the rest of it."

"Yeah, but you didn't stop there, did you?"

"I couldn't. The paper was worth half my grade in the course. I spent months on that."

"Of course you did," Ben Sr. said seriously. "I've never known you to write anything longer than a few pages. This was sixty-five pages long. You've almost got enough to publish a book on the subject. Do you really believe all those Presidents were part of some great conspiracy?" [45]

Gideon looked his father in the eyes, matching the intensity of the gaze he found there. "Yes, I do. Maybe not all of them agreed to it at first, but no one since Calvin Coolidge has really pushed back against the progressive socialist agenda in any meaningful way.

"One interpretation suggests JFK tried to fight against it, as did Nixon, and look what they got for their trouble.[39] So whether they were part of it or not, the rest certainly didn't fight it."

"But you think President Towers is fighting it?"

"Yes. He's cut so many unnecessary regulations, pulled the government out of controlling the internet, and he just announced he's trying to take down the Federal Reserve."

"I thought the Federal Reserve was there to make sure banks are stable."

"Exactly," Gideon said. "Preventing any industry from failing requires outside interference, even with banking. It's all part and parcel of the same agenda. First they centralized the banking industry, then they removed the gold standard. It's all part of an agenda to globalize the money systems."

"You lost me on that one," Ben Sr. said. "You're starting to sound like that conspiracy theory radio guy, Xander Johnson, or something like that. He's always complaining about the globalist conspiracy."

Gideon shook his head. "I don't believe everything that guy says, and I didn't get this from him. Isaiah chapter ten tells us what the goals of the conspiracy are."

"It does? Where?"

Gideon stood up and went to the wall lined with stuffed bookshelves. It wasn't hard to find his father's quadruple combination or quad. It contained the Holy Bible, The Book of Mormon, the Doctrine and Covenants of the Church of Jesus Christ of Latter-day Saints, and a small collection of other writings called The Pearl of Great Price. He flipped through the Old Testament as he walked back to his seat. "Right here. Go ahead and read verses thirteen and fourteen."

"13 For he saith, By the strength of my hand I have done it, and by my wisdom; for I am prudent: and I have removed the bounds of the people, and have

robbed their treasures, and I have put down the
inhabitants like a valiant man:

"14 And my hand hath found as a nest the riches of
the people: and as one gathereth eggs that are left, have
I gathered all the earth; and there was none that moved
the wing, or opened the mouth, or peeped." [46]

Ben Sr. stared at the pages for a while after he'd finished reading. "I'm sorry, but I don't see what you're talking about."

"These verses are the Antichrist boasting about his accomplishments just before he is destroyed by the Right Hand of God," [47] Gideon explained. "The bounds of the people means the borders of countries."

"So that's the tie into the globalists that Johnson always complains about."

Gideon nodded. "Robbed their treasures means he will take over the monetary systems of the world, controlling everyone's ability to buy and sell."

"But then the world would just switch to the barter system."

"He's taken care of that, too," Gideon replied. "The mark of the beast will be required for anyone to buy or sell." [48]

"There are so many different interpretations of that verse. What makes you think your version is right?"

"Because I don't know exactly what it is. That's not what matters. The beast hasn't risen yet, so he hasn't decided what his mark is. But we know what it does, what it is for. It allows the Antichrist to control the commerce of the world."

Ben Sr. gave a deep sigh and leaned back in his chair. "I've never bothered much with studying all these prophecies. I figure the Prophet will warn us what the mark of the beast is, or who the Antichrist will be. We just have to follow the Prophets."

"That's a good first step," Gideon said, "but this class has opened my eyes to a deeper way of thinking. We've been commanded to study these prophecies, to be prepared and prepare the world for the Lord's Second Coming."

"Where do you get that idea?"

"From Joseph Smith. He revealed God's word on this topic in Doctrine and Covenants Section forty-five, verse thirty-nine."

Ben Sr. flipped through the pages of his scriptures until he found the right verse. "And it shall come to pass that he that feareth me shall be looking forth for the great day of the Lord to come, even for the signs of the coming of the Son of Man." [49]

"I, for one, want to be able to say I fear the Lord."

Ben Sr. stared at the page, running his finger over the verses before and after multiple times. "I've read this chapter a dozen times before, and it's never struck me like this."

"That's why we have to keep reading the scriptures."

The Shadow Council Protects Their Investments

January 3rd - Washington, D.C.

Peyman Ahmadi took his seat in the spacious conference room beneath the Smithsonian. He'd seen many of these underground conference rooms, but this one happened to be attached to an underground city. One of the few that remained a secret. He thought he was the first to arrive, but someone was already sitting in his seat.

It took him a moment to recognize the man who'd recently been Ten, but it looked like Peyman's fortunes were looking up. Ten had become Thirteen, meaning Peyman was now promoted to Twelve. Promotion of any kind, even through the demotion of another, was one step closer to the head chair. He took the seat designated for Twelve with a smile to the new lowest ranking man in the room.

It wasn't long before the rest of the Council filed in, and One dove right into the meeting. "You may have noticed there have been a few seat changes around the room. Seven, would you like to share with the others why that is?"

The big Texan stood up in his usual three-piece suit. Seven, who used to be Four, swallowed before he said, "The stock market fell farther than expected, and it somehow helped Towers' candidates get elected. We've lost our controlling majority in the House and the Senate."

"Have you devised a plan to correct this error?" One asked.

"We've drafted a dossier filled with damaging personal details about . . ." He paused when One hung his head.

"That's not going to work," One said. "Someone already tried it with lies. Now we can't even use the truth to blackmail him."

"Then we have no other choice but to eliminate him," Seven said.

"Are you mad?" Three said. "Spencer Michaels is even worse than Towers. You can't let him take office."

Seven started shaking as he said, "Then we'll have to take care of both."

There was silence in the room as One stared at Seven, who continued shaking for a moment before he was able to get it under control. At last, One said, "Do you think you can handle that? Or do we need to find someone else?"

"No!" Seven shot back right away. "I can do it. I *will* do it. Consider it done."

One nodded. "Good. Make sure you get it done before he dismantles the Federal Reserve. I shouldn't have to remind you it's been one of our best tools for over a century. How long can you keep that bill from passing?"

"Today's vote in the House was close," Seven replied, his usual confidence returning, "but we were able to secure Congressmen Baldwin as Speaker of the House. He is a sort of protege of mine. If he continues to serve us well, he may be a future candidate for this council."

"Politicians never get on this council," Three said in his southern drawl. "You know that."

"That's only because they never keep up with their proficiency levels, preferring political power over all others. Baldwin says he has already achieved level fifty-four."

One jotted something on a notepad. "I'll be looking into that, of course."

Seven nodded.

Peyman suspected the Texan had already verified Baldwin's last proficiency test, or he wouldn't have brought it up.

"No matter how proficient he may be, Baldwin is supported by a slim majority of Republicans in the House. I think we can stall for three months in the House and two tops in the Senate. I don't think we can hold off this new wave of elected officials any longer than that."

"That will have to be enough time," One said.

"I assure you, it will be," Seven said. "They won't live to sign that bill."

The Pope's Overture of Love

January 6th - New York City

Pope Ferdinand walked into the offices of the World Evangelical Alliance and shook Peter Banachek's hand. "Thank you for accepting my invitation, Secretary-General."

Peter motioned for the Pope to take a seat. "I must say I was intrigued by your call." He walked around his desk and sat down. "What is it exactly you hoped to accomplish?"

"A great deal," the Pope said. "As Secretary-General, you represent and guide over six hundred million people of faith worldwide. I've read your statement of faith. The statement I signed in 2017[50] shows there is nothing incompatible between your group and the Catholic Church."

"Nothing incompatible!" Peter shouted.

Two guards rushed into the room, guns raised.

"Stop!" the Pope said. "He is not a danger to me."

The guards lowered their weapons and backed slowly out of the room.

"I want no more interruptions," the Pope said. "Is that clear?"

"Yes, Holy Father," they said in unison as they closed the door.

"Now, where were we?"

"You were telling me how you've changed the doctrine of the Catholic Church to conform to the Evangelical beliefs."

Pope Ferdinand shook his head. "Nothing quite so grand. Have you read the statement released in 2017?"

Peter nodded. "If you're referring to the joint statement between the Catholic Church and the Lutheran World Federation released on the five hundredth anniversary of Martin Luther nailing his thesis to the door, then I'd say I've studied it closely."

"Do you understand the spirit in which it was written?"

"You seek unity for the body of Christ. That is truly a noble enterprise. I can't say though, that I could persuade six hundred million people to rejoin the Catholic Church, even if I wanted to."

The Pope shook his head. "That's not what I'm asking at all."

"Then be specific. What are you asking?"

"First, for your signature on the document, showing that you agree with its aims and intentions. Secondly, a promise not to poach from other religions who also sign the document. Thirdly, and this part is negotiable, I'd like you to call a General Assembly and allow me to address them."

Peter blinked several times before he said, "You want to address our General Assembly?"

The Pope nodded.

"We haven't held one of those in ten years."

"I'm aware of that. The purpose of these assemblies is exactly what we are discussing between our two sects of Christianity. The assembly seems like the perfect opportunity to explain the agreement to the leaders of your organization."

Banachek stared at him for a long time, unsure what to say. Finally, he said, "I'll have to consult with the other leaders. This can't be my decision alone."

The Pope smiled as he stood. "Of course. I would expect nothing less. Contact me when you have a decision."

David & Moroni's BIG Project

January 11th - Near Panguitch, Utah

Moroni Whitefeather drove into the hidden green valley. It was an idyllic setting, situated between two mountains, with a river flowing through the middle. He hadn't been to the valley in more than a year, and David Andrews had undoubtedly been busy.

A shining seven-story building stood in the center of the valley. The skeleton of a matching building being constructed nearby spoke of more to come. Moroni parked his car in the lot directly in front of the completed one.

David Andrews stood there to greet him with a broad smile on his face. The two old friends hugged and laughed.

"You've been busy," Moroni said.

"As have you!" David shot back. "How was your trip to Australia?"

Moroni frowned. "Waste of time. The Greenford's aren't right for the program."

"You said the same thing after your meeting in India," David said as they walked toward the building.

"True. That earthquake striking the next day was unsettling. Still, I met a very promising young missionary I hope will join us someday. His name was Shumway, I think. That reminds me, his parents live not far from here. I'd better stop in and introduce myself tomorrow. I want to see if they have any other promising children."

"Sure, sure," David said. He stopped a few feet from the door. "You really love your job, don't you?"

Moroni chuckled. "I get to see the world, meet interesting people, and offer them a better future. What's not to love?"

They both laughed.

"Are we going inside or what?"

"Of course!" David said. "But the tour starts here."

"Oh, is this an official tour? I didn't know you were doing those yet."

"This will be the second," David confirmed. "I got the Redds moved in yesterday. Harold and Patricia both show great potential as future leaders, perhaps the best recruits so far."

"It'll be a long time yet before I'm ready to settle down and stay in one place," Moroni said.

"Good! We've got too much work to do for you to just sit around here. As our best headhunter, I felt it was time you got to see in person what we've been talking about for so long."

They both smiled until Moroni said, "So you were giving me a tour?"

David nodded. "Of course, of course. So many distractions. Well, the first feature I want you to see is the windows that cover the exterior walls. Go ahead, take a closer look."

Moroni walked over and leaned his face in close to the glass. What looked like tinted windows from afar was actually micro circuitry embedded in the glass. "Is this a display screen?"

"No," David said. "Guess again."

Moroni straightened up. "You know technology isn't my area of expertise."

"They are solar panels. Windows that let between ten and thirty percent of the light through and produce more than a hundred watts of electricity per square yard in full sunlight."

"Really! It must have cost a fortune."

David shook his head. "This is just one of the wonders I'm going to show you today. Almost all of them have been or will be manufactured on-site from raw materials. We're shipping in what we need for now, but soon we'll start building the production facility. It won't be long before most of our raw materials come as byproducts of the food we raise."

"So when you said self-sufficient, you really meant it," Moroni commented. "Right down to replacing every piece of the city."

David nodded. "Now you're catching on. Come on in. There's lots more to see."

Scott Studies Criminology

January 12th - Berkeley, California

Scott Knox kept poking around the dark website with the bounty list. He was fine taking money to show up and shout chants with everyone else. That was harmless, a protected right, even. But the acts he was considering now were all illegal in one way or another. He knew the person behind the list had a good reason for each one, though precisely what that was Scott couldn't always tell.

As he scrolled up to the top for the eighth time that night, he noticed a link in the top right corner.

Forum

That's all it said. He clicked on it, filling the screen with a list of topics. Everything from the best bottles to use for a Molotov cocktail, to how to throw a punch, and what to say if you are brought in for questioning. One topic practically begged him to open it.

How to avoid being caught

He clicked on it and found thread after thread of people discussing all the different methods law enforcement used to catch criminals. There was a whole thread about setting up a Virtual Private Network, and Scott laughed. He'd been doing that for most of his web browsing for years.

Then he saw one on facial recognition and had to share it. "Kevin, listen to this. Our government uses facial recognition software so sophisticated that it can see right through the average ski mask."

"What! You've got to be kidding. Where did you find that?"

"It's on that website. You know, the one with the list of bounties. It says the latest versions of facial recognition can reconstruct the basic features of the face right through a mask, glasses, and a fake beard." [51]

"Really?"

"Yeah," Scott said. "It's got a link to the news article describing it."

Kevin got up from the table and walked around to stand behind Scott. "Well, do they also tell you what kind of disguise to wear?"

"It has a few suggestions, but it says they haven't been fully tested."

"Still, it's got to be better than nothing. What else is on there?"

"I'm not sure," Scott said defensively. "I just found this section of the site."

"Well, it makes me glad we didn't throw those bottles at the protest last week, or we might be in jail by now."

"So what you're saying is me chickening out actually saved us?"

Kevin gave a slight chuckle. "I'm not sure I'd go that far."

Scott scowled up at him. "I'll let you know if I find anything else of interest on here."

Kevin nodded. "Sounds good. I've got loads of studying to do anyway."

"Yeah," Scott shot back. "You'll need that business degree for when we go straight."

They both chuckled at the joke.

Gideon Gets Guidance

January 20th - Notre Dame, Indiana

Gideon Shumway arrived at the church building half an hour before the Sunday services were scheduled to begin with a burning question in his heart. Watching his grandfather die right in front of him put the fear of God into him like nothing else ever had. Fifteen years of Sunday School, four years of Seminary during high school, and two years on a mission preaching the gospel all felt like background noise to the question weighing on him now.

His grief was even affecting his relationship with Karen. She was trying to be supportive, but he'd cut back their dates from three nights per week to one. Even those few hours they spent together every Friday night was a strain as he tried to keep a smile on his face and enjoy their time together.

The chapel was empty, just as he'd hoped. He'd prayed every morning and every night for the past several weeks, pleading with God for answers and getting none. So today he came early, hoping the answers would come more quickly in a church. Visiting the temple was an all-day event for him, and he hadn't found a free day yet.

"Oh, God," he whispered, "I need to know if my grandfather is okay. Did he live a good enough life to …" Someone sat down next to Gideon. He looked up and saw a tall man with dark hair. He had the look of a Native American. Gideon had never seen him before.

"I can see I've interrupted a very deep thought," the man said. "For that, I apologize. I just felt like I needed to talk to you."

A sense of calm spread through Gideon's heart. Somehow, he knew this man had come in answer to his prayer. He felt a burning desire to speak to this man in private. He looked around and saw a few others were starting to find their seats, even though there were more than twenty minutes before the meeting would begin. "Perhaps we could go somewhere more private?" Gideon suggested.

The man smiled. "An excellent suggestion. My name is Moroni."

"I'm Gideon." They both stood and exited the chapel, shaking a couple of hands along the way. He found it interesting that both their names came from the Book of Mormon.

It wasn't hard to find an open room. As soon as Moroni shut the door, before Gideon even had a chance to sit down, the man said, "Now tell me, what's troubling you?"

"My grandfather died a few weeks ago."

"I'm sorry for your loss."

Gideon nodded and pressed on. "Thanks. I've been getting a lot of that. What I can't seem to get are answers. I just can't seem to shake the question from my mind."

"Which question is that?"

"Will he be exalted?"

Moroni heaved a long sigh. "I'm not sure that's the right question to be asking."

Gideon frowned at this. Why shouldn't he be able to know? Couldn't God tell him if his grandfather was destined for eternal glory? But then the peace swept over him again, making him forget why it was so important to know that. "Then, what is the right question?"

"You've faced death on a very personal level, and it has brought the subject of salvation to your heart. But is it actually your grandfather's salvation that you're anxious about?"

The thought struck Gideon like a bolt of lightning. A dozen scriptures popped into his mind ranging from "work out your own salvation" [52] to "this life is the time for men to prepare to meet God." [53]

"Of course," he said. "I just didn't want to face the possibility that my own salvation might be in question."

"That sounds like the right place to start. Now let's see if we can get you some answers."

Scott Plays with Fire

February 12th - Washington, D.C.

Scott Knox stood outside the Capitol Building, shivering under his thick coat. It was frigidly cold that morning, but his nerves had more to do with the bottle of gasoline concealed in his pocket. Kevin was right beside him with a bottle of his own. They each had body cameras carefully concealed on their coats.

Everyone around them was shouting, "Down with Towers! Save the Fed!" to protest the bill still in committee. It was hard to believe they were actually drafting legislation to dismantle the Federal Reserve, an institution that had prevented another Great Depression for most of the last century. Every time Scott raised his fist in the air, the bottle bumped against his side. As if he needed another reminder it was there.

Everyone around them was wearing either a red hat or a red scarf, and there was another, even larger group wearing blue hats or scarves a couple hundred feet away. Every rally or protest Scott had attended in the past several months was divided into these two camps, and the amount of red or blue kept increasing. No one he could see in either group was wearing both red and blue. No blue gloves or blue coats could be seen among the Republican protestors, even their jeans were black instead of blue.

"Are you gonna do it this time?" Kevin asked.

"Down with Towers! Save the Fed!" they shouted with the crowd.

Scott had chickened out at the last three protests, all at the State Capitol in California. He probably would have done it, but he'd hesitated, and once Kevin threw his, there was no way Scott was going to single himself out. He was willing to support the cause but wasn't prepared to go to prison, even for a hundred Litecoin.

"Come on," Kevin said. "They're never gonna even know we were here."

"Are you sure?" Scott said.

The chanting of "Down with Towers! Save the Fed!" interrupted their conversation every ten seconds, giving Scott time to consider his responses.

Kevin rolled his eyes. "We flew from California to Ohio, then took a Waymo from there to D.C., just like you insisted. It cost us more for the Waymo than I paid for my flight."

"Yeah, but the Waymo doesn't know who we are," Scott explained. "Flight records are public knowledge.

"Is that why we dumped all our electronics in a locker in Cincinnati and bought burner phones?"

Scott nodded. "And we set up a brand-new cryptocurrency wallet to pay for the ride here."

"You're paranoid, man."

"Of course I am!" Scott said.

"Down with Towers! Save the Fed!"

"This could cause a riot," Scott continued. "I don't want anyone to know we were anywhere near here. I don't want to leave any financial records for someone to follow later."

"It's called cryptocurrency for a reason," Kevin said. "I still don't understand why we had to create a separate wallet."

"Just because they can't tell who owns the wallet, doesn't mean they can't track the activity of it. If we create too many clues by using the same cryptocurrency wallet all the time, it'll eventually give them enough evidence to hunt us down."

"Now you're just stalling," Kevin said. "If you don't do it today, you're never going to do it."

Scott knew he was right. This was his last chance, and he needed the money. Litecoin had taken a small dive over the weekend, and he'd lost ten percent of his money. He knew it would recover, but in the meantime, he had bills to pay. "Let's do it."

"Down with Towers! Save the Fed!" they shouted one final time, before ducking down near the edge of the crowd. They both pulled their red hats down over their faces, revealing them as the ski-masks they actually were. They turned on their body cameras.

"Down with Towers! Save the Fed!"

Scott pulled out the bottle filled with gasoline, opened it, and shoved the rag inside. He made sure the cloth was soaked before he pulled out the lighter and lit the other end. Kevin was doing the exact same thing. There was no turning back now.

They stood up together and lobbed the bottles toward the blue hats.

There were shouts and screams as the bottles shattered on the grass at least thirty feet from the nearest person, and the flames spread.

"Who threw that!" several people shouted.

Scott and Kevin blended into the center of the crowd as best they could before ducking down and removing their ski masks and standing up again.

As they did so, Scott saw someone in a blue ski mask run out of the crowd of blue hats, screaming, "Go home, you Nazis!" He threw his own flaming bottle, which smashed only a few feet away from the crowd, splattering a dozen people in burning gasoline.

Screams and panic ensued as some helped put out the flames while others ran after the guy who threw the Molotov cocktail, and everyone else scattered.

The thrower vanished into the crowd of blue protestors as the red hats tried in vain to penetrate the other group. A fist-fight broke out, and more than a dozen red hats were knocked to the ground. Enraged, the rest of the red hats swarmed over, despite being clearly outnumbered.

Police sirens filled the air as fire-hoses quickly sprayed down the clashing crowds.

Scott and Kevin turned and ran the other way, along with nearly half the red hats. Police began swarming in from every angle, and the runners all picked up speed, especially Scott and Kevin. They still didn't want to go to jail, even if they would make $800 a week.

*   *   *

Gary Sanders sat for twenty minutes in the underground conference room, waiting for One to arrive. The worst part of the wait was not having access to his electronic devices. After all, they didn't want Google Maps tracking their movements in and out of such secretive facilities.

One burst through the doors. "What could be so important you can't wait for the quarterly meeting?"

Gary stood as soon as the doors started moving. "Forgive me, One. I saw an opportunity and felt the need to get your approval."

One walked around the table to his customary seat, making a big show of sipping his coffee before setting it down and motioning for Gary to sit. "It must be a tremendous opportunity to require my personal verbal approval."

"It is, sir." Gary sat down. The butterflies in his stomach felt more like eagles. If he got this wrong, he was a dead man.

"I assume this relates to your promise to remove the twin problems?"

Gary nodded. "Yes. The main difficulty is getting the targets in the same place at a known time."

"Why should that be hard? Just hire two assassins to take them out at the same time."

Gary shook his head. "If one of them is delayed, the other would lose their opportunity. Plus, doing so would reveal a greater conspiracy, and I did not dare risk even that level of exposure."

One nodded. "I see you've given this some thought. That's good. Go ahead then, tell me your plan."

"Well, Leon Cologne is preparing a personal trip into space."

"Yes, I'm aware of that. How does it relate?"

"If I am permitted to sabotage the flight," Gary said slowly, "it will create a favorable series of events."

One shook his head as he interrupted. "You are not allowed to interfere with that launch in any way."

Gary's heart sunk. This was the only plan he could come up with.

"We're already taking steps to make sure he will never return," One added.

A massive ball of nerves was suddenly released. Convincing One to let him sabotage the launch was the most challenging part of the plan. "Can I assume then, that your methods will cast doubt on the safety of his entire program?"

"Of course," One said. "This private space exploration stuff has to stop. Is that what you came in here to propose? You want us to get Towers and Michaels on that flight? Because I don't think that's going to happen."

"Not at all, sir. But the aftermath of such an event is very likely to bring both targets to the same stage at the same time."

"I suppose that's possible. That's really your area of expertise, is it not?"

Gary nodded. "Yes. It seems this meeting was unnecessary after all. Just know that the success of my plans is dependent on the success of putting an end to the private space exploration sector."

"Believe me, it is far more important to end this nonsense about space colonies than to accomplish the task I've assigned you. We will not fail."

"Then neither shall I," Gary concluded as he stood to leave.

Gideon's Salvation Paradox

February 14th - Notre Dame, Indiana

Gideon Shumway sat at his kitchen table looking over the list of scriptures Moroni had given him. He'd read all of them three times and spent as much time on this as he had any of his actual classes over the last three weeks. The concept of spiritual justification wasn't foreign to him, but he'd always thought of it as something that happened in the next life.

He wanted to know for himself where he stood with God. Moroni insisted that he had to understand justification first.[54] Yet some of the verses were contradictory.

"What 'cha working on?" Duane asked. He set his umbrella against the wall.

"Hey, Duane. I'm trying to reconcile the contradictions in these passages of the New Testament."

"Which ones?" Duane set his backpack on the floor and took a seat next to Gideon.

"Titus 3:7 and James 2:21." [55] Gideon pushed his Bible over to Duane. "Titus says we're saved by grace, and James says it's through works."

Duane smiled. "Those do appear opposites, don't they? People have been arguing about this for over five hundred years."

Gideon chucked at this comment. "Yeah, I guess this was one of the reasons for the Protestant Reformation, wasn't it?"

"Still, let's dive in and see what we have here." Duane bent over the Bible and read, "That being justified by his grace, we should be made heirs according to the hope of eternal life."

"Right. Saved by grace."

Duane shook his head. "No, it says justified by grace. That's not necessarily the same thing as being saved."

"It isn't?"

"No. Look, what does it mean in your religion to be saved?"

Gideon paused a moment, trying to remember some quote or scripture to answer the question properly, but decided to just blurt it out. "Being saved means returning to the presence of Heavenly Father and dwelling forever in His presence. It means progressing forever until the perfect day."

Duane stared at him and blinked several times. He didn't say anything, and Gideon began to wonder if he'd said something wrong.

"You believe in different levels of heaven?" Duane asked.

"Yes," Gideon said. "You should know that. Aren't you a comparative religion major?"

"We haven't covered Mormonism in that much detail yet." Duane cleared his throat before continuing. "Being justified doesn't mean you automatically rise to the highest level of heaven. It just means you aren't cursed to an eternity in hell."

Gideon pondered this a moment. He'd never studied the Muslim concepts of heaven and hell, but if they believed in more than two levels of happiness and misery in the next life, he wondered what other concepts they might have which more closely matched his own religion.

Refocusing on the discussion at hand, he said, "I see what you're saying. Justification means your sins are forgiven. In the Church of Jesus Christ, we believe we are forgiven of our sins through baptism, which gets us into the Church and Kingdom of God. But there are still other things we have to do to achieve the highest glory."

"There it is," Duane said. "You've answered your own question."

"I have?"

Duane nodded. "Do you really believe that the act of being buried in the water and coming out again can wash away your sins? If so, why aren't people rebaptized on their death beds?"

Gideon shook his head. "No, of course not. No matter how much work we do, someone has to pay the price of justice. For us, that was Jesus Christ. His atonement paid the price for our sins and allows Him to grant mercy."

"But, you still believe you have to go through the physical ordinance of baptism?"

"Yes."

"Then, through your works, you gain access to the grace of God."

Gideon stared at Duane. He'd just explained a difficult concept more clearly than any of his seminary or Sunday school teachers ever had, and he wasn't even Christian, let alone Mormon. Still, the words rang true in his heart. He knew it was right.

What's more, it changed everything for Gideon. Processing the ideas out loud, he said, "God asks us to do a few simple things to show our devotion, which then gives us access to mercy through the atonement of Christ. I can never be enough on my own, no matter how many good works I do, yet I cannot claim mercy if I don't take those simple steps which He asks."

"Exactly."

A fire burned in Gideon's heart, stronger than he'd ever felt, even while preaching the gospel as a missionary. "I don't have to be perfect to be justified. I just have to ask God to honor the commitments I've already made to Him."

"Now you've got it. What class is this for, anyway?"

"None," Gideon replied as he stacked up his books. "This is for my own edification. I'd better hit the shower. I'm supposed to pick up Karen in thirty minutes."

Maria: Master of Investigation

February 15th - Washington, D.C.

"I've taken all the media coverage of the protests for the last three years and poured it into the facial recognition software," Greggor Talvert said.

Maria Croix sat next to him, watching the faces flash across the screen. She'd come to Talvert's office with the promise of good news. "Did you find any matches?"

Without overtime approval, it took Talvert six weeks to create this program. She knew he could have done it in one if his regular duties had been offloaded to others. She'd just about given up hope of ever finding the Christmas Eve flame slinger.

"It'll take another week to fully process what we've got so far, but I've already identified ten people who have been at more than a dozen of these rallies in different cities."

"What are their names?"

Talvert swallowed hard. "I have no idea."

"I thought you said you'd identified them."

"Well, I can show they were at several rallies, but to put a name to the face will take longer. I've already set up a search of the national criminal database for these people, and by Tuesday, I'll have it coded to automatically start that search for anyone else who was at an unusual number of rallies. But it's going to take time."

Maria shook her head. "Why are you only searching the criminal database? Why aren't you searching the DMV records?"

"Because they haven't committed a crime," Talvert said. "I assumed you'd want to interview these people."

"Of course I want to interview them," Maria shot back. "I'm not going to throw them a party!"

"Right," Talvert pressed on. "So those in the criminal database will be easier to haul in without risking lawsuits for false arrest."

"Exactly."

"Plus," Talvert added, "searching the DMV records will take significantly longer. If this method doesn't give us the leads we need, we can expand the search."

Maria patted him on the back. "We need more people like you, Talvert. Let me know when you've connected one of these faces to a name."

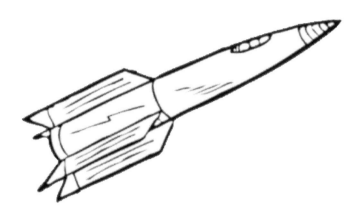

Leon Goes for the Gold

February 15th - Hawthorne, California

Liz Smith sat three feet from the podium, trying to sort out how she'd gotten here. Less than a year ago, she'd earned her bachelor's degree in business. She'd hoped being a personal assistant to a CEO in a small company for one summer would give her a better handle on how a business runs while she decided what kind of business she wanted to start. Then, somehow, her resume wound up in Leon Cologne's hands, and he offered her a ridiculously large salary for a two-year commitment.

Her nightly dinners with Leon had continued over the last six months, with most of the conversation centered on the ISS. They'd been joined by his two children a few times, and on those nights, the conversations became more personal. She looked forward to her time alone with Leon each day. She also caught herself smiling every time she saw him.

Leon swept into the room as dozens of cameras started flashing, and several dozen reporters shouted his name, pelting him with questions. He ignored them all and walked right up to the podium. He grabbed it and shouted, "Settle down, or I'll have the room cleared. We go live in two minutes."

There were a few murmurs of surprise, but then all talking ceased. Liz had kept a tight lid on what the press knew. Clearly, her efforts were successful. As far as they knew, this was a standard quarterly business update, which meant none of them had arranged to broadcast it themselves. They shouldn't even be aware he would be airing the meeting on YouTube. Nothing grabs the attention of the public faster than an unplanned announcement.

She smiled as she saw several of them texting, probably scrambling to get someone at their networks to show the feed live. Everything Leon did was ostentatious, as far as the paparazzi were concerned. Today would be no different.

A few gasps broke the semi-silence as the representatives of the five space agencies in charge of the International Space Station walked into the room and up to the podium. That was precisely the reaction Liz had hoped for. No one in the press knew why these people were here, and only a few of them even recognized who they were. Leon took the time to shake each of their hands and show them to their seats.

One reporter was heard shouting into his phone, "I don't care who you've got booked! This story is huge! Hello? Hello?"

"Sorry to cut you off," Leon said to the shouting reporter. "I just activated the jamming devices. We're live in thirty seconds."

Liz's tablet vibrated. One text made it through before the jamming. It read, *"CNN just went live. Fox News and The Blaze are promising to do the same."*

Silence finally fell over the room, only a few seconds before the green light turned on.

"Thank you all for joining me today," Leon said. "As some of you have noticed, I have brought five extraordinary friends with me for this announcement. Six weeks from now, I will be visiting their home among the stars."

The reporters gasped again.

"Yes, you heard me correctly. I've worked out an arrangement with these fine folks to host myself and five friends aboard the International Space Station for one week. The recent successful launches have shown the world that privatized space travel is not only possible, but it is also safe. Now some of you might be wondering who I'm going to take with me on this historic first journey. Well, honestly, I'm not sure yet. We've narrowed down the candidates to fifteen people, all of whom are already training for the experience. As you might expect, there's the issue of cost. What we've worked out is that each person selected will present their weight in gold to pay for the ride."

Laughs broke out around the room.

"I know, the idea seems a bit ridiculous, and I know very few people will be able to afford it right now. But that's always been the way of things with new technology. In twenty years, we'll get it down to your weight in silver, then copper, and perhaps in our lifetime, we'll get the cost down far enough that it will rival the cost of a trip to Disneyland."

He waited as there was more laughter, mixed in with some applause.

Clearing his throat, he continued, "Once all the candidates have met the qualifications set forth by the ISS Oversight Committee, we will announce those who are going. That announcement will take place in about a month. Any questions?"

Gideon Hears a Voice

February 17th - Notre Dame, Indiana

As Gideon Shumway sang "We'll Sing All Hail to Jesus' Name," he thought about all his sins up to that moment in time. The phrase in the second verse struck home. "He called upon the sin-bound soul To join the heav'nly throng." [56] Tears started pouring down his cheeks as he realized this applied directly to him. Jesus didn't care about those sins anymore. Gideon only had to let them go and "sin no more" to be forgiven.

After the hymn, the bread was blessed and passed. Gideon took his small piece and thought about the Atonement, about Christ giving up His life for others so that all would rise again.

All.

That meant everyone, including his grandfather. Including himself.

The water was blessed and passed, and the phrase, "That they may do it in remembrance of the blood of thy Son, which was shed for them," [57] rang in Gideon's mind. Jesus bled from every pore to complete the Atonement.[58] He'd suffered every pain and anguish of body and soul as payment for sins. Not just for everyone's sins, but for Gideon's sins specifically. The price had already been paid.

As Gideon drank the tiny cup and placed it back in the tray, he heard a voice say to him, "Gideon, thy sins are forgiven thee. Be thou sanctified." [54]

He didn't have to look around to know it was the voice of an angel. It filled his entire body and brought peace to his heart. More tears poured down his cheeks as he knew God had forgiven him.

When he was able to compose himself, he pulled out the notebook Moroni told him to always carry and wrote down the phrase, 'Be thou sanctified.'

That afternoon, Gideon wrote an email to Moroni, describing his experience. Less than an hour later, Moroni responded.

> *Gideon,*
>
> *Congratulations on your amazing spiritual experience! As you've probably guessed, this is only the first step of your spiritual progression. Having your sins forgiven is the process of being justified. When you have sanctified your life, you can receive the Baptism of Fire we spoke about.*
>
> *You should also know that temptations will increase. God is not the only one who has taken note of your change of heart. Be careful of your friends, and do not slack in your scriptural studies or prayers.*

Will Scott Burn It Down?

February 27th - Boulder, Colorado

Scott Knox stood outside the home of Senator Ball's private residence, surrounded by about fifty Republican protestors yelling, "Topple the Towers! Keep the Fed's powers!" Half of them had their ski masks down, which wasn't that unusual, given the temperature was barely above zero. Kevin was there with him, of course, which was good because today's bounty required two men to accomplish. There were also half a dozen uniformed officers standing between the protestors and the home.

Senator Ball was the author of the bill to dismantle the Fed, which was set to hit the Senate floor within the week. From the list Scott saw online, there were similar rallies outside the homes of every Republican and Independent supporting the bill, but this one paid the most.

"Topple the Towers! Keep the Fed's powers!"

"This is the big one," Kevin said.

"Our most lucrative contract yet," Scott agreed.

"Topple the Towers! Keep the Fed's powers!"

They would get ten percent of whatever property damage they were able to inflict on the house. Scott was reasonably sure the home was insured, and he knew if they hadn't taken the contract, someone else would have.

"Topple the Towers! Keep the Fed's powers!"

"This one is going to take careful timing," Scott said as he opened up the Waymo app on his phone and requested a pick up two blocks from the house. He waited a moment for the system to assign a car to the request. "It's eight minutes out."

"Topple the Towers! Keep the Fed's powers!"

"You know what we have to do next," Kevin said.

"Of course I do," Scott said. "I won't back out. I think I've proven that already."

"Topple the Towers! Keep the Fed's powers!"

They waited one more minute before they both shouted, "Down with Ball! Kill the bill!"

The group copied the new chant, "Down with Ball! Kill the Bill!"

They reached into the inner pockets of their thick coats and pulled out the bottles filled with gasoline.

"Down with Ball! Kill the Bill!"

As they started the chant a third time, Kevin lit the fuse and flung the bottle as they shouted, "Kill the bill!"

Before the first bottle even hit, Scott threw his at the same spot. The first one smashed against the window, and the heat of the fire shattered the glass. The second bottle flew right inside. Scott wasn't sure at first if the bottle had broken, but the flames inside the home showed him he'd hit his mark perfectly. The house was on fire inside and out.

At the same time, the cops drew their Tasers and fired them into the crowd. Eight people went down.

The majority of the protestors started screaming and running in every direction they could away from the house and the authorities, while the cops rushed in and laid cuffs on everyone they could.

Scott and Kevin ran hard and fast, easily outpacing the slowest members of the group. They hoofed it for two blocks where the promised Waymo car waited. As they hoped, it was self-driving. They jumped in, closed the door and buckled their seat belts, while Scott set his phone on the console to confirm he was the requester. Within seconds the car took off, weaving around the few people who had run in this direction and kept pace with them.

Additional patrol cars were already appearing, but they were rushing to the scene or detaining the runners, rather than setting up a perimeter.

"I think we made it!" Kevin shouted as he reached to pull off his ski mask.

"Not yet!" Scott shouted.

"Why?"

"These cabs have cameras." Scott pointed to the in-cab camera aimed right at them. He pulled out his pink-noise generator and turned it on, ensuring the microphones would only record static. The gentle whooshing felt almost oppressive in the confined space, but they quickly adjusted to it.

"So? No one is going to know which cab we used."

"Are you joking? There's going to be an investigation! You don't think they'll be interested in every car that left the area?"

"Man, you are super paranoid," Kevin said. "We've done this half a dozen times already, and no one has caught us yet. Besides, this mask is itchy with all the extra padding sewn in it."

"I'm not paranoid, I'm careful. We live in the age of constant surveillance. That extra padding keeps the cameras from getting a good match on facial recognition. Besides, this time it wasn't just tossing a fireball on an empty lawn. We attacked the home of a Senator. That's the federal level. The FBI or CIA, or maybe even the Secret Service is going to be looking for us. Don't blow this now."

Kevin sighed. "Alright, smartypants, what's the plan?"

"This car will take us to a shopping area. Very public, easy to blend in. Then we just find a place away from prying eyes, change clothes, and get another cab using your phone."

"Is that why you wouldn't let me turn it on?"

"Yes!" Scott said. "I don't want them tracking it until I've ditched my burner."

"Burner phones logged in with fake accounts, false names, masks, and misdirection. Where did you learn all this stuff?"

Scott laughed. "There is a discussion forum attached to the bounty list, talking about how to avoid getting caught."

"So that's why we flew into Colorado Springs and drove up to Boulder?"

Scott nodded.

"Was it really necessary to ditch all our electronics at the airport?"

"Yes. Absolutely. Don't worry, we'll pick them up before we leave."

"Good. That iPhone 15 wasn't cheap. "

Maria: Finding the Cocktail

February 28th - Boulder, Colorado

Maria Croix walked through the rubble of Senator Ball's home, trying to get a feel for who would do something like this. A large part of the front wall of the house was lying on the front lawn, surrounded by pieces of the ceramic tile roof. The drywall was gone, exposing the charred black remains of the studs holding up what was left of the second story.

The couch was nothing but a pile of springs and nails with the remains of a toilet from what she assumed was an upstairs bathroom lying on top of it. The glass top of the coffee table lay shattered on top of a toasted carpet or rug. It was hard to tell at this point.

"Tell me again how it happened," Maria said to the local fire chief.

Over the last two weeks, she'd assembled quite a list of faces, but had very few names to put with them. New faces were coming

193

in every week as more and more protests turned violent. The few names she could put to faces didn't help much, as she had no evidence of them doing anything illegal. Still, none of that compared to, or even hinted at what happened here.

"Normally, a report on this would take a week," he began.

"I don't care about normal," Maria said. "This was an attack on a United States Senator." She wished there was a video of the attack, so she could run it through Talvert's list of faces.

"I understand that," the chief shot back. "That's why I'm here to discuss it with you instead of writing up the report."

She gave him a scathing look before turning back to the remains of the house.

"Anyway, we had plenty of witnesses, which doesn't happen often. The first Molotov cocktail smashed against the front window, here." He pointed to what used to be the living room. "The heat from the first bottle shattered the glass, allowing the second bottle to smash through and splash gasoline on the couch, carpet, and coffee table, which were immediately engulfed in flames.

"There was barely enough time to evacuate the home before the flames ate through the ceiling to the second story. By the time we got here, flames were pouring out of every window facing the street, as well as the roof. We got the flames out pretty quick, but the damage was done. The home has to be torn down."

"Does this look like the work of amateurs or professionals?" Maria asked.

The chief sighed. "Ten years ago, I would have said only professionals would have known the first bottle wouldn't make it inside. But I've interviewed a dozen firebugs in the last five years who say they learned it all on YouTube."

"Do you think this was the work of a pyromaniac?"

He shook his head. "No. Definitely not."

"No?" Maria raised one eyebrow at this. "What makes you so certain?"

"They worked as a pair, for one thing. That's extremely rare. Add to that the crowd who watched them do it, right in front of a police presence. They didn't have time to stand around and watch it burn. No, this pair doesn't care about the fire. They only care about the damage to the home."

"You're willing to swear to that in your report?"

"Of course."

Maria smiled. "Good. That's exactly what I need to make sure we find the pair who did this."

Gideon Takes Karen on a Date

March 1st - Notre Dame, Indiana

Gideon Shumway knocked on Karen Emmett's door, eager for their date. They were scheduled to see *X-Men: Dark Phoenix*.

The door opened, and Nancy stood there. "Come on in, Gideon. She's almost ready."

Gideon stepped inside and bounced a little on the balls of his feet. The cloud that had hung over his head since Christmas was gone. He wasn't done grieving his grandfather's death, by any means, but he did feel much better.

Brenda eyed him with a wry smile on her face. "You look happy for once."

Gideon gave her a smile in return. "Thank you! I am happy."

She chuckled and headed into the bedrooms. Less than a minute later, Karen came out, a big smile on her face, her cheeks very rosy. "Brenda's right. You do look much happier."

Gideon bowed to her for effect. He stood back up and looked her in the eyes and offered his hand. "Thank you for noticing. Shall we go?"

She giggled, then took his hand as he led her to his car. He was a perfect gentleman that night, opening the door for her everywhere they went. He held her hand through the whole movie, letting her squeeze it tightly during the scarier scenes.

Halfway through dinner, Karen finally asked, "I have to know what happened to you."

"What do you mean?"

"I mean, you're so much more alive. Last week you were so depressed. You've been depressed since your grandpa died, and then suddenly, you're bouncing all over the place, opening the door for me, holding my hand, actually listening when I talk. So, tell me what changed."

Gideon set down his fork, unsure where to begin. He studied her face, trying to decide how much of this she would understand. He finally said, "I found closure."

"With your grandpa's death?"

Gideon nodded. "Watching him die right in front of me shook my faith, made me reevaluate everything I thought I understood about God. Now I feel solid in my faith again."

Karen frowned, which left Gideon confused. She didn't look happy for him. "So, what does that mean for us?"

"What do you mean?"

"Gideon, do you remember the first time you asked me out?"

He blushed and looked down at the table. "That's going to be a difficult one to forget. You shut me down hard."

"I knew who you were from the first week of last semester. I watched you and asked my friends about you. They told me you were Mormon, and Mormon's don't date girls outside their church."

"Well, that's generally true, but not always."

"I just need to know one thing if we're going to keep dating." She stared at him, looking more serious than he'd ever seen her.

"What is it?"

"Are you hoping I'll convert for you?"

Gideon shook his head slightly. "No. I'm not dating you because I'm hoping you'll change for me. I like you the way you are."

"But you do hope we'll get married someday?"

"Well," Gideon blushed again, trying to decide what the right answer was. "Eventually, I suppose. That is the purpose of dating, after all."

"Not for most guys," Karen replied. "You're the first guy I've dated that didn't want to have sex on the first date. That's the reason you got the second one. I don't believe in sex before marriage."

"Neither do I," Gideon replied quickly.

"Well, I would hope so. Otherwise, I'd be really insulted."

"Insulted?"

"Never mind. I'm really happy you found closure about your grandpa. And I'm glad we had this little talk."

"Me too," Gideon said, though he was left a little confused. Something his father said to him a few years ago surfaced in his memory.

"Son, I have to tell you that women are confusing," Ben Sr. said to him before he left for senior prom. "You won't always understand what they say. So, whenever that happens, just know that if they're happy, you don't need to understand them."

He'd never needed that advice before, but now he was glad he had it.

The Muslim Mahdi's First Act of Terror

March 3rd - Warsaw, Poland

Mohammad Ali Malik sat staring out the window of his room in the Castle Inn. He had an excellent view of the entrance to St. John's Archcathedral as midnight mass ended. It was a risk to be so close to the action, but this was his first major operation, and he wanted to see how well his men performed.

It was his destiny to become Mohammad Al-Mahdi, the savior of the world, who would unite all of Islam under one banner, and from there, subjugate the world to the will of Allah.[59]

The crowd began to fill the street, pleased with themselves for proving their devotion by attending weekly mass. They had no idea what true devotion was, but some of them were about to learn.

Screeching tires announced the arrival of the car with the first team, and the crowd instinctively bunched together.

"Allāhu Akbar!" a man shouted just before opening fire with a machine gun. He fired off several dozen rounds before the gun jammed.

Ali smirked at the minor setback. The car sped away as the rest of the crowd ran outside to see what had happened. That's when the second team took action. This was a team of one, a man who blended into the crowd with a thick jacket on. Ali stood and walked into the next room. As much as he wished he could watch this next part, he was too close.

The explosion shook the room and blew in the windows, which allowed him to hear the screams. He smiled as he walked back to the window to inspect the damage and await the body count.

Only one thing bothered him about the attack, and that was the death of the suicide bomber. It wasn't the death itself which occupied his thoughts. The man was guaranteed to enter paradise. No, it had more to do with the limited number of followers he'd recruited so far. Until their numbers grew, he would have to teach his men to do things a bit differently.

Scott, the Money Will Be Worth It

March 15th - Washington, D.C.

Scott Knox was bundled up in several layers to fight off the freezing temperatures of the unseasonably bitter cold weather. Kevin was also bundled up so well that no one would be able to identify either of them on camera. Their previous attack on the traitor, Senator Don Ball, had caused an increased level of security. Yet despite his caution, the Senator continued to walk from his favorite restaurants back to the Capitol Building.

"Why did we take this bounty?" Scott asked. "We got paid well for the last one, better than we could possibly get paid for this one."

"Is it all about the money for you?" Kevin asked. "I thought we were trying to stop this bill from going through. Besides, if we put him in the hospital long enough, this bounty will pay better. Ten thousand dollars for every day he can't participate in Senate hearings or committees."

Scott just shook his head. "There is no way we are going to put him in the hospital for a full week, let alone put him out of commission for a full ten days."

"That Kentucky Senator was laid up for three weeks." [60]

"Yeah," Scott said as he shrugged his shoulders, "but they caught the guy who did that."

"If we do this right, they won't have anything to hold us on."

"I don't know …"

Kevin stared at him as if trying to decide the best thing to say. "You've got the easy part on this, but if you want to abort, just say so. I can't do this job without you."

"I'll do it," Scott said, "but we need to be more careful about which bounties we take."

Kevin nodded. "Agreed." His phone buzzed. "There's the signal. Ball is leaving the restaurant. Only one bodyguard."

"Just one? This is going to be a piece of cake." Scott started running.

Kevin waited two seconds before running after him yelling, "Come back here, you creep!" They ran half a block with Kevin spewing out the vilest insults he could imagine.

Scott ran right in front of the Senator, then turned sharply to the left. He looked over his shoulder to see if Kevin did his part.

"You're not going to get away that easy!" Kevin yelled as he ran right at Ball.

Someone stepped in front of the Senator, presumably the bodyguard. "Stop!"

Kevin slammed right into the guy, knocking him into Ball and kept going.

Scott didn't have time to see how badly Ball was hurt. The news reports would tell him later. Right now, he had to keep running. There was a cab waiting around the next corner. He hopped in. He was disappointed to see this one had a human driver.

As Kevin joined Scott in the back seat, the driver asked, "Anyone else coming?"

"No," Scott said. It was hard to remain calm and avoid tipping off the driver that anything was going on.

The driver started driving. "BWI is thirty miles away. If it were me, I would've flown out of Reagan."

"We'll keep that in mind on our next vacation." Kevin's tone was condescending and sarcastic at the same time.

"Well, excuse me," the driver replied. "I usually like to talk to the guys I pick up. You want to spend the next half hour in silence, that's fine with me."

"I hope so," Scott said. "That's what we want."

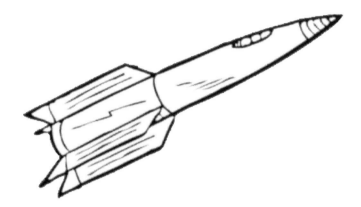

Liz's Golden Ticket

March 15th - Hawthorne, California

Liz Smith walked into Leon Cologne's office, pleased to see him behind his desk, intently studying his computer screen. Keeping him productive was her primary task. Every time he wandered away, it meant months of additional work to launch another widget or gizmo. That was all well and fine when it kept the company profitable and on the cutting edge of technology.

However, right now, they were planning to send six billionaires into space. Something they could only accomplish if Leon stayed focused. Their nightly dinners had turned into interviews of the world's wealthiest people—specifically, those who were applying to join Leon for the week-long excursion to the International Space Station.

It was nice meeting the wealthiest and most influential people in the world, but she missed the time alone with him, away from the distractions of the office.

"Leon," she said softly when he didn't look up from his screens.

"Ah, Liz." He focused on her, looking her up and down. "Am I late for a meeting?"

She shook her head. "No. I just wanted to let you know the two industrial scales for the media event have been moved into place."

"That reminds me, I have a question for you. How much do you weigh?"

"Excuse me?" Liz thought he was joking, but not even a hint of a smile showed on his face.

"Your weight, or more precisely, your mass. I need to know your mass."

Something caught in Liz's throat as she tried to figure out how that could possibly be relevant. Did he expect her to get on that scale in front of the media?

"Come on, don't be shy. I'm going on national television next week, where my mass will be displayed to the whole world. If I'm going to bring enough gold for both of us, I'm going to need to know your mass."

She gasped. "You want to take me with you to the International Space Station?" She'd dreamed about being an astronaut as a child, but it was a long-lost ambition. Seeing Earth from space would undoubtedly be unforgettable.

"Of course. Didn't I make that clear?" Leon studied her face as if trying to read a foreign language. "After all, this was your idea to begin with. Besides, I'm going to need you up there to keep me on task."

"Then, this has nothing to do with only two women applying to be among the first space tourists?"

"Why is that a problem?"

She smiled at his ignorance of the human condition. He was one of the smartest people on the planet, but like most engineers she'd met, there were certain aspects of life they simply couldn't grasp until it was spelled out for them. "You're trying to create a fully self-sustaining colony on Mars. You're going to need an equal number of men and women. Showing a bunch of men going into space isn't going to encourage women to volunteer to move to Mars."

Leon's face reflected her smile, the long-familiar twinkle appearing in his eyes. He shook his head slowly. "I never would have thought of that. Where would I be without you?"

"From what I've seen, you'd probably be in orbit right now, in a tiny capsule, all alone."

He laughed, and Liz couldn't help but join in. "Seriously, though," he said, cutting off her laughter, "do you want the seat beside me? Because if you do, I'll need to know your mass."

"Yes! I'll go with you. There's just one thing I need you to do for me."

"Name it."

"When I get on that giant scale you bought, on live television in front of the world, you'd better be on it with me."

"Why?"

"That way, no one will actually know my weight. Just our combined weight."

"Sure. I can do that." The thought pleased him, and his smile turned into a smirk.

Maria is Recruited

March 19th - Washington, D.C.

Maria Croix stormed into Barry Malevich's office, the head of the National Joint Terrorism Task Force, waving a thick file folder over her head. "Two weeks! I've been waiting two weeks to get in here, and this is the list of what's happened since then."

Barry looked up from his computer screen at the noise and stood to offer his hand. "You must be Maria," he said calmly. "I've heard of your, uh, bold manner."

She ignored his offered hand and slammed the files onto his desk. "Did they also tell you how vital my investigation is? Do you know how many new attacks have been linked to this same group in the two weeks you've kept me waiting?"

She'd wasted three weeks trying to convince the Secret Service to pursue the matter before Director Janson finally told her it was a case for the JTTF. Then she got in touch with Malevich, only to have him sit on it for two weeks while they reviewed her evidence before granting her an audience.

"Seventeen confirmed," Barry said. He pointed to one of the chairs on the other side of his desk.

"Try thirty-five," Maria shot back, refusing to sit, "including last Friday's attack on Senator Ball."

"I suppose that file folder contains the evidence linking all these actions to a single organization?" Barry asked as he reached for the files.

"It's all the evidence I've collected so far." Her volume fell to a normal level as Barry opened the file and began flipping through. "The reason I'm coming to you is to get the resources I need to find the missing link. I know I'm close to finding the man behind it all."

"I'm sorry, but I don't see the link. What group are you blaming for all this?"

Maria shook her head as she finally sat down. "I don't have a name for them yet, but I've linked 273 people who've attended violent rallies in at least five different states each. These thirty-five latest incidents all had at least one of those 273 in attendance. The only way that's possible is if someone is financing them."

"Have you brought these people in for questioning?"

"A few," Maria admitted. "None of them said anything of value. Some looked genuinely shocked at the idea that they could get paid to attend those rallies."

"Has there been unusual activity in their bank accounts?" Barry pressed as he continued to flip through the files.

"No, but that only proves they must be funded by someone."

Barry looked up at her, and the files dropped to his desk. "Exactly how is a lack of activity proof of collusion?"

"These people are traveling to different states to attend these rallies. Some have gone from California to Florida, others from Texas to Chicago."

"So you've said."

"There's no evidence that they purchased airfare. That kind of travel should have drained their meager bank accounts, but none of them are missing a single payment. They aren't going broke, but as far as I can tell, they aren't getting rich either."

"This man here," Barry said, pointing to the file, "Norman Gifford. It says he flew from Albuquerque to New York, where he was seen at a rally where a Molotov cocktail was used to start a car fire."

"Yes. That was March 2nd," Maria said, nodding. "The resulting clash between the protestors and the police left ten people hospitalized, including two cops. Only three people were arrested, and they were all locals."

"Who paid for his ticket?"

"I don't know. I'm being stonewalled on that one."

Barry scanned the file again. He slammed his finger down on the paper. "ShapeShift."

"Yeah, it's one of those crypto whatzits that don't respond well to threats," Maria said. "They won't even transfer me to a manager without a warrant. I can't even prove whether the account was his or someone else's."

Barry stood up with a smile. "How many of these plane tickets did you track to ShapeShift?"

"Only four," Maria said. "The others were from Poloniex, Bitstamp, Coinbase, and half a dozen other currency exchanges. None of them will tell me who the accounts belong to."

"Don't you see? You found the connection."

"I have?"

"Yes!" Barry walked over and placed one hand on her shoulder. He was at least a foot taller than her, yet she didn't feel like he was trying to dominate her with his height. It was a friendly gesture. "You said there wasn't unusual activity in their bank accounts."

"Right."

"And most of them are paying for their airfare using cryptocurrency."

"Which makes it impossible to know where the money comes from," Maria said. She was starting to get frustrated now. She'd had the same argument with her analysts more than a week ago.

"Which means they are being paid in cryptocurrency."

Her eyes went wide when she realized what he was implying. "That's the connection," Maria said, thinking out loud as the pieces fell into place. "Someone is hiring these protestors with cryptocurrencies, hiding behind the encryption so we can't see who they are."

"I think my team can take it from here. We have more experience in tracking cryptocurrency."

Maria glared up at him. "You're not taking me off this case! I've put my neck out there too far on this one for you to just grab the ball and leave me hanging out to dry!"

Barry frowned and backed up a step. Then he laughed. Maria's glare became a scowl as she prepared to launch into one of her infamous tirades. But he cut her off by saying, "That's what I was hoping you would say. I love your passion. You'll fit right in at the JTTF."

"Fit right in? What are you saying? I came to you for help, not for a job."

"The JTTF is made up of many agencies," Barry explained, "including the Secret Service. Don't think of it as a new job, think of it as a promotion, with upward mobility opportunities."

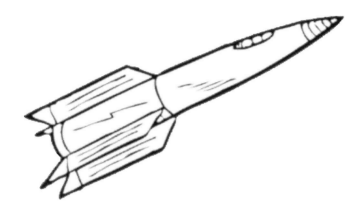

Liz is Prepping

March 20th - Hawthorne, California

Liz Smith gasped as she walked into the small warehouse temporarily converted into a stage. A large green screen stood behind two industrial scales with a huge LCD display ten feet in the air between them. Gray rocks and dirt added to the lunar landscape.

This was the only part of the ISS project on the Hawthorne campus, where she had no input, involved as she was in the negotiations between the five countries, which all had to agree on the requirements imposed on the potential astrotourists. She would have preferred a faux Martian landscape.

"Okay, Bill, get on the first scale," a man wearing a beret said through a megaphone. It was comical how much he looked like a stereotypical movie director. He had to be Tartan Quincy

A burly man over six and a half feet tall stepped up. The display showed *189.5 kg* over his head.

"Frank, Tom, both of you get on the other one," Quincy said.

As the other two much smaller men stepped on the other scale, *173.2 kg* appeared above them for a few seconds. The screen then flashed, *12.3 kg short* over the whole thing.

"Perfect. Now we need to find something to balance it out. Grab those weights."

Liz cleared her throat when she was just a few feet behind him.

Quincy jumped and turned around. Then he scowled and said, "This set isn't open yet!"

She scowled back at him. "I'm Liz Smith. Nothing on this campus is closed to me."

All the anger melted from his face in an overly dramatic performance of penance. "I'm so sorry, Miss Smith. I didn't realize it was you."

"The press will be arriving in thirty minutes. Are you prepared?"

"We're doing a final check of the programming right now."

As he spoke, the stagehands moved the weights onto the scale with the two men. Above them, the number on display went down until it said 0.2 kg over. Then it shifted to *Payment Achieved.*

"You see? Working perfectly."

"And the green screen overlay?"

He walked over to a small monitor to the side of the set, facing away from the stage. "See for yourself."

She smiled at Leon's sense of humor. It looked like the stagehands were standing on the scales on the moon. "This is what the world is going to see?"

"It's a little over the top for my taste," Quincy said as he rolled his eyes, "but I wasn't given artistic license to change it, so here we are."

"So I can give Pinkerton Security the green light to inspect the equipment?" Liz asked.

"Remind me why they have to check everything?"

She folded her arms and scowled at him. She'd already gone over this in half a dozen emails over the last month. "For the last time, we're bringing in thousands of pounds of gold for this event. I couldn't persuade Leon to use gold-painted lead bricks, so we must have security. If they lose a single ounce of gold, it'll damage their reputation. They have to test your measurement systems and double-check that no one added a hidden trap door or any other harebrained scheme to steal some of this gold."

The thought of over twenty-five million dollars' worth of gold in a single building made her shudder. The temptation for theft was so high that she wouldn't be surprised if a mob tried to break down the doors to get inside. Leon insisted Pinkerton could handle the security needs. Either way, this was going to be an event no one would forget any time soon.

Scott & Kevin Take the Next Step

March 21st - Berkeley, California

Scott Knox laid low for several days listening to the news, but his attack on Senator Ball didn't get more than a few sound bites. Only the conspiracy news even suggested the attack was anything but a chance encounter. Initial reports said the Senator would be back on the Senate floor by Monday, which would have meant no payout. But after almost a week, he was still in the hospital.

Kevin spent the time catching up on his business classes. Neither of them even talked about attending more rallies, too fearful of being recognized. But now that almost a full week had passed, they were both itching to find their next bounty.

"Have you seen this one?" Kevin asked. He sounded shocked and excited.

Scott knew that could only mean his friend had finally noticed the big one. He walked over to the computer, just to confirm.

"Yup. I've seen it. Ten million each to kill the President and Vice-President and a ten-mill bonus if they die on the same day."

"How long has that been up?"

"Several weeks, I think. I first noticed it the morning after we burned down the Senator's house."

"Well, how come no one's claimed it?" Kevin asked. "A bounty that high, you'd think someone would…"

Scott grabbed the mouse and clicked on the bounty. Unlike the others, which disappeared as soon as someone accepted the mission, this one showed five usernames listed as bounty hunters hoping to claim the reward. Each one registered the date when they planned to strike.

"Whoa," Kevin said as he finished scanning the list. "How come you didn't tell me about this sooner?"

"Because I thought it was a trap," Scott said. "You know, you put your name up there, and the next day the Secret Service knocks on your door to arrest you."

Kevin laughed. "If the Secret Service knew about this site, we'd have been arrested long ago. This is deep in the dark web, my friend. Trust me, we aren't any safer by not putting our names in the hat. Besides, we always use a VPN to access the site. They can't trace it to us."

"Wait, you're serious? You really want to kill someone for money?"

"No," Kevin said. His eyes went wide with excitement. "I'm gonna take this bounty for a boatload of money! And I'm going to change the fate of the country at the same time."

"Believe me, I've thought about it, but every time I check it, all the dates are taken. Monday was supposed to be the first attempt, but I didn't see anything on the news about it."

"They've scheduled two attacks every month. Oh look, there's one available at the end of May. Are you in this with me, or not?"

"I don't know." Scott hated President Towers and was glad to see so many people willing to take him out of the picture, but the idea of pulling the trigger himself created a knot in his stomach. "I don't even know how to fire a gun."

"That's what makes this perfect. No one would ever suspect us."

Scott shook his head. "That doesn't inspire me with confidence. Have you ever even held a gun before?"

Kevin shrugged. "What difference does that make?"

"You're seriously going to commit to killing the President of the United States without ever having held a weapon. You have to be the worst assassin in history."

"Come on, there have to be five other failed attempts for us to even have a shot." Kevin paused as his gaze unfocused. That was his thinking face. "Besides, how hard can it be?" He lifted both his arms for emphasis. "I mean, anything we don't know we can learn on YouTube. Also, there's no way we could be the only ones in on this plot."

"What do you mean?"

"You remember how in D.C. there was a spotter to tell us when Ball left the restaurant?"

Scott nodded. "Who did that come from, anyway?"

"It was another bounty on the list, down in the section you ignore because they don't pay much." Kevin clicked on the last available date. "See? It says on May 26th that Towers and Michaels will both be at the Brown Convention Center in Houston. It even suggests the best place to set up our shots. How would they know these things if someone else hadn't already accepted the lesser bounty and given them this info?"

Scott pondered this. All the bounties on the President and VP had details that could only be obtained by someone on the inside, such as the route of the Presidential motorcade through a small town. He'd never stopped to consider where all that information came from. The May 26th date had five times as many details as any of the others.

"How come no one else has volunteered for this?" Scott asked. The more he saw, the more possible this scenario appeared, which was both thrilling and scary.

"Maybe they only listed it an hour ago. Plus, it's a two-man job, minimum. How many two-man teams do you think there are on this site?"

Scott scanned the rest of the information.

> *Bounty Hunters will be provided with Press Credentials for the event, as well as detailed security arrangements at least two weeks prior. Possible scenarios include:*
> *1. Sniper shot from 1/4-mile distance.*
> *2. Remotely triggered explosives.*
> *3. Close-range fire during a press conference.*
> *As always, video recording evidence is required to collect the bounty.*

As near as he could tell, all that would really be required of them was to be in the right place at the right time with enough training to make a shot from fourteen hundred feet.

"Come on, we can do this!" Kevin said, echoing Scott's thoughts.

"You're serious?"

Kevin nodded. "Of course I am. Look, I'm signing up, throwing our names in the hat."

Scott wrinkled up his face at this. The knot in his stomach kept getting bigger. "I didn't think you had it in you to…"

"We," Kevin interrupted, "are going to do this together. All the information we need is here."

"Yes, I see that. What I mean is how can you justify murder."

Kevin turned around and stood up to look him in the eye. "You hate Towers more than I do. How many times have you ranted that he ruined your life? How many times have you said you wished he were dead?"

"Yeah, I wish he were dead, but I don't want to be the one to pull the trigger."

Kevin rolled his eyes. "Don't tell me, after all this time, you're still holding on to a shred of morality."

"What?"

"How many criminal acts have we committed together?"

"I don't know, but…"

"We burned down a house together," Kevin pressed. "We put a man in the hospital. Either of those could have killed him."

"Yeah, but no one died."

"But they could have, and you were still willing to do it."

Scott swallowed hard. The reality of what he'd been doing the last few months nearly swallowed him whole, yet he felt compelled to keep moving forward. He'd gone from wishing someone else would do it to seriously being tempted to pull the trigger himself in less than ten minutes.

Each step felt natural, even right, but when he considered it as a whole, it felt wrong. He shook off the thought, unwilling to face the darkness contained there. He had to keep going. "Two months. You think we'll be ready to do this in two months?"

Kevin smiled widely. "We'd better be. I already accepted the bounty."

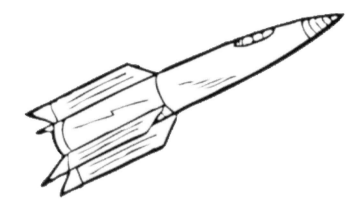

Leon's First Love

March 28th - Hawthorne, California

Liz Smith sat in her favorite armchair in Leon Cologne's office. She'd spent so much time here the last six weeks that it was starting to feel like her office. Leon was lying on the floor again, staring up at the same display of stars she'd seen him stare at several times a week. Mars rose from the floor and slowly climbed the wall, a bright red dot among the dimmer stars.

Leon's eyes followed its slow progress up the wall and onto the ceiling without saying anything. As it moved closer to the middle of the room, he said, "I'm glad you're going with me into space."

"Well, we can't have you getting lost up there."

He laughed. "Yes. You really do keep me on track. I'm not sure what I'd do without you."

Yellow flags started popping up in her head. The statement was laden with so much desire and longing that she sat up straighter in her chair. She had to distance herself from him emotionally and remind him why she was really there. "You'd find another recent graduate of business college to get your coffee."

He sat up and looked at her. "You don't have to do that anymore. I can get anyone to do that. You've proven you're much more than a Personal Assistant."

She swallowed hard. The yellow flags turned into screaming red sirens as certain things clicked into place. All the dinners she'd shared with Leon, meeting his children, the interest he'd taken in her personal life were all adding up. This man didn't go anywhere without her knowing about it, and he didn't tell her he'd spent two hours at Harry Winston's last week. There could be only one reason he would leave a visit to a high-end jewelry store off his calendar. "I don't like where this is going."

Surprise and fear flashed briefly in his eyes.

It was so different than his usual manner that she gasped slightly.

"Once more you see right through me," Leon said. He walked over to his massive desk and opened the top drawer. He pulled out a small box. "Perhaps you've guessed what's in this."

Liz nodded.

"Then you know I want to wait a few more days to give it to you."

She swallowed and nodded again as a tear rolled down her cheek. She managed to squeak out, "I can't."

His face fell, and he quickly put the box back in the drawer. When he looked up at Liz, a single tear rolled down his cheek. "I'm never going to find another woman like you."

Liz couldn't restrain her own tears any longer. She wanted to run out of the room, but her legs refused to obey.

"Can…" Leon said, choking on the words. He took three deep breaths before saying, "Can you at least tell me why?"

She pointed to the bright red dot starting to make its way down the other wall. It was a little blurry through her tears, but she could still make it out. "That is your first love. I knew that the first week I started working here. I can't leave Earth and go to Mars. I just can't."

He closed his eyes and nodded slowly. He swallowed hard before saying, "I thought you were onboard with the whole plan, the colony on Mars, the new life we'll create there, all of it."

"No," she squeaked out. "I can't leave my family, my friends, everything I've ever known, and go to another planet with no chance of returning."

He nodded as more tears poured out. "Will you still join me on the space station?"

Without even thinking about it, she shook her head. It took a moment for her brain to catch up with what her body knew instinctively. How could she spend a week in close quarters with him after this? She felt a sudden urge to visit her parents in Virginia. With all the emotions roiling in her mind, she needed her mother's advice, her mother's embrace.

"I understand. There are half a dozen people ready to take your place. We can say you got a cold and couldn't go."

She nodded at this. The true story of why she wasn't going into space would be major headlines the whole time Leon was gone. A minor illness was completely believable. "To sell the story, maybe I should take sick leave, starting tomorrow, so people don't ask if you've been exposed."

"Yeah. That will work."

Target: The Fourth Black SUV

March 28th - Springfield, Missouri

Macy Jones gripped her steering wheel as she waited for the text message. She was so nervous, having never done anything like this before. Her phone buzzed. She glanced down at it.

4th Blk. Now.

She hit the accelerator and pulled out onto the side road. She'd practiced this four times over the last week, and today was the big day. She'd intentionally worn down her brake line until the brake fluid was entirely gone. That way, it would look just like the incident a couple years ago, just in case she failed.[61] It also meant there was no backing out now.

"Fourth black SUV," she told herself. "He's in the fourth black SUV." It became her mantra as she hit fifty-five, twenty miles per hour over the posted limit.

She came up to the curve and veered left, her muscle memory taking over. The bumps and jostling of driving her truck over the grass and into the weeds was nothing new. She was seconds away from earning ten million dollars! The thought made her accelerate a little more as she plowed through the weeds.

"Fourth black SUV. He's in the fourth black SUV."

The hill dropped off sharply, and she turned to compensate. By the time her right front tire went into the concrete ditch, her truck was almost parallel with it, allowing her to smoothly drive up the other side. A flurry of black SUVs was coming right at her, and she aimed for the fourth one.

Bam

The jolt spun her so hard she lost hold of the wheel. The world twisted around her, then tilted as first one tire, and then another went off the road into the ditch. She barely caught a glimpse of the fourth black SUV as it sped past, untouched.

"Damn!"

President Towers' vehicle, along with many others, sped away, leaving her hopes of cashing in on the big one in the dust. Two black SUVs stopped in front of her, next to the one that had rammed her, and soon she had ten guns pointed at her.

Dazed, but not confused, she unbuckled her seatbelt and slowly got out of the truck with her hands in the air. She barely heard them shouting for her to get on the ground, but she still obeyed.

As they put the cuffs on her, she wondered if the attack on V.P. Michaels was going any better.

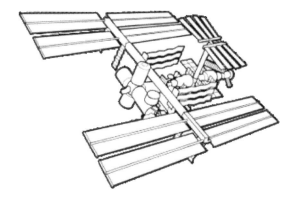

The Advent of Space Tourism

April 6th - Alexandria, Virginia

Liz Smith watched the media circus that covered Leon Cologne's successful launch of the first astrotourists aboard the new Big Falcon Rocket, their docking with the ISS, and the many hours of footage showing a bunch of billionaires having a week-long party in space. She'd cried on her mother's shoulder for the first two days, but the worst was past. She'd never even considered marrying Leon, and she didn't really understand why he felt like marrying her.

"Houston, this is Tourist One. We are loaded and prepped for departure," Leon's voice said on the speakers. Their week in space was over, and they were all packed up and ready to head home.

The response came a couple seconds later. *"Roger that, Tourist One. You are cleared for departure."*

"Tourist One departing." Leon pushed a button, and the camera angle shifted to outside the station.

Their capsule remained firmly attached.

"Tourist One, we are showing no joy on that departure. Can you confirm?"

"Confirmed, Houston. We are still attached. Please advise."

The camera switched back inside. Leon was still smiling, but several of the others were not.

"What's the matter?" John Banks asked. *"Why aren't we going anywhere."*

"Houston advises you repeat the departure command."

Leon could be seen pressing the same button several times. *"It's sending the command, but nothing is hap…"*

The sound and video feed both cut off, and there was a blank screen for a second.

"Tourist One, come in," the Houston voice said.

The video switched to mission control in Houston. *"Command, we've lost contact with Tourist One."*

"All communications with the ISS have been lost," a new voice said.

Patty Parker's face broke in. *"It looks like there's some sort of communications break down with the International Space Station, and Houston has cut us out of the feed while they research the problem."* Commercials replaced the news broadcast.

"What's going on?" Liz asked the room. "Why aren't they on their way back yet?" Her heart was pounding, and nothing was making sense.

"I don't know, honey," her mother, Janet said. "I'm sure they'll get it fixed in a moment."

Liz gripped her chair while she waited. She never thought a three-minute commercial break could take so long.

"This is horrible news," Patty Parker said as the program came back on. *"We've got live footage from amateur astrophotographer, Ken Markowitz, who specializes in filming the ISS."*

A very shaky image of the ISS came on the screen, and something looked very wrong, though Liz couldn't tell what. It did nothing to ease her growing panic.

"Our experts are telling us these plumes here," eight red ovals appeared on the screen, highlighting areas of the station, *"are maneuvering jets for the ISS, intended for short bursts. For some unknown reason, they are operating continuously. Still no word from Houston as to what this could mean, but we have Dale Greensborough, former NASA engineer on the line with us. Dale, what can you tell us about these jets?"*

"This is the worst possible scenario I can imagine, Patty," Dale said as a photo of him came up on the screen. *"If they can't get those maneuvering jets turned off in the next two minutes, the station could deorbit."*

"Are you saying the ISS could fly off into space?"

Patty's question echoed the one on Liz's mind. Would Leon be lost in space? Would she have to watch as he slowly ran out of air?

"No." Dale paused a moment before he said, *"It will impact the atmosphere, be torn to pieces and crash to the Earth, only God knows where. Probably in the ocean."*

Liz tried to swallow, but her throat was too tight. "No. It can't be."

"Are you telling me this could be the end of the International Space Station?" Patty asked.

"This is NASA we're talking about," Janet said, turning to face Liz. "I'm sure they'll work something out."

"It certainly looks that way," Dale said.

"You're only saying that because you didn't see all the death threats Leon got over this!" Liz rose to her feet, unable to sit still.

"What about the people on board the station?" Patty asked. *"Can they save the station, or get to safety?"*

"Death threats?" Janet repeated, rising to stand next to her daughter. "What are you talking about?"

"If they are aware of the problem, and cannot stop it," Dale continued in the background, *"I'm sure they're headed to the escape capsule they keep docked for just such an emergency."*

"I work for one of the richest, most powerful men in the world," Liz explained as she started pacing back and forth. "He gets death threats for everything."

"Can you tell us what might have caused this?" Patty asked.

"As his Personal Assistant, I handle all of that," Liz continued, pacing faster. "He probably isn't aware of how many people threatened to cause his rocket to explode on the launch pad."

Dale paused, creating dead air. Just as Patty opened her mouth for another question, Dale said, *"I'd rather not guess on this one, Patty."*

"You knew all that, and you were willing to go up with him?" Janet asked, her eyes wide with fright.

"The world is watching with bated breath, Dale," Patty said. *"Isn't there anything you can add?"*

Liz stopped in front of her mother and looked her in the eyes. "Yes, Mom. I was. We can't live our lives in fear."

"Let me clarify," Dale said. *"I would only be speculating at this point, and even to do that, I'd have to get clearance. I'm sorry, but those jets have already been firing for too long. That station is coming down. I've already said more than I should. I'm sorry."*[62]

There was an audible click.

Liz turned to the television. "Did he just say what I think he said?"

They both stood in silent anticipation.

"Well, that was Dale Greensborough, former NASA engineer, and part of the team who designed the ISS," Patty Parker said. *"It looks as though the International Space Station is indeed dropping from orbit, and if Dale is correct, it's already too late to save the station."*

"No! This can't be happening!" Liz ran out of the room. She couldn't do it. She couldn't watch any longer, knowing that Leon was on board. She ran up to her room, flung herself on her bed, and cried.

Several hours later, Janet woke Liz up when she sat on the bed. "Liz, I think you need to dry your eyes and wash your face."

Liz looked up at her mother as her nightmares were replaced by the equally horrifying reality of the last few hours. "Why? What possible reason is there for me to look presentable?"

Janet hesitated, which only made Liz's heart race again. Her mother never was good at delivering bad news. "The ISS has already entered the atmosphere, and there's no sign of anyone being alive."

"That's what I was afraid of," Liz said slowly. "But you didn't answer my question. What else has happened?"

"Well…"

"Spit it out, Mom."

"Apparently someone found out about Leon's visit to Harry Winston about a week before you announced you weren't going. There's a pack of reporters outside, and they all want to hear your story."

Liz heaved a huge sigh. "Give me five minutes."

Janet nodded and left the room.

Liz stood up, clutching her pillow tightly. She'd faced reporters before, but never when her grief was so fresh. And never when they were there to ask about her personal life.

She gave the pillow one final squeeze before dropping it back on the bed. As she did so, she swallowed her problems, and her brain kicked into action mode. She'd spent months dealing with the media for Leon, and now it was almost second nature.

She went into the bathroom and scrubbed her face three times before applying makeup. Just enough so that it looked like she wasn't wearing any. Then she marched down the stairs to the front door and flung it open to face the vultures.

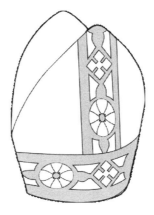

Pope Ferdinand's Stepping Stones

April 7th - Hanover, Germany

Pope Ferdinand entered the conference room of the World Communion of Reformed Churches. The responses to his invitations were much slower than he'd hoped. This was only the second religious leader in six months who'd been willing to see him.

What's worse, the World Evangelical Alliance had refused to call a General Assembly until the exact nature of the relationship between the two groups had been thoroughly negotiated, which could take years. He had much higher hopes for the World Communion of Reformed Churches.

President Jawcria Dweck sat at the head of the table with a scowl on her face. He didn't know why she looked so sour or who any of the others in the room were.

"Thank you for meeting with me," the Pope said.

"It is hard to refuse the invitation of someone in your position," Jaweria said. "I must say I was confused by your request."

The Pope smiled at her, doing his best to hide his displeasure at having to reach out to a female minister. He tried to think of her as one of the nuns, but she certainly wasn't dressed like them. At least her clothing was modest. "I thought I made myself very clear. I am here to invite you to join the growing number of churches who have agreed to end the great protest and reunite the body of Christ."

Jaweria shook her head. "We could never ignore the last five hundred years of hatred and murder to be reunited with the Catholic Church."

"And I am not asking you to," the Pope said as he took a seat at the foot of the table.

"But isn't that what you've come to request?" Jaweria asked. "You want us to renounce the Protestant Reformation, one of the founding ideals of our organization. Without that, what would be left of us?"

"No organization can truly prosper if its sole purpose is to oppose something or someone else."

Jaweria laughed. "You must know that's not the sole purpose of our group."

"Yes, I do. All I'm trying to do is set a tone of mutual understanding and acceptance," the Pope said, quoting from their own Mission Statement. "I would like to find some unity and renewal in worship, theology, and spirituality. Together we can restore justice and eradicate poverty. All that is required is a healing reconciliation which will surely lead to peace for the body of Christ and the transformation of both churches and society." [63]

He knew these were the principles that united the various churches in the World Communion of Reformed Churches. In essence, he was asking to have the Roman Catholic Church join them with equal status to the other members. Jaweria paused, and Pope Ferdinand knew he'd chosen his words well. He studied her face as he waited for her reply.

"What exactly did you have in mind?" Jaweria asked at last.

Pope Ferdinand smiled. The hard work was done. The rest would just be working out the details.

President Towers Demands Answers from NASA

April 7th - Houston, Texas

President Daniel Towers marched into the conference room, walked past his seat at the head of the table, and stared at the group of scientists and advisors who'd been assembled to handle this crisis. "Alright, who's got the answers I need?" he asked.

He'd spent the whole plane ride to Houston arguing with Karl, his head of security for the last fifteen years. Karl felt that jumping in so quickly after a tragedy like the loss of the International Space Station sent the wrong message. The scientists, he explained, were all better off figuring this out themselves.

But Towers couldn't ignore the deaths of six billionaires, half of whom were his close friends. The fact that a dozen cows in Kansas and three of NASA's finest were also lost was enough to ensure Towers would not relent.

This was no time to stand on the sidelines while a team of professionals came up with some lie to tell the public. This was the time to get the truth before someone had a chance to spin it.

232

One of the men at the table cleared his throat. His tie was slightly askew and had half a dozen coffee stains on it. His stark-white shirt looked like it was brand new. "We're still sorting through the telemetry provided by the satellite network to see what went wrong. I have my best team going through all the telemetry line by line."

Towers focused on the one who spoke. "What's your name?"

"Dr. Terry Hatfield. I monitor all ISS telemetry and station health."

"Well, Terry," Towers said, starting out calmly, but building in volume as he spoke. "How long is it going to take for you to tell me why the ISS came rocketing out of the sky and crashed in rural Kansas?"

"Based on the Markowitz video," Terry said, seemingly ignoring Towers' anger, "the maneuvering jets fired in a particular pattern, designed to deorbit the space station."

Towers paced back and forth around the room as they talked, purposely making everyone uncomfortable. "And why did they fire?" Their calm manner only infuriated him. He'd used this technique dozens of times to intimidate his employees into confessing their mistakes. But these three seemed immune.

"That's what the telemetry data should tell us," Terry said calmly.

"Fine," Towers said, speaking as much to the wall as the people in the room. "Who can tell me why those jets exist in the first place?"

"Dr. Norm Russell, Mr. President. I'm in charge of the designs for the ISS. Those jets were designed for a controlled re-entry at the end of the space station's useful life." His white shirt was rumpled, as if he'd slept in it, but the crisp, bright colors of his tie suggested it was brand new. Clearly, someone had done a poor job of making these scientists presentable for the President's arrival.

"The station was designed to do this?" Towers asked, standing right behind Norm. "Is that what you're telling me?"

"Yes," Norm said. "Though the command wasn't supposed to be given for another five years, at least, and certainly not with anyone on board."

"And why did we lose contact with the station when that happened?" Towers asked. *Why did they all refuse to show any sign of intimidation?*

"That I can't answer," Norm said.

"I can, Mr. President. I'm Dr. Victor Franks, head of communications. The satellites we use to communicate with those in low Earth orbit received a command to remove the ISS transponder codes from their approved broadcasts. This was programmed in as part of the deorbit routine." Victor wore a tweed sweater. Considering the hot and humid climate, it was probably there to hide whatever was wrong with his shirt.

"Are you telling me you didn't have a backup system?" Towers asked.

"Of course we did," Victor said, "but the station crew still on board would have to know there was a communication problem and switch over to ground-based communication. I was monitoring the other bands, but nothing ever came through."

"Any thoughts on why that might be?" Towers asked.

"I hope it's because they were too busy trying to override the deorbit command or get to the escape capsule."

"Is there any evidence anyone made it to the escape capsule?" Towers asked. His glares went unheeded. He'd never seen a group of people so immune to intimidation. Didn't they know he could end their careers?

"Unfortunately, it never detached from the station," Terry said. "If anyone was in there, they would have burned up before being sucked out into the sky when the capsule breached."

"Then what about Tourist One?" Towers asked. "Why weren't they able to detach and land safely?"

No one spoke. Towers glared at each of them in turn, but they all just stared back impassively.

Terry's phone buzzed, and he looked down at it. "Just got the preliminary from the telemetry analysis. It looks like the command to detach Tourist One was improperly programmed. That's definitely what set off the deorbit command."

"Improperly programmed?" Towers' temper rose once more. "Are you telling me this all comes down to a couple of poorly written lines of code!" His voice echoed around the room, but he was beyond caring.

"Yes, that's what the preliminary report says," Terry replied calmly.

"I want the name of the person who wrote that line of code, and I want him in this room right now!" Their calm demeanor over the deaths of his friends was infuriating.

"That would be Leon Cologne, Mr. President," Victor said as he stared at his computer screen. "Terry, can you send those codes to me?"

"Why?" Terry asked. "What are you thinking?"

"Well, I've got the command lines on my screen for detaching Tourist One," Victor explained. "There's no way they could have triggered the deorbit command."

"Okay, I sent it."

Towers watched the exchange between the three nerds. He had to admit, they knew how to deal with a difficult situation. If he wasn't so angry over this whole incident, he might have been pleased with their performance. It was the kind of thing Karl would mention to him later.

"Yeah, this line of code is completely different from what I approved two months ago," Victor said. "Only one line is different, and it's written in hex."

"What are you saying?" Towers had no idea what hex was, but it didn't sound friendly.

"I'm saying this was either an enormous blunder caused by a small error in the code or a deliberate attack. The change in code caused Tourist One to broadcast the command to the station, rather than to the specific subroutine for detaching."

Towers glared around the room. "Are you saying Leon Cologne sabotaged the International Space Station?"

"It certainly looks intentional," Terry said. "Though I can't say for sure it was Mr. Cologne who changed the program. Either way, I don't see how we can continue working with SpaceX."

"Why?" Towers asked.

"It was either their faulty programming or lack of security which caused this disaster," Terry said. "We may never know which, but we do know that either answer poses too great a risk to continue with things the way they are. "

"Exactly what are you saying?" Norm asked.

"Most of our projects relied on that station," Franks replied. "Without it, we'll be scrubbing every launch for the next six months. I think there's a telescopic satellite set to launch in September. But all our astronauts will have to be put on indefinite leave. This disaster has basically halted all operations until we can replace the ISS."

Terry cleared his throat, cutting off whatever Franks was about to say next. Terry then looked President Towers in the eyes and said, "I'm saying no matter what the investigation finds, my recommendation will be to terminate our contract with SpaceX, effective immediately."

Scott & Kevin Sharpen Their Sharpshooter Skills

April 11th - Richmond, California

The Rangemaster reviewed Scott Knox's targets after two solid hours of shooting. "These scores look really good. You've made remarkable improvement."

Scott smiled. "Thanks. It's a lot more fun than I thought." He was picturing President Money's smug face on the target every time he fired. He would make that man pay for ruining his life.

"I think you're ready for the 200-yard range. What do you think?"

Scott tried not to look too eager. He'd spent every morning for the past two weeks learning how to care for and fire his rifle. Plus, he spent his afternoons watching YouTube videos on how to correct for wind and range. "I think I might be up for that."

"Same time tomorrow?"

Scott nodded as he packed up his rifle and eavesdropped as the instructor reviewed Kevin's scores. They pretended not to know each other here, as a precaution. This was the only range within fifty miles that had a 200-yard range. Scott was here quite frequently for hours at a time. Kevin came when he could, which sometimes overlapped with Scott's practice schedule.

They were both aware that three attempts had been made on Towers already, though only one even made the news. Macy Jones was under arrest for her attempted assassination of President Towers. By the time she got to trial, Towers would be a memory. Perhaps then the judge might be willing to buy her story about brake failure.

"Your pattern isn't as tight as it could be," the instructor told Kevin.

"The gun keeps jumping out of my hands," Kevin complained.

The instructor sighed loudly. "Look, just like any sport, marksmanship requires commitment. Coming in twice a week, you aren't going to remember your previous lesson. Sure, you can clean and fire your rifle, but you can't really get a feel for it if you don't use it more frequently."

"I know," Kevin replied, "but I've got exams coming up."

"We all have lives to lead. But if you want to move up to the 200-yard range, I need to see you in here more often to achieve the tighter clustering. Otherwise, you'd just be wasting your time trying to hit a more distant target."

Scott tried to hide his smile as he left. That would undoubtedly put an end to Kevin's boasts about being a natural.

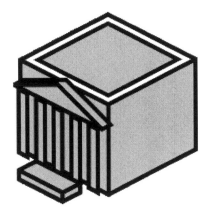

Maria's Help is No Help

April 16th - McLean, Virginia

Maria Croix walked slowly to the podium in a room packed with law enforcement officers from many different states, and a variety of agencies. Her last four weeks working with the National Joint Terrorism Task Force, or JTTF for short, had been some of the most fulfilling in her career. "Thank you all for coming," she said. "We have a lot of ground to cover and not a lot of time."

She paused to make sure everyone in the room was focused on her before continuing. "There has been a sharp rise in the level of violence at political rallies around the country. While this would be easy to dismiss as political unrest, we have uncovered evidence that many of the protestors are being paid to commit violence at these rallies."

"Someone is paying them to throw Molotov cocktails and burn down homes?" a young man in an NYPD uniform asked.

"Yes," Maria confirmed. As she'd hoped, there was a ripple of murmurs throughout the room.

"Why haven't we been told about this before?" one woman shouted.

"We're still trying to connect all the dots," Maria continued. "That's why you're all here. We need the help of local JTTF's to track down POI's and determine whether they have committed a crime or are only witnesses to a crime. I have compiled a list of 429 people from thirty-four different states. We have positively identified these people as attending rallies outside their home states without any visible means of paying for their transport. It will be your task to narrow down the list in your area, looking for those who might be capable of committing crimes for hire."

"How are they getting paid?" the NYPD officer asked.

"We believe the organizer is using cryptocurrencies, which they are in turn using to pay for transportation," Maria said. She'd already faced dozens of questions in other meetings about how absurd it sounded, or how it didn't constitute proof of any crime. Any hope she had of avoiding such questions here vanished as several hands shot in the air. She took a deep breath and plunged into the now-familiar list of explanations.

"Look, I know it isn't much of a connection," Maria admitted. "We've already looked into whether these are people who got rich by purchasing cryptocurrencies a few years ago and now have too much time on their hands."

Half the hands went down.

"For those few for whom we have a name, this doesn't appear to be the case. We are still working to track the transactions to a single main source, individual, or group."

Most of the remaining hands lowered.

"As you might imagine, there is a lot of red-tape involved in trying to discover the identities of someone who may have paid someone else to do something which might not have been a crime. To break this wide open, we need to find someone who will talk. There are almost five hundred people involved in this. Offering money for criminal activity must have attracted at least a few people who've already committed a crime in the past. We are looking for those few. Perhaps traveling out of state was a parole violation. We need someone we can question who is willing to talk to avoid penalties."

When she finished, only one hand remained in the air. It was attached to a short bald man sitting near the back in a three-piece suit. She couldn't make out his badge, other than to see there were three letters on it. She pointed to him, and he stood.

"Which acts of violence have you conclusively linked to this group?"

She barely resisted grinding her teeth. The question was so pointed she knew the man had to be a plant from the FBI, who'd objected several times to this entire line of inquiry. Speaking in as even a tone as she could manage, she said, "The Christmas Eve burning of the White House lawn. The destruction of Senator Ball's home. The attack on Senator Ball himself. Property damage at the homes of half a dozen other Senators. Physical injuries to several members of Congress. These acts have all been loosely tied into this investigation."

"Then you don't have the smoking gun," the FBI man said.

"I've been authorized to find it," Maria said. "That's why you're all here."

"You want us to waste our time and JTTF resources trying to prove your conspiracy theories?" the man asked loudly.

"My evidence was enough to convince Director Malevish," Maria said with a smile. "If you have a problem with these orders, take it up with him. For the rest of you, you should be receiving an email shortly with the faces of those we are fairly certain live in, or have ties to the jurisdiction of your local JTTF's. The first task is to put as many names to these faces as possible. If any of them are on parole or have a criminal background, no matter how buried, bring them in for questioning."

The bald man finally sat down, and Maria continued with her presentation. "Now, there are ten people of great interest who we know have committed crimes at these rallies. We are prepared to charge them with inciting to riot, property damage, or worse. Once we can prove they were paid for the actions, the charge becomes domestic terrorism.

"Our efforts to identify them have so far failed. If you have one of these ten people in your area, put as many resources into identifying and locating them as you can. For these men, I'll personally come to observe the interrogation."

She spent the next hour explaining the details of what she needed. That was followed by another half hour of questions and answers. Thankfully those were all about procedure, and stayed on topic.

As she was enjoying some well-deserved refreshments, the bald man came up to her, and she saw he was only two inches taller than her. He held out his hand.

Maria reluctantly accepted it.

"You handled yourself well up there," he said. "I'd apologize, but I needed to witness your reaction under pressure for myself. After all, you do have a reputation. Reports are one thing, but first-hand experience is something else." A quick look at his nametag revealed he was Trey Watkins with the CIA.

Maria eyed him warily as she tried to ignore the implied insult. "I didn't think the CIA was part of the Joint Terrorism Task Forces on American soil."

"Strictly an advisory capacity," Trey said. "If we get foreign chatter about something happening on American soil, we pass it off to you. Today, though, I'm here specifically to offer you a job."

"I have a job," Maria said. "I like my job protecting the President."

"But it won't last forever," Trey said. "One way or another, this case will end your career with the Secret Service."

"How do you figure?" Maria asked.

He smiled in a way that sent a shiver down her spine. "If you find and take down this group, it will justify all the effort and time you've put into it. They'll insist you work with the JTTF full time."

"I don't think I like what you're implying."

"Think of it this way then." Trey's wry smile vanished. "While you're here, someone else is filling your position with the Secret Service. If you succeed, why wouldn't the JTTF try to grab you up?"

"And if I fail?"

"If you fail, the President dies, and you're a failure with the Secret Service. Why would they want you back then? Either way, you've proven your skills to the CIA. We'll want you on our team, no matter how this plays out."

His words had barely sunk in before he turned and vanished into the crowd. She tried to pursue him, but he was gone. So far, nothing tied to the Presidency besides that first Molotov cocktail at the White House. But if the CIA knew something linking the group she was tracking to a threat against the POTUS, she had to know it.

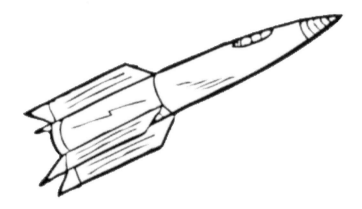

An Offer Liz Can't Refuse

May 1st - Hawthorne, California

Liz Smith walked into the same conference room where only seven months ago, the idea of traveling to the International Space Station was pitched to the ISS Oversight Committee. Somehow the room felt much smaller now that there was so much more weight on her shoulders. Leon's death left a power vacuum and a very complicated will, which for some reason, placed her in charge of finding his replacement. But how do you replace an eccentric visionary genius?

She had five lawyers surrounding her with expertise ranging from liability to business evaluation and contract law. They were the best in their fields.

Three Secret Service agents were positioned around the room, looking stiff as boards. It had taken forty-eight hours to secure the facility with these agents poking their noses into places they didn't belong. More than once, she had to threaten to sue them and the

President just to get them to put on the proper protective gear to enter the clean rooms. Not to mention forcing them to wait several hours to ensure their clearance levels were high enough to see what was inside.

Two more Secret Service agents entered, followed by five members of the ISS Oversight Committee. Right behind them were four unknown men in suits, one of which Liz thought she recognized from the news somewhere. He stayed by the door, and President Towers walked in, right behind him.

"Alright, everyone, have a seat," Towers said. "We've got a lot to cover today, and I've got a full agenda."

"Mr. President," Liz said as she sat down. "It is truly an honor to have you join us for this meeting."

"I've taken a personal interest in this fiasco, young lady," Towers replied. "Now, let's get down to business, shall we?"

"Yes, lets," Brian Morley said. He was SpaceX's lead attorney and had instructed Liz to let him do all the talking today. "We are challenging your claim that it was our faulty code, which caused the crash of the ISS. Our code passed inspection through all the proper channels before it was built, and again before it was launched. There is no possible way Leon Cologne changed the code in the docking module prior to liftoff, nor could he have done so during flight."

"We concede that point," one of the unknown suits said. He sat next to President Towers. "Dr. Terry Hatfield, NASA Operations. We did verify that your code passed all inspections and tests prior to liftoff. However, we also found a virus planted in the reusable fuel module, which modified the code in the docking module when it achieved an altitude of ten thousand feet."

"What's your evidence?" Brian demanded.

Hatfield shoved a folder across the table. "This is a copy of the report I received last night. Obviously, you'll need time to review it before we come to some sort of settlement."

Brian started scanning the folder.

Liz felt the tension in the room rise several notches while Brian read. The silence continued for several minutes until she couldn't stand it anymore. She had to interject. "Even if we find this report to be accurate, that makes this a case of intentional sabotage by parties unknown. That doesn't make Leon or SpaceX responsible for what happened."

"I think you'll find the level of sophistication in this virus shows it could only be an inside job," Hatfield said. "It is our claim that an employee of SpaceX constructed the code for this specific purpose, which makes this fiasco the responsibility of SpaceX."

Liz opened her mouth to respond, but Brian put a hand on her arm. He stared at Hatfield and said, "And if we are unable to refute your evidence, what exactly are you asking for?"

"The ISS cost $150 billion to build with five years left in its usable life," Hatfield said. "That means, without considering the possibility of scavenging parts before decommissioning, the station had a value of $28.8 billion. At last check, SpaceX as a company is worth $26.4 billion. We propose that NASA, which is already the chief customer for SpaceX, take immediate and total control of the company."

"That's outrageous!" Liz said.

"Is it really, Miss Smith?" Hatfield asked. "Many of your employees are former NASA. They'll come back to work for me pretty quickly once SpaceX declares bankruptcy. Then we'll purchase all your facilities at a discounted rate. Why not save everyone the trouble and disruption and sign over the company voluntarily?"

"Because you haven't established our liability," Brian shot back. "Even if you could, we could restructure under Chapter 13. There's no reason to believe this would be the end of SpaceX."

"With the death of Leon Cologne, you've got no visionary genius at the helm," President Towers said. "If you can find someone else prepared to take the reins of the company and get a new International Space Station built within five years, we'd be willing to discuss a payment plan."

Liz clamped her jaw shut. She had to trust her lawyers to discuss this and not let her emotions make the situation worse.

"How long?" Brian asked.

"I'm sorry?" Hatfield asked as his wide grin vanished. "How long for what?"

"How long will you give us to search for a replacement visionary who can build a new space station at a discount of $28.8 billion?"

"Well, we aren't prepared to discuss those terms at the moment…"

"Then give us one year," Brian said. "If we do find SpaceX to be contractually liable, it will take us a full year to find a suitable replacement for…"

"Three weeks," President Towers interrupted. Every eye turned to face him.

"That's hardly enough time to find the right candidate and allow them to give notice at their current employment," Brian replied.

Towers shook his head. "You've already made a short list of possible candidates. I know, because that's what I would do. This is a dream position, so whoever you find would have no problem leaving their current job without notice, even if you have to go outside of SpaceX to find a suitable replacement, which I doubt you will. Anyone who supports Cologne's vision strongly enough to take over should already be working for you. As for ownership of the company, right now, the company's liabilities exceed its value, so there really isn't anything to sell."

"Three weeks hardly seems like enough time to evaluate the evidence and find who is truly responsible for the sabotage," Brian said.

"Perhaps I'm not making myself clear," President Towers said. "I'm giving you three weeks to come up with a better plan than having the director of NASA take over SpaceX as another division. No one will lose their job, and business will continue as usual, except that the company will be owned by NASA instead of being privately held. If, after three weeks, you refuse to comply, NASA will terminate all contracts with SpaceX and begin building all new materials and designs in-house once more."

"I see," Brian said as he stood.

Liz stood at the same time.

"Mr. President, we have a perimeter breach," the closest Secret Service Agent said softly.

"That's my cue to leave," President Towers said.

"We will review your offer and get back to you quickly," Brian said.

"Pathway is clear. Mogul is on the move," an agent said.

"Do that," Towers said to Brian as he walked down the hallway. "If I have to visit you again, I'll be even less pleased than I am now."

Everyone else waited until the Secret Service agents left, followed by the members of the ISS Oversight Committee, who had strangely remained silent through the whole exchange.

Liz followed Brian out of the room, trailed by the other SpaceX lawyers.

She exited the elevator on the top floor, sure she'd ruined everything with her emotional outburst. She knew Daniel Towers never reacted well to being pushed, and her words had definitely pushed him. He'd pushed back, hard.

"By the way, you did a great job in there," Brian said as they entered Cologne's office.

"I did?"

Brian nodded. "The paperwork they gave us said nothing about possibly appointing a replacement or a payment plan. They wrote it up to say they would terminate contracts with SpaceX effective immediately if we didn't give them the company today. You bought us three weeks."

Liz's phone rang. She picked it up in a bit of a daze. "Liz Smith, speaking."

"Miss Smith, this is Mark Johnson with security. I'm just letting you know we have ambulances and police en route."

"What happened?"

"Some nut tried to shoot his way through the front door, screaming 'Death to Towers.'"

"Was anyone injured?"

"Two of our security officers and three Secret Service Agents are injured," Mark said. "The shooter is dead."

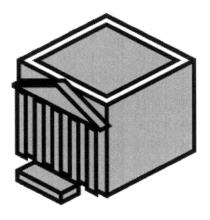

Maria's Dark Web

May 1st - McLean, Virginia

An email from Dennis Harrison marked *URGENT* popped up on Maria Croix's screen. She paused five seconds for the virus scanner to review the email before it gave a tiny green check.

The last two weeks had been filled with reports from around the country. Most of the interviews yielded nothing. Half a dozen people had chosen to go back to prison on a parole violation rather than reveal anything while the rest were let go. Only one interview had given them even a scrap of information, and Harrison was the man assigned to capitalize on it.

As soon as Maria clicked on the email, there was a knock at her door. "Who is it?"

"It's Dennis. I need to talk to you immediately."

"Come in." She glanced down at the contents of the email.

"We've found the connection! Here is the link. Do not click it until I get there."

The link was a long URL that started with numbers instead of words.

"We've done it!" Harrison shouted as he sat down. "We've gained access to the site we got in exchange for waiving a parole violation."

"Exactly why shouldn't I click on this link without you here?" Maria asked.

"Because first I have to log you in through a VPN."

"VP what?"

"Virtual Private Network. It masks your location information. If you try to login to this site from a government server, it will launch a virus, and a pretty nasty one, too."

"We have the best anti-virus software available," Maria said. "I think we can handle it."

Dennis gave a snort of a laugh. "That's like saying we have the best antibiotics available, so we don't need to use clean needles."

"I thought our software could block anything."

"No." He shook his head. "It can only block what it recognizes as a virus. Anyway, the virus isn't the point. I've got you on the VPN. Go ahead and click on the link."

Maria did, and a website popped up with three options. Log In, First Time Here, Flee to Safety.

"You've got to click First Time Here on every new computer, or it will lock your computer out of the website," Dennis said.

The procedure to log in took another five steps, any one of which, if done wrong, would have locked her out or launched the virus on her computer. When the site came up, it displayed a list of upcoming political rallies around the country, with a date and time, followed by an extra decimal, ranging from 0.03 to 0.45.

"This is the big breakthrough?" Maria asked. "What is so spectacular about a list of planned rallies?"

Dennis scowled. "It may look like just a list of rallies, but you see those decimals on the far right of each listing? That's how much Litecoin someone will be paid to attend."

"You're saying if I go to the rally in D.C. on Saturday, I'll get what? 0.1 Litecoin? That doesn't sound like much."

"That's an hourly rate. It actually comes out to about forty dollars an hour."

"Wow," Maria said as the number sank in. "Whoever is funding this must be rich. How much are they spending per rally?"

"We don't know how many people at the rallies are paid to be there, and rallies in important places pay better, to cover the cost of travel."

"How much?" Maria repeated.

Dennis swallowed hard. "We've estimated it between fifty and two hundred thousand dollars per rally."

"Two hundred thousand?"

Dennis nodded. "This proves what you've been saying all along. The violence at these rallies is being coordinated by someone paying them to throw bottles of gasoline."

Maria shook her head. "Look again. Nothing on this site says anything about illegal activities. Other than those who violate their parole to participate, I don't see anything illegal about it."

"What? How can that be?"

"This is America, where we still have the right to peaceably assemble to protest perceived wrongs by our government. There isn't anything saying someone can't pay people to swell the size of the crowd."

"But can't we argue that the violence of the crowds means they are inciting to riot or something?"

Maria shook her head. "No, I'm afraid not. If I heard that man right, and I know I did, he was paid specifically to throw that flaming bottle on the White House lawn on Christmas Eve. That tells me there's another list, a much shorter list, with an even bigger price tag for breaking the law. No one spends a quarter-million dollars on a violent rally without making sure violence will break out."

"Are you saying what we've found is worthless?"

"No!" She stood up and started pacing behind her desk. "Goodness sakes, no. This is extremely valuable. Now we have a starting point. Have the techs analyze the site. I need to know the history of who signed up for what rallies." Dennis started to object, but Maria held up her hand and kept going. "I know, there's probably some reason why you can't do it. Look, just get what information you can. Don't bother trying to retrace usernames to actual people. I just need to know who went where, and especially those who suddenly dropped off the list. Got it?"

"I've already sent the work order to the techs. But I don't understand. If none of this is illegal, what will that analysis give us?"

"Leverage."

Scott Practices Sharpshooting at ¼ Mile

May 10th - Berkeley, California

Scott Knox spotted his target through the scope, took a deep breath, let it out, and squeezed the trigger. There was a click, rather than a bang. This was a relatively secluded part of the forest, but he didn't dare risk using actual bullets out here. A moment later, his phone called out, "Five inches to the left."

He swore softly. That was the difference between success and a total miss. He cocked his rifle, knowing that the dry-fire round was still ready to go. Each time he fired, the specialized device stayed in the chamber and shot out a laser pulse instead of a bullet. His target was positioned in front of a prepaid phone hanging from a tree branch about a quarter-mile away and several hundred feet below him. The phone was running an app for detecting the laser on the target paper.

The app and target came pre-made, as a packaged set with the laser-emitting bullet. The hardest part of the whole thing was synching the two phones and adding the audio announcement. After all, the system wasn't designed for such long-distance shooting.

He squeezed the trigger again.

"Four inches to the left," his phone called out.

"You're improving," Kevin said as he came out from around a tree. "How long have you been out here?"

"Six hours or so," Scott said. "Still haven't actually hit the target yet."

"Take a break and give me a shot," Kevin said.

"Did you bring your rifle?"

Kevin shook his head. "Not tonight. I just came up here to let you know I was finished. I thought you were going to meet me back at the apartment. We need to celebrate!"

Scott shook his head. "I'll celebrate when we get this right. We've only got ten days before we fly out."

Kevin nodded. "I know. But I'm done with finals now, so we can spend all day every day out here until we're ready. But right now, we need to keep up appearances and go out and celebrate."

Scott took another shot.

"Two inches above," his phone said. That at least would wound his target, if not kill him.

He turned to Kevin and laughed as his last comment sunk in. "Appearance? Do you think we're under surveillance?"

Kevin shrugged. "You never know. I'm speaking more about my friends. They're expecting to celebrate with us tonight, and if I don't go, it'll look suspicious."

"And you accuse me of being paranoid."

"I guess you've rubbed off on me. We're going after a much bigger target this time. Being famous and all is fine, but I'd rather not spend the rest of my life in jail. No amount of Litecoin is worth that."

"Fine," Scott said. He knelt next to the case and started stripping apart the rifle. He'd gotten it down to ninety seconds.

"Hey! What happened to letting me have a shot?"

"What happened to 'No one fires my rifle but me'?" Scott shot back.

Kevin scowled at him. "On the range. Did you forget that part?"

Scott waved toward the distant target. "This *is* the range. Now, are you going to stand here complaining, or are you going to grab the target, so we can head to dinner with your friends?"

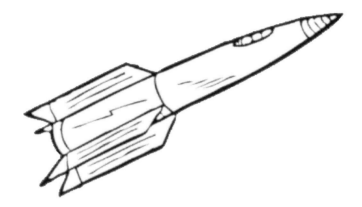

Liz Completes Her Search for Leon's Successor

May 10th - Hawthorne, California

Liz Smith looked up from her paperwork as Brian Morley entered her office. She was trying not to get used to calling it *her* office, as she was only here until she found Leon's replacement, and she didn't have very long to do that. "What is it?"

"We have to eliminate Terrance Mansfield as a candidate," Brian said.

"Why?" The list was getting dangerously short now.

"He's Australian."

"So? Leon was born in South Africa."

Brian took a seat across from her and plopped his tablet down on the desk. "True, but Cologne was also a United States citizen. Mansfield is here on a work visa."

"Then we'll use the expedient and necessary clause to get his U.S. citizenship pushed through."

"That's how we got his visa. However, a deeper background check showed his cousin moved to Syria to join the Global Islamic State, a radical group trying to pick up where ISIS left off."

"Mansfield is a Muslim?" Liz asked.

"I have no idea," Brian shot back. "That's not the point."

"No, it's not." She stood up and started pacing. The chair became uncomfortable after a couple of hours, and she wasn't sure if it was because the chair was designed specifically for Leon's ergonomics, or because of the weight on her shoulders. Either way, she needed to stand. "We don't have many people left to evaluate. Simmonds flat out refused, Hangelton failed the background check. He shouldn't even be working on a NASA contract with his past. Grainger was diagnosed with Bipolar Disorder last month. I've eliminated everyone else from our list."

"Bipolar?" Brian repeated. A wry smile crept onto his face. "That explains a few things."

"I'm serious. I think we're going to have to give in to their demands."

"Still, Bipolar Disorder wouldn't keep Grainger from taking over, would it? I mean, he could be the next Howard Hughes."

Liz shook her head. "I'm afraid his case has become life-threatening. He's in the hospital. Besides, I checked. They don't give government clearances to those who experience periods of depression."

"We've still got ten days. Maybe something will come up. We're not done with our internal investigation on the sabotage."

Liz clicked on the star projector that Leon was so fond of. The slowly moving points of light reminded her of him. Especially the bright red one. "Even if we found proof it was a NASA employee who planted that, it doesn't change the fact that we're not going to find a suitable replacement. I started compiling that list six months ago at Leon's request. He wanted to train someone to run the company from here after he went to Mars. I can't come up with a new list in ten days."

"What are you saying? You just want to give up?"

Liz walked to the window and looked out over the campus. Thousands of employees were counting on her to find them a new leader. If she couldn't find one soon, they would begin losing bids on new contracts, followed by reevaluation or elimination of existing ones. At least if NASA took over, they'd all keep working. "I'm saying I want to give the hard-working men and women of this company a future."

"Then why don't you take over? I'm sure you know enough about how to run this company…"

Liz laughed. "Me? Run SpaceX? There's no way. I mean, sure, I could administrate, make sure all the various departments kept running properly, and all that. I can run the business side of things, but I can't review the designs and functions of the products we make. I don't know them well enough. I'm not an engineer.

"No, the heart and soul of this company was Leon Cologne. He drove us all forward, always reaching for the next step. He was like a kite in a strong breeze, and I was just the string, keeping him tethered to the ground."

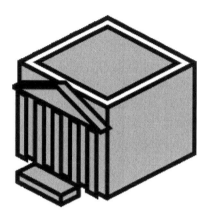

Maria Buys Access

May 11th - McClean, Virginia

Maria Croix slammed the door as she entered the interrogation room carrying a stack of files as a prop. Everything she had on Jason was available electronically on her tablet, but a thick stack of papers was more effective in instilling fear. "Inciting to riot, damaging public property, assaulting an officer of the law, and conspiracy to commit murder. Did I forget anything?"

"You forgot to tell me what all that has to do with me," Jason shot back.

He wasn't the first interview they'd conducted in the last week based on the information they'd gathered from the dark website offering money for rallies, but it was the first one she'd conducted herself.

Maria gave a wry smile. "Those are the charges you're facing. Or, perhaps I should just lump them all into one and charge you with domestic terrorism."

He laughed. "You don't have enough proof to hold me, so you threaten to pull the terrorist card? It sounds like you're just drumming me up for information. What do you want to know, and what are you offering?"

"So that's how it is?" Maria asked, raising one eyebrow. "Right down to business, you can't be frightened by anything?"

Jason shook his head. "I've got nothing to lose."

"Well, that's not exactly true, is it?" Maria shot back.

He laughed before he said, "I'll wager I'm getting paid more than you are to be here."

First down, Maria thought. "The trouble with that thinking is that you were living with your parents when you threw that Molotov cocktail on the White House lawn." He was one of five people she suspected of that act, five she knew were at the rally, or at least in the city that day.

"So? What do my parents have to do with it?"

He didn't object. That was almost an admission of guilt. "Well you see, you paid rent to your parents after taking payment for a potential terrorist attack, which means . . ."

"That wasn't rent!" Jason shot back. "I was just helping with their bills."

Maria smirked. Once more, he failed to deny throwing that bottle or receiving funds for illegal activities. "It amounts to the same thing. They are involved in this terrorist plot, and I'll have to detain them until we can get to the bottom of this whole thing."

The color drained from Jason's face. "You can't do that, can you?"

"We take domestic terrorism very seriously. Anyone who receives money as proceeds from a terrorist act must be detained and questioned, to determine their level of involvement."

Jason swallowed hard. "Well, there has to be some way that we can work this out, without involving them."

Maria paused and stared at him, weighing his fate. "I suppose we could claim you were a paid informant."

His eyes lifted at those words. "Informants don't go to jail, right?"

"Of course not," Maria said, "as long as they report on *all* their activities and everything they learned. You can't leave anything out, or we'll have to charge you with any other crimes we uncover on our own."

"And informants are anonymous, right?" Jason asked.

Maria nodded. "Of course they are. We can't have your name on the news letting everyone know you were working for us. I just need you to write down everything you know about the events on Christmas Eve and any other related incidents." She pushed a pad of paper and pen closer to him.

He started writing right away. Maria suppressed a smile. Two minutes later, he turned the paper around and handed her the pen.

Only the top sheet of paper had anything written on it. Maria shook her head. "I don't think that's nearly enough information."

"No, it's not. Read it."

She read it out loud. "I, Jason Mantiford, have been employed by the Joint Terrorism Task Force as a paid informant at a rate of… Are you expecting me to fill in your pay rate?"

Jason nodded his head.

"You realize that by accepting this money, you'll have to surrender whatever money you received for illegal activities during this time?"

"Then you should make it at least ten thousand per month, or we're going to have a problem."

"How so?" Maria asked as she scanned the rest of the agreement.

"Because that's how much I've been earning, and I've already spent a large chunk of it. I don't want to violate the agreement, after all."

Maria gritted her teeth and said, "Fine. Ten thousand per month. I'll have to get approval for that, but if the information you give is valuable enough, it shouldn't be a problem." It was almost as much as she made. She quickly read over the rest of the agreement and signed it, hoping he was worth the risk. After all, they weren't really going to pay him, just legitimize his ill-gotten gain.

By the end of the day, she had plenty of information from Jason. Unfortunately, he refused to admit to throwing that Molotov cocktail on the White House lawn. He did admit to throwing others, just not that one.

Scott & Kevin See the Truth of The Dark Eagle

May 16th - Berkeley, California

Scott Knox and Kevin Smith sat at the table in their apartment, staring at the maps, pictures, and schedules surrounding the upcoming event. They'd just returned from a three-day campout filled with nearly constant long-range rifle practice. Both of them were now able to hit their mark from a quarter mile, more than half the time.

The schedules and detailed plans had been posted to the bounty site while they were gone, labeled as Operation Dark Eagle.

"Why do you suppose they call it Operation Dark Eagle?" Kevin asked.

"Well, our national symbol is the eagle," Scott replied, trying to find some logic to it. "Even the presidential seal has an eagle on it. I guess it refers to how evil Towers is."

"So President Towers is the dark eagle?" Kevin asked.

"Sure. I guess so. At least, that's the best I can come up with."

Kevin laughed. "You have absolutely no idea, do you?"

"No more than you. That's not the point, though, is it?"

"No." Kevin refocused on the paperwork laid out before them. "Let's see what we're up against."

"President Towers will arrive first," Scott said, "in an armored motorcade. Then VP Michaels will arrive fifteen minutes later."

"Then we can't hit Towers as he walks into the building," Kevin concluded. "We've got to wait until Michaels gets there."

"But once Towers is inside, we can't get a clean shot."

"Unless one of us is also inside."

"No way," Scott said as he waved his arms over the pile of papers. "First of all, we'd never get inside with a gun."

"I'm sure we could manage it somehow," Kevin shot back. "I mean, we have to have someone on the inside to give us this much detail about the President's security plans."

"First of all, I don't think they'd help us sneak in a gun. Whoever is getting us the press credentials and Towers' security itinerary is already sticking their necks out enough."

"We could try," Kevin shot back. "The worst they can say is no."

"Secondly," Scott shot back, "even if we did get our guns inside, we'd never make it out of the building alive." Scott studied Kevin's face for a moment. It looked like Kevin didn't care if he got caught. "I'm not agreeing to any plan where either one of us gets caught or killed."

"They wouldn't kill me," Kevin shot back with a smile. "They'll want a very public trial."

"They'll also want to know who your accomplice was that shot the VP. I am not going to jail over this."

"But we'd be legends! I mean, how many people have killed a sitting President?"

"Two," Scott said flatly, "and they both died. I'm not going to die for this."

"Okay. Which is why I propose we trigger the fire alarm."

"What good will that do?" Scott asked.

"The security analysis says that in the case of a fire, the President will exit here," Kevin pointed to a side exit, "giving us the perfect opportunity if one of us is in this room." He pointed to the layout of a nearby office building.

"While the other one is here," Scott said, pointing to a hotel, "positioned to take out the VP."

"Exactly."

"Is there anything in here about why both of them will be in Houston?"

Kevin stared at him with a blank expression before saying, "Why would that be important? We know they're going to be there." Something caught his attention, and he got up from the table.

"What is it? What's wrong?"

"He's on television, right now," Kevin said as he turned up the volume.

"We're still looking into the situation," Towers' said, apparently answering a question. *"Either way, Spencer Michaels and I will be making the announcement in Houston, Texas, as part of the Space Tech Symposium."*

"See? There you go," Kevin said, muting it again. "They are going there for some space conference."

"Did you catch what they will be announcing?"

"What else? They're going to announce plans for a new space station."

Scott nodded. He supposed that made sense, but something about it felt wrong. Unable to pin it down precisely, he put the matter out of his mind. Towers and Michaels would both be there. That was the important thing.

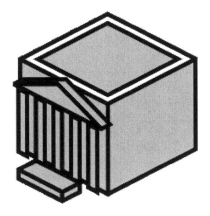

Maria Interrogates Cyberpunk256

May 17th - McLean, Virginia

Maria Croix poured over the reports from the last month. Fifteen different task forces around the country had identified thirty-five of the individuals on the list, and three of them had violated their parole by leaving the state for a rally. Still, none of them admitted to being paid, other than Jason.

"We've got him in interview four," Dennis Harrison said as he burst into her office without knocking.

Any other news would have earned Dennis a reprimand. Instead, Maria just grabbed her tablet and followed him out the door and through the winding cubicle maze between her office and the interrogation rooms. She waited to ask questions until they were both in observation room four, looking through the one-way glass at a short, balding man with glasses.

"*This* is Cyberpunk256?" Maria asked, referring to him by the online handle.

Dennis nodded. "We've confirmed he was the only one home during the majority of his posting activity. Honestly, his son looks like more of a threat, but we're sure it's him."

"How long has he been in custody?" Maria asked.

"Three hours," Dennis said. "This guy's a local."

"Three hours, and this is the first time I've heard of it?"

"Don't blame me. The guy was picked up on disorderly conduct and spent two hours in a drunk tank before the cops bothered to check for arrest warrants."

"Has he said anything?"

Dennis shook his head. "No one's asked him anything. I knew you'd want to be the first one in there."

"Okay. Grab three coffees. I don't want him wriggling out of this one by claiming he was too drunk to understand his rights."

"Not likely," Dennis said. "He blew a 0.04."

"He's barely buzzed? What was the disorderly conduct for?"

"Peeing in a public fountain."

Maria rolled her eyes and shook her head at the idiocy of the average criminal. She glanced through the report while Dennis went to get the coffee she'd requested. Cyberpunk256, a.k.a. Harold Robinson, looked like a typical citizen. His online postings as Cyberpunk didn't match the psychometrics of his Facebook profile.

Dennis came in with the coffee, and Maria signaled him to follow her into the interrogation room. She sat down across from Harold and said, "Thank you, Dennis. You may go."

"What's all this, then?" Harold asked.

"Coffee," Maria said as Dennis closed the door behind him. "Just in case you're still a little drunk."

"I didn't pee in the fountain because I was drunk. I did it to protest the fluorine the government is putting in our drinking water."

"You mean fluoride. It's to protect your teeth."

"No. I mean fluorine," Harold said as he took the first coffee. He sipped it and smacked his lips. "That's good coffee."

"You were telling me about fluorine?"

"Yes! It's a known neurotoxin which results from combining fluoride and chlorine."

"Was it the neurotoxins that caused you to boast about killing the President? Or was that in protest to his policies?"

"Wait, what?"

"Two days ago, you posted to a monitored dark website how you were going to kill the President tomorrow."

"I did?"

Maria pushed her tablet over for him to see. "You posted, and I quote, 'I'm going to take down the Towers before he takes down the country. He's just a pawn of NWO.' Are you going to waste my time denying you wrote this?"

"Cyberpunk256? This is my neighbor, Chuck. He's always bragging to me over the fence about the money he's making attending rallies. He even boasted about toasting the White House lawn on Christmas Eve."

Maria's hands involuntarily squeezed into fists. This was the first lead in months relating to the act which had set her on this path. She could hardly believe her luck if it turned out to be true. She forced her hands to relax before saying, "This was posted from your IP address. How do you explain that?"

"What's an IP address?"

"We know your modem was used to access this site on multiple occasions."

"Oh, that," Harold said.

"Yes, that."

"Chuck sometimes uses my Wi-Fi when he has trouble paying the bills on his internet. I can't really stop him, so we both just pretend I give him permission."

"Well, I'm sure we can get Chuck in here to discuss that. Does he have a last name?"

"Of course he does. Doesn't everyone?" Harold laughed.

Maria kept her expression blank to show she was not amused.

"Charles Varley. Man, I heard the police have no sense of humor, but can't you lighten up just a little?"

"I'm not a police officer, Mr. Robinson. I'm a federal agent and part of a Joint Terrorism Task Force." She got up and walked out of the room, letting those last words sink in.

Maria's Dark Web Discovery

May 23rd - Washington, D.C.

Maria Croix scanned through the dark website Charles Varley had given them after three days of interrogation. Apparently, his plans to kill the President included a ten-million-dollar reward for success. The three days of interrogation weren't the hard part. It was the three days of waiting while the techs figured out how to gain access to the site without alerting the owner.

Now that she had full access to the backbones of the page, she was trying to take it all in. Everything was here, the proof she'd been right and hadn't wasted the last six months of her life. There really was someone financing the start of a war. Rewards were listed for throwing Molotov cocktails, punching an officer of the law, and even doing anything that triggered a riot.

It didn't matter that the user-names were all random strings of letters and numbers. Putting actual names to them would come in time. Right now, Maria was more interested in the pattern of behavior.

She was about three hours into her investigation, writing down notes about which user-names accepted which bounties when she came across the listing for burning down Senator Donald Ball's home. It was followed quickly by another for putting him in the hospital, and a third to mess up his treatment to keep him there. The third bounty was listed in draft mode, meaning it had never been posted to the site. She clicked on the first two bounties, and quickly found they were claimed by the same person; user X5J2KR1.

She searched for all the bounties taken by X5J2KR1 and found several dozen. The payouts were well over a hundred thousand dollars, with only one left unresolved. She reached for her cup of coffee as she clicked on the last one.

The coffee ended up on the floor. Maria barely noticed as she scanned through the list of seven attempts to kill President Towers and Vice-President Michaels. She tried to line up the dates with the incidents she'd heard about.

March 18th didn't bring anything to mind, but March 28th matched with the attempted ramming of the Presidential motorcade in Missouri. With this evidence, that woman would be in jail for the rest of her life. Again, April 7th didn't match, and she wondered how much she'd missed by stepping away from her position in the Secret Service. The fire in Towers' penthouse on April 20th had made big headlines, as did the shooter in California who managed to break into SpaceX headquarters on May 1st. Charles Varley was scheduled to try something the day they picked him up. One assassination attempt was still in the future.

X5J2KR1 was scheduled to kill the President and Vice President in Houston, Texas, on May 26th, only three days away. She grabbed the unsecured phone and started dialing. She just hoped her contacts in the Secret Service would still take her call.

A Presidential Bounty

May 24th - Washington, D.C.

President Daniel Towers sat in the Oval Office reading over the latest draft of the bill to dismantle the Federal Reserve. It had passed the House of Representatives by one vote. On Monday, it would go for a vote in the Senate where he was sure it would pass.

"Mr. President, I need a moment of your time," Lucas Janson said. He was the Director of the Secret Service.

Towers looked up, then down at the clock. "Is it 10:00 already? Come on in, Lucas. Have a seat."

Lucas closed the door behind him and sat down. "I got an email from one of my agents last night with some concerns about the security in Houston."

"What kind of concerns?" Towers asked.

"She claims someone has taken a contract out for assassination. She's still compiling all the data, but she says it's linked to six other attempts on your life."

Towers chuckled. "How much am I worth?"

"Twenty thousand Litecoin."

"Litecoin? Contract killers are taking cryptocurrencies now? What will they think of next?" Towers cleared his throat. "What does that translate to in dollars?"

"Just over ten million."

"Cheapskates," Towers said. "I don't think I'd take any threat seriously for less than one hundred million."

"Do you want to see the report? I don't think there's much to it, but we might need to postpone your announcement on Sunday."

Towers stood up, angered by the suggestion. "I've never backed down to a bully before, and I'm not going to start now!" He slammed one fist on the desk. Lifting the same hand, he pointed at Lucas. "It's your job to make sure I'm safe. You've done a terrific job so far, and I'm confident you'll do just fine in Houston as well. You said this was connected to the other attempts?"

Janson nodded.

"Those were all weak half-baked attempts by amateurs. If this threat is anything like the others, you and your men won't have any problem with this one either."

"Do you want to see the report?" Janson offered.

Towers shook his head. "No, this bill to dismantle the Federal Reserve is more important right now. I might be signing it on Tuesday, and I want to make sure they got all the details right before we fly down to Texas."

President Towers in the Crosshairs

May 26th - Houston, Texas

Scott Knox paced in his hotel room where he'd been holed up for the past six days. His life was completely upside-down from where he wanted it to be. In less than an hour, President Towers' convoy would arrive, followed fifteen minutes later by Spencer Michaels' convoy. Scott's assignment was to shoot Michaels, but he'd spent the last week questioning everything.

Kevin had been his friend since third grade, and they'd always agreed on almost everything. At least, that's what Scott thought before he moved out of Kevin's apartment and cut off all communication for the last week. For the first time in months, the voice in the back of his head was louder than Kevin's, and all the reasons that led him to stand there, holding a long-range rifle, were falling apart in his mind.

The news played in the background, but the words they were saying caught his attention.

"President Towers is expected to make an announcement today about the future of NASA," Patty Parker of Fox News said. *"Ever since the crash of the International Space Station on April 6th, Democrats have argued to shut down NASA permanently, claiming space exploration is simply too dangerous."*

"April 6th?" Scott repeated to himself. "But I took this bounty more than two weeks before that. How did they know Towers and Michaels would be here today, making an announcement? How could they know the ISS would crash before the billionaires even launched?"

His thoughts became dark, and his mind refused to process the idea. "I've got the gun, I've got the skills. I just have to take the shot, and I'll have my revenge and my fortune."

Talking with yourself was one thing, but arguing with yourself was quite another. Still, this was a crazy situation. A little eccentric behavior was understandable.

It took a moment for his previous train of thought to reach the station of its inevitable conclusion. "They crashed the ISS, just to get them both here."

"No!" he shouted back at himself. "It doesn't matter. Towers is dangerous. He has to be eliminated."

Why is it your place to make that decision? the voice in his head replied.

"Someone has to. If I don't, someone else will." He'd gone to Sunday School every week as a child and sat through Seminary. After high school, he'd stopped going to Church, plagued as he was by too many doubts. He still wasn't sure whether that voice in his head was the Holy Ghost, his conscience, or just his doubts. Right now, he didn't care. He had a job to finish.

A scripture popped into his mind, unbidden and unwelcome.

Woe unto them that call evil good, and good evil;
that put darkness for light, and light for darkness; that
put bitter for sweet, and sweet for bitter! [64]

"No! Towers is the evil one. He's ruined my life, and he's ruining the country. He's the dark one. I have to kill the dark eagle."

You are about to shed innocent blood. There is nothing darker, nothing more evil.

At that thought, he stopped in his tracks and looked down at the gun in his hands. Up to now, he'd caused some chaos, some property damage, even injured a sitting Senator. He could forgive himself for all those things, but taking the life of someone he barely knew was so far beyond anything else he'd done that Scott didn't know if he would ever recover.

The gun fell from his fingers and clattered to the floor. The world twisted around him, and suddenly everything made sense again. He'd allowed himself to be drawn into this plot by Kevin. Their hatred had fed off each other for months, thinking that they had to use any means necessary to achieve their goals. But killing was never his goal. He and Kevin were following someone else's agenda, someone whose name was still a mystery.

"I have to stop this," he said to the empty room. He looked around for his phone and realized he only had a burner, which didn't have Kevin's burner phone programmed into it. "I have to get a hold of Kevin. Think! Think!"

They'd worked so hard to create distance between them, so no one would suspect they were working together, and now the only means he had of communicating with Kevin was his gun.

He grabbed the gun off the floor, checked the scope to make sure it wasn't knocked out of alignment by the fall, and went over to the window. Kevin was in a nearby office building, he just had to find the right window. By now his friend would have removed the glass and started dialing in his sights for the shot.

There had to be some way to spot him, some way to stop him. If he shattered the window hiding his friend from the Secret Service, Kevin would have to abort the operation. No one would die, and with luck, they'd both get away.

He glanced down for a second, and his heart sank. The Presidential motorcade was already parked, and the VP's motorcade was approaching the convention center.

He checked the time. Forty minutes had slipped by since the last time he'd checked, and there was no time to waste. Now was the time to act. If he shattered the window of Kevin's room, they could walk away from this nightmare. However, if he shot Michaels and allowed Kevin to shoot Towers, they'd both be fifteen million dollars richer by morning.

But he'd lose his soul.

The debate started up in his mind again, but he pushed it aside. There was no more time for debate, as any delay would eliminate his options.

He removed the glass from the window and focused on his intended target. He'd only have time for one shot.

The fire alarm from the convention center was loud enough for Scott to hear, timed perfectly to go off just as Michaels was walking in. As expected, his team turned around and started heading back to the safety of the armored vehicles.

Scott took aim and fired.

*   *   *

Maria Croix pulled up behind the Presidential motorcade and started power walking towards the Brown Convention Center. She reluctantly left her firearm in the glove compartment, because it was always a bad idea to be armed when walking unannounced toward the President's position. She passed two cars before someone stepped out from between them, blocking her path. They were getting lax in their security without her.

"I'm sorry, but you'll have to use a… Maria?" the agent said.

"That's right. Maria Croix, Special Agent with the Secret Service." She showed him her badge.

"What are you doing here?"

It took her a moment to remember the man's name. He'd been one of the dozens of agents she'd directed while working at the White House. "Agent Shaw, right?"

He nodded.

"I'm here because of a POTUS triple one," Maria said. "Walk with me." She tried to walk past him, but he moved to stand in her way.

"I'm sorry, I can't let you past this point without proper clearance."

"Listen, Shaw, I've just spent the last three days trying to convince everyone that there is actionable intelligence which clearly shows the President's life is in danger. Call it in, or let me through, but don't just stand here while he dies."

He held one hand up to his ear. "I've got Special Agent Maria Croix here, claiming to have credible intelligence of an immediate POTUS triple one."

Shaw paused, nodded, and said, "I'll let her know." He put his hand down before saying, "Director Janson received your message two days ago. The President himself rejected your evidence. I can't let you through."

"Look, just take me to the ASAIC. I can explain it to him."

Another motorcade drove past, and they both turned to look at it.

"We can do that after the VP's motorcade has passed," Shaw said. "Right now, I have to make sure no one interferes with it, and that includes you."

"Then let me pass so I can explain it to someone who isn't too busy to help." She tried once more to walk around him, but he placed his arm on her shoulder to hold her back. Her first instinct was to grab his hand and make him sorry he touched her, but if she did that, the rest of the agents might get trigger happy, and Shaw wasn't a bad fighter himself. He wouldn't go down easily.

"You need to sit tight," Shaw said. "My superiors don't currently believe your intelligence is actionable. If I act on it against their wishes, it'll come back down on me. You don't want that, do you?"

"You don't want the President to die, do you?"

"There are snipers on every roof within half a mile of here. I think we've got it covered."

Maria sighed. Their overconfidence would be their downfall.

Sirens started going off, and they both turned to look at the building. She was standing close enough to hear Shaw's earpiece buzz, "We've got a fire alarm. Going to exit strategy Alpha. Mogul is on the move."

"Hoosier and Hummingbird are pulling back," a second voice said.

Hoosier and Hummingbird referred to Vice President Michaels and his wife. Maria knew it was protocol to evacuate all the essential assets, even for something as small as an unexpected fire alarm.

All the cars in the Presidential motorcade started up as President Towers exited the building, surrounded by Secret Service agents. A gunshot rang out with a double echo.

Dan Towers' head whipped suddenly to the side, and he disappeared as three agents jumped on him, forming a human shield.

"Shots fired!" a dozen agents called out at once.

Maria's heart skipped a beat as she watched the Secret Service fail in their duty for the first time in more than fifty years.

"Mogul is down! Repeat, Mogul is down!" an agent near the President shouted.

"Shooter sighted at one o'clock high," another agent called out.

Every agent with a gun pulled it out and aimed at the building across the lawn, about a quarter-mile away. Twelve stories up, there was a window missing, revealing a man holding a rifle. Maria regretted leaving her gun in the car.

"It's too far," Shaw said. "I don't have a clean shot."

"You're just going to let him get away?" Maria shouted as she pounded on Shaw's chest.

Shaw grabbed her arms. "He won't get away." He spun her around to face the office building again. "The snipers will make short work of him."

Even before Shaw finished speaking, three shots rang out in quick succession. From this distance, it was hard to tell what happened, but she was sure the shooter was hit at least once, knocking him back, with his legs hanging out. As if in slow motion, the shooter slid out the window and fell, his body tumbling to the ground.

The whole thing was over in seconds, though it felt like hours. Half a dozen agents ran over to the fallen shooter while the Vice Presidential motorcade took off.

"Hoosier and Hummingbird are away," Shaw said.

Rage welled up inside Maria, and she searched for an outlet. There were still dozens of armed agents nearby, so she just spat out, "How are your superiors going to feel about you now?"

"Don't even think of bringing me into this," Shaw shot back. "I was doing what I thought was best and following orders as well. If you are going to pick a fight over who should have listened to you, leave me out of it."

"Maria! What are you doing here?" Agent Jenkins said behind her.

She turned around to face him. His face looked as dour and serious as her own with tears starting to form. "Trying to save the President's life, of course."

"You mean you knew this would happen?" he asked accusingly. "Why didn't you say something or call someone?"

"I sent you an email yesterday when I couldn't get through to Director Janson," Maria shouted back. "I've been screaming it to everyone and anyone I could reach in the Secret Service for three days, and no one listened to me."

"I've been on duty or aboard Air Force One for two days," Jenkins explained. "I haven't had a chance to check my email."

"Is he alive?" Maria asked.

"No." Jenkins shook his head as he choked back more tears. "The shooter got in a good clean headshot. Towers is gone. Vice President Michaels made it away safely."

"How could he get such a clean shot by firing through a window?" Shaw asked.

"I don't know," Maria said. "I'm sure the forensics team will tell us."

Sirens drowned out the conversation as more Secret Service agents showed up. In less than a minute, the press tried to pour out of the convention center while an ambulance came to take President Towers' body. The Secret Service was only partially successful at keeping the press inside and opted instead to block their view of Towers by standing around him as he was lifted onto a gurney and loaded into the ambulance.

Less than a minute after the ambulance left, a plethora of Houston Police, Texas State Police, and Texas Rangers started pouring in. The next ten minutes was organized chaos with Jenkins coordinating all the various groups.

From all the conversations, Maria was able to gather that the shooter was dead, and all buildings within a quarter-mile radius were on lockdown until they could be searched. Even with all the local law enforcement helping, it would take hours.

Jenkins sent a team of Rangers to search the convention center before he turned back to Maria. "Well, since you're here, can you help us with the search?"

"You want me to help you search the building where the shooter was?" Maria asked. That was against protocol since she wasn't on active assignment here.

"No, I was thinking you could join the team searching the hotel, over there. You might find the place he spent the night."

Maria nodded. "Anything I can do to help."

*   *   *

Scott Knox watched his friend fall to his death, certain that he'd caused it, but no idea how. He'd only shot the window. He stood there, frozen with shock as he watched. Kevin seemed to fall for an eternity, inching ever closer to the ground. Every detail suddenly became exquisite, and he saw the blood trailing behind the body, the glazed look of a dead man in Kevin's eyes as he fell, the shouts of the Secret Service down below.

When the body finally hit the ground, Scott turned his attention to the growing crowd around President Towers. That wasn't right. He was supposed to be in his vehicle by now, speeding away from the scene. The only reason there would be a crowd was if Kevin had fired at the same time he did. He'd seen the muzzle of his friend's rifle sticking out of the window just before he'd squeezed the trigger.

The reality of what had happened shot through him like lightning, and he realized he needed to move. Fast. He tore down his rifle, packing it into its case in seconds. He replaced the glass, grabbed his burner phone and his suitcase, and headed out, leaving the *Do not disturb* sign on the door.

He ran to the stairs and climbed up three flights breathing heavily only on the last few steps. Thankfully that was all the farther he had to go. His second hotel room was on the fifteenth floor. He'd checked in here two days ago. As they'd planned, he took out his rifle case and hid it in the ceiling along with the gloves he'd worn. Then he hopped in the shower to wash away any possible gunpowder.

He'd just finished getting dressed and sat down to watch the television when someone knocked on the door.

"No, thank you," he said. "No housekeeping today."

"I'm not housekeeping," a female voice said through the door. "Open in the name of the law."

Scott swallowed hard and opened the door. Part of him knew this was expected, even part of the plan. The Secret Service would search the hotel, which was why he had a second room. "What's going on?"

The short woman pointed to the television. "Isn't it obvious? Someone just shot the President. Maria Croix, Secret Service." She flashed her badge.

"I know that. It's on every channel. I saw you already got the shooter. So why are you here?" The images on the TV had already confirmed what his mind had deduced. By shattering the window of Kevin's room, he'd given the Secret Service snipers a massive target to aim at. He'd also removed the one thing that would have protected his friend from the bullets, which had to travel nearly a quarter of a mile to reach their target.

The woman stared at him for a second. "We're searching every room in this hotel, in case he had an accomplice."

Scott stepped aside and let her in, his heart pounding as he said, "Go ahead."

She stepped inside, looked around briefly, then turned to Scott. "How long have you been here?"

"I got here two days ago."

"Purpose of your visit?"

"I'm here for the Space Tech Symposium and the President's speech. I suppose today's events have been canceled now?"

"Definitely."

"Well, in that case, I'll be checking out today."

"Take that up with the front desk," the agent said. "What's your name?"

"Harold."

"Does that come with a last name?"

"Steinberg."

"I'm going to need to see some ID."

Scott pulled out his wallet, with a fake ID for Harold Steinberg from Idaho. He'd paid over a thousand dollars for that tiny piece of plastic, all for this very moment.

The agent swiped the license through a machine, and three seconds later, the results came up on her screen. "Alright. This checks out. Stay put for at least a few hours, unless you want to be strip-searched on your way out."

Scott's eyes went wide at the suggestion, but he said nothing.

"If you think of anything to add to the investigation, give me a call." She handed him her business card along with the fake ID and left as she said into her wrist, "Room 1524 is clear."

He glanced down at the card and was surprised to see she wasn't Secret Service at all. The card said Maria Croix, Joint Terrorism Task Force.

*   *   *

Maria returned to the twelfth floor after helping finish the search of the rooms. There were three dozen empty rooms which the hotel showed as occupied. All but one had luggage and other signs that the occupants would be back soon. But room 1243 was completely empty, and she needed to know why.

The occupant hadn't checked out, though it looked like no one had slept there last night. She let herself in using the master key the concierge gave her and stood in the room, trying to decide where to look first.

Look. That was where Maria needed to start. She walked to the windows and looked down. She could barely see the spot where Towers' died. It wasn't a clean shot. Not even an expert marksman would have perched here to take out the President.

She searched the room a second time, looking in every drawer and closet, turning over the mattress, and even looking in the ceiling. The tiles were easily moved and easily reached by standing on the table, even for her.

After an hour of searching, she found nothing. It didn't make sense. Why would someone be checked into this room, yet be the only room without any sign of habitation?

Frustrated, she went back to the window and ran her hand along the glass, trying to picture a second shooter here. There was no evidence yet to suggest an accomplice, but the bounty had been for both Towers and Michaels.

Her fingers found a bump where there should be smooth glass. Leaning in closer, she saw a piece of the window had been meticulously cut out and hastily replaced, just big enough for the end of a rifle. But where was it aimed?

Two potential targets were evident to her. She could easily have hit the building where the actual shooter had been. But why would anyone do that? They would have to know the shooter was there and what he was planning to do.

Her gaze fell to the ground, at the second obvious target. From here, she also had a clear shot to the door of the convention center where VP Michaels had been. Perhaps that had been the plan, but one of them had backed out at the last minute. It happened all the time in first-time teams.

Weren't there two men involved in the attack on Senator Ball's home? Weren't there two men involved when Senator Ball was put in the hospital? If the second man of the team wanted to pull out at the last minute, perhaps the only way he could communicate with his accomplice was with his gun.

"This is Agent Croix requesting an additional forensics unit be sent to room 1243 of the Embassy Suites."

"I thought that building had been cleared," Jenkins replied.

"I've found evidence of a possible accomplice."

Gideon's Prayer is Answered

May 26th - Notre Dame, Indiana

Gideon Shumway returned home from church feeling exhausted and hungry. Normally, he only fasted on the first Sunday of the month. Lately, Gideon had been fasting every week, trying to learn what God wanted him to do with his life. He wasn't sure that he was where God wanted him or doing what God needed to be done. All through the three hours of church services, these thoughts swirled around in his head.

The chorus of the opening hymn of Sacrament Meeting kept repeating in his mind.

> I'll go where you want me to go, dear Lord, Over mountain or plain or sea; I'll say what you want me to say, dear Lord; I'll be what you want me to be.[65]

Gideon went into his bedroom and shut the door. Duane wasn't home, but Gideon wanted to make sure he wasn't interrupted. He knelt by his bed and started praying, speaking to God as if He were in the room, and as a friend. Gideon spent twenty minutes explaining everything that had happened to him, about his possible football career and how much that meant to his earthly father.

Only then did he ask the question that had been on his mind all day. "God, I'm willing to go where you want me to go, do what you want me to do, say what you want me to say, and be what you want me to be. What should I do with my life?"

A warm feeling in his heart grew and spread until it felt like his whole body was on fire. A bright light shone through his eyelids, and he opened his eyes to see the cause.

An angel was standing above his bed.[54]

Gideon tried to say something, but he was full of fear, freezing his tongue.

"Gideon, do not be afraid, for I am a fellow servant. God has heard your prayers."

Endnotes

1. August 20th, 2017 - Damascus, Syria
   Mufti A.H. Elias and Mohammad Ali ibn Zubair Ali
   http://www.islam.tc/prophecies/masdaj.html (As of 2015)
   The full text is too long to include here. For further study on
   this topic, visit http://www.islam.tc/prophecies/
   Physical description of the Imam Mahdi:
   1. He will be tall;
   2. He will be fair complexioned;
   3. His facial features will be similar to those of Rasulullah
   (Sallallahu Alayhi Wasallam);
   4. His character will be exactly like that of Rasulullah;
   5. His father's name will be Abdullah;
   6. His mother's name will be Aamina;
   7. He will speak with a slight stutter and occasionally this
   stutter will frustrate him causing him to hit his hand upon his
   thigh.;
   8. His age at the time of his emergence will be forty years;
   9. He will receive Knowledge from Allah.

2. August 20th, 2017 - Damascus, Syria
   There are many signs which are to precede the appearance of
   the 12th Imam. For a brief overview, visit
   https://en.wikipedia.org/wiki/Signs_of_the_reappearance_o
   f_Muhammad_al-Mahdi

3. August 20th, 2017 - Damascus, Syria
   Deadly rocket fire hits near Damascus trade fair
   https://www.i24news.tv/en/news/international/153417-
   170820-injuries-reported-after-rocket-strikes-much-awaited-
   damascus-business-fair

4. August 21st, 2017 - Sublimity, Oregon
   A total solar eclipse from coast to coast. The sight of a lifetime! https://www.greatamericaneclipse.com/

5. August 21st, 2017 - Sublimity, Oregon
   Eclipse Map — April 8, 2024 Total Solar Eclipse
   https://www.timeanddate.com/eclipse/map/2024-april-8

6. August 21st, 2017 - Marion, Illinois
   Joel 2:31 (KJV)
   The sun shall be turned into darkness, and the moon into blood, before the great and the terrible day of the Lord come.

7. August 21st, 2017 - Marion, Illinois
   September 23rd, 2017 - Mt. Hamilton, California
   Revelation 12:1-2 (KJV)

8. September 19, 2017 - Mexico City, Mexico
   The 1985 Mexico City earthquake struck in the early morning of 19 September at 07:17:50 (CST) with a moment magnitude of 8.0 and a Mercalli intensity of IX (Violent). The event caused serious damage to the Greater Mexico City area and the deaths of at least 5,000 people.
   http://en.wikipedia.org/wiki/1985_Mexico_City_earthquake

9. September 19, 2017 - Mexico City, Mexico
   The 2017 Central Mexico earthquake struck at 13:14 CDT (18:14 UTC) on 19 September 2017 with an estimated magnitude of M_w 7.1 and strong shaking for about 20 seconds. Its epicenter was about 55 km (34 mi) south of the city of Puebla. The earthquake caused damage in the Mexican states of Puebla and Morelos and in the Greater Mexico City area, including the collapse of more than 40 buildings. 370 people were killed by the earthquake and related building collapses, including 228 in Mexico City, and more than 6,000

were injured.
http://en.wikipedia.org/wiki/2017_Central_Mexico_earthqu
ake

10. September 23rd, 2017 - Mt. Hamilton, California
    End of World in 2012? Maya "Doomsday" Calendar
    Explained
    Monument text's "poetic flourish" confuses modern minds,
    experts say.
    https://news.nationalgeographic.com/news/2011/12/11122
    0-end-of-world-2012-maya-calendar-explained-ancient-
    science/

11. September 23rd, 2017 - Mt. Hamilton, California
    New Apocalypse deadline? Grigori Rasputin predicted the
    end of the world to come on August 23, 2013
    http://www.daniel-irimia.com/2013/01/01/new-apocalypse-
    deadline-grigori-rasputin-predicted-the-end-of-the-world-to-
    come-on-august-23-2013/

12. September 23rd, 2017 - Mt. Hamilton, California
    The blood moon prophecy is a series of apocalyptic beliefs
    promoted by Christian ministers John Hagee and Mark Biltz,
    which state that a tetrad (a series of four consecutive lunar
    eclipses—coinciding on Jewish holidays—with six full moons
    in between, and no intervening partial lunar eclipses) which
    began with the April 2014 lunar eclipse is a sign of the end
    times as described in the Bible in the Book of Joel, Acts 2:20
    and Revelation 6:12. The tetrad ended with the lunar eclipse
    on September 27-28, 2015.
    http://en.wikipedia.org/wiki/Blood_moon_prophecy

13. September 23rd, 2017 - Mt. Hamilton, California
Nibiru: How the nonsense Planet X Armageddon and Nasa
fake news theories spread globally
http://www.telegraph.co.uk/news/2017/09/21/nibiru-
nonsense-planet-x-armageddon-nasa-fake-news-theories/

14. September 23rd, 2017 - Mt. Hamilton, California
Helaman 14:3-5
3 And behold, this will I give unto you for a sign at the time
of his coming; for behold, there shall be great lights in
heaven, insomuch that in the night before he cometh there
shall be no darkness, insomuch that it shall appear unto man
as if it was day.
4 Therefore, there shall be one day and a night and a day, as if
it were one day and there were no night; and this shall be
unto you for a sign; for ye shall know of the rising of the sun
and also of its setting; therefore they shall know of a surety
that there shall be two days and a night; nevertheless the
night shall not be darkened; and it shall be the night before he
is born.
5 And behold, there shall a new star arise, such an one as ye
never have beheld; and this also shall be a sign unto you.

15. September 23rd, 2017 - Mt. Hamilton, California
Saturday's Venus-Jupiter Encounter May Explain Bible's Star
of Bethlehem
https://www.space.com/33866-venus-jupiter-conjunction-
star-of-bethlehem.html

16. September 23rd, 2017 - Mt. Hamilton, California
Luke 3:21-23
21 Now when all the people were baptized, it came to pass,
that Jesus also being baptized, and praying, the heaven was
opened,

22 And the Holy Ghost descended in a bodily shape like a dove upon him, and a voice came from heaven, which said, Thou art my beloved Son; in thee I am well pleased.

23 And Jesus himself began to be about thirty years of age, being (as was supposed) the son of Joseph, which was the son of Heli,

17. September 23rd, 2017 - Hawthorne, California
Bill Gates bought land to create a futuristic city with the latest technology integrated from the ground up.
http://www.foxnews.com/tech/2017/11/12/bill-gates-firm-buys-arizona-land-for-80-million-to-create-smart-city.html

18. September 23rd, 2017 - Near Panguitch, Utah
Vision of Sols Guardisto in 1923.
As printed in Prophecy; Key to the Future, Pages 199-201
I saw further on, instructions given whereby the places of refuge were prepared, quietly, but efficiently by inspired elders. I saw Cardston and the surrounding foothills, especially West and North, for miles being prepared for a refuge for your people, quietly but quickly.

19. October 1st, 2017 - Las Vegas, Nevada
Las Vegas shooting: What is the Route 91 Harvest festival? The Route 91 Harvest festival, near the Mandalay Bay, was the scene of a shooting spree that left at least 50 dead and injured 400 more.
https://www.usatoday.com/story/life/2017/10/02/las-vegas-shooting-what-is-route-91-harvest-music-festival/722394001/

20. October 1st, 2017 - Las Vegas, Nevada
   Reza Pahlavi, Crown Prince of Iran; born 31 October 1960, is
   the last heir apparent to the defunct throne of the Imperial
   State of Iran and is the current head of the exiled House of
   Pahlavi.
   https://en.wikipedia.org/wiki/Reza_Pahlavi,_Crown_Prince
   _of_Iran

21. December 14th, 2017 - Ventura, California
   The Thomas Fire, considered the largest fire in California's
   modern history, has finally been fully contained.
   The U.S. Forest Service confirmed on Friday (12 January
   2018) that the blaze was at 100 percent containment.
   http://abc7.com/thomas-fire-largest-fire-in-ca-history-100-
   percent-contained/2934699/

22. December 14th, 2017 - Ventura, California
   Firefighter dies while battling Thomas fire in California
   A California firefighter has died while battling the Thomas
   fire that is threatening the Golden State's Ventura and Santa
   Barbara counties, officials said.
   The firefighter was an engineer with the California
   Department of Forestry and Fire Protection from San Diego,
   said Cal Fire director Chief Ken Pimlott in a press release
   Thursday.
   Authorities identified him as Cory Iverson, 32, of Escondido,
   California, and said he had a 2-year-old daughter and his wife,
   Ashley, is currently pregnant.
   He was an eight-year-veteran for Cal Fire.
   http://abcnews.go.com/US/firefighter-dies-battling-thomas-
   fire-california/story?id=51801005

23. December 14th, 2017 - Ventura, California
    Ash falls like snow as tens of thousands flee Thomas fire
    By CHRISTOPHER WEBER
    Ash fell like snow and heavy smoke had residents gasping for
    air Monday as a huge Southern California wildfire exploded in
    size, becoming the fifth largest in state history and driving
    celebrities from a wealthy hillside enclave.
    Tens of thousands have fled their homes as flames churn
    through foothill towns near Santa Barbara, the latest flare-up
    after a week of wind-fanned wildfires throughout the region.
    http://www.dailynews.com/2017/12/11/thomas-fire-
    consumes-about-360-square-miles-becoming-states-5th-
    largest-blaze/

24. September 20th - San Mateo, California
    Waymo is a self-driving technology company with the
    mission to make it safe and easy for everyone to get
    around—without the need for anyone in the driver's seat.
    Our journey started at Google in 2009, and we became
    Waymo in 2016.
    https://waymo.com/

25. September 23rd - Vatican City
    For more information on St. Ferdinand III of Castile, patron
    saint of the Spanish Army's Corps of Engineers, see
    http://en.wikipedia.org/wiki/Ferdinand_III_of_Castile

26. September 23rd - Vatican City
    Ferdinand II (1578–1637), a member of the House of
    Habsburg, was Holy Roman Emperor (1619–1637), King of
    Bohemia (1617–1619, 1620–1637), and King of Hungary
    (1618–1637).
    His acts against Protestantism started the Thirty Years' War.
    As a zealous Catholic, Ferdinand wanted to restore the

Catholic Church as the only religion in the Empire and to suppress Protestantism.
http://en.wikipedia.org/wiki/
Ferdinand_II,_Holy_Roman_Emperor

27. September 23rd - Vatican City
The Reformation, specifically referred to as the Protestant Reformation, was a schism in Western Christianity initiated by Martin Luther and continued by John Calvin, Huldrych Zwingli, and other early Protestant Reformers in 16th-century Europe. It is usually considered to have started with the publication of the Ninety-five Theses by Luther in 1517
https://en.wikipedia.org/wiki/Reformation

28. September 23rd - Vatican City
"The animosity and resentments left by the Reformation only began to heal after the Second Vatican Council in the 1960s, with the start of an ecumenical dialogue aimed at promoting Christian unity.
"There are still some doctrinal disputes. But Pope Francis says that while theologians iron out their differences, the two churches can work together on social issues like caring for the poor, migrants and refugees, and combating persecution of Christians."
https://www.npr.org/sections/thetwo-way/2016/10/31/500057532/in-show-of-unity-pope-francis-marks-500th-anniversary-of-protestant-reformation

29. September 23rd - Vatican City
Homily of Pope Francis at Basilica of St. Paul Outside the Walls, Saturday, 25 January, 2014
As we find ourselves in his presence, we realize all the more that we may not regard divisions in the Church as something natural, inevitable in any form of human association. Our

divisions wound Christ's body, they impair the witness which we are called to give to him before the world. The Second Vatican Council's Decree on Ecumenism, appealing to the text of Saint Paul which we have reflected on, significantly states: "Christ the Lord founded one Church and one Church only. However, many Christian communities present themselves to people as the true inheritance of Jesus Christ; all indeed profess to be followers of the Lord but they differ in outlook and go their different ways, as if Christ were divided". And the Council continues: "Such division openly contradicts the will of Christ, scandalizes the world, and damages the sacred cause of preaching the Gospel to every creature" (Unitatis Redintegratio, 1). We have all been damaged by these divisions. None of us wishes to become a cause of scandal. And so we are all journeying together, fraternally, on the road towards unity, bringing about unity even as we walk; that unity comes from the Holy Spirit and brings us something unique which only the Holy Spirit can do, that is, reconciling our differences. The Lord waits for us all, accompanies us all, and is with us all on this path of unity.

30. September 30th - Washington, D.C.
Authors' Analysis:
If President Donald J. Trump is taken out and Vice President Mike Pence is quickly taken out, the next in line is the Speaker of the House, currently Paul Ryan.
https://en.wikipedia.org/wiki/United_States_presidential_line_of_succession

31. October 5th - New York City
Ezra Taft Benson, October 1961 General Conference, Pg 69
Concerning the United States, the Lord revealed to his prophets that its greatest threat would be a vast, world-wide

secret combination which would not only threaten the United States but seek to overthrow the freedom of all lands, nations and countries. In connection with the attack on the United States, the Lord told his prophet there would be an attempt to overthrow the country by destroying the Constitution.

32. October 5th - New York City
Joseph Smith, 1844, as recorded in the autobiography of Mosiah Lyman Hancock.
"There will be two great political parties in this country. One will be called the Republican, and the other the Democrat party. These two parties will go to war and out of these two parties will spring another party which will be the Independent American party . . ."

33. October 15th - Notre Dame, Indiana
See Appendix A
The Apocrypha was included in the original 1611 King James Version of the Bible and was removed from the Non-Catholic King James Bible in 1885.

34. October 15th - Notre Dame, Indiana
See Appendix A
Many scholars believe that this Ezra's Eagle Prophecy is speaking of Rome as the Eagle, because Rome used the Eagle as its national symbol. I have read material saying that Hitler's Nazi Germany is the Eagle, because the Nazis used the symbol of the Eagle. However, America also uses the Eagle as its national symbol. It's clear that everyone who knows this prophecy is trying to match up the Eagle, but careful consideration must be paid to the full prophecy of Ezra's Eagle in both chapters 11 and 12. Not just "looking for a convenient Eagle," as the scholars have done.

35. November 6th - Notre Dame, Indiana
    2 Esdras 11-12
    2 Esdras is the second book of the prophet Ezra, sometimes called 4 Ezra. It was once included in the King James Version of the Bible but was later removed due to questions about its origins. The full text of these two chapters is too long to include here. You can read it at:
    http://www.pseudepigrapha.com/apocrypha_ot/2esdr.htm
    http://www.kingjamesbibleonline.org/2-Esdras-Chapter-11/

36. Thanksgiving Day - Notre Dame, Indiana
    2 Esdras 11:1-2, 11
    1 Then saw I a dream, and, behold, there came up from the sea an eagle, which had twelve feathered wings, and three heads.
    2 And I saw, and, behold, she spread her wings over all the earth, and all the winds of the air blew on her, and were gathered together.
    11 And I numbered her contrary feathers, and, behold, there were eight of them.

37. Thanksgiving Day - Notre Dame, Indiana
    2 Esdras 12:13-16
    13 Behold, the days will come, that there shall rise up a kingdom upon earth, and it shall be feared above all the kingdoms that were before it.
    14 In the same shall twelve kings reign, one after another:
    15 Wherefof the second shall begin to reign, and shall have more time than any of the twelve.
    16 And this do the twelve wings signify, which thou sawest.

38. Thanksgiving Day - Notre Dame, Indiana

    2 Esdras 11:12-17

    12 And I looked, and, behold, on the right side there arose one feather, and reigned over all the earth;

    13 And so it was, that when it reigned, the end of it came, and the place thereof appeared no more: so the next following stood up. and reigned, and had a great time;

    14 And it happened, that when it reigned, the end of it came also, like as the first, so that it appeared no more.

    15 Then came there a voice unto it, and said,

    16 Hear thou that hast borne rule over the earth so long: this I say unto thee, before thou beginnest to appear no more,

    17 There shall none after thee attain unto thy time, neither unto the half thereof.

39. Thanksgiving Day - Notre Dame, Indiana

    January 2nd - Nephi, Utah

    2 Esdras 12:18-21

    18 In the midst of the time of that kingdom great struggles shall arise, and it shall be in danger of falling; nevertheless it shall not fall then, but shall regain its former power.*

    19 And whereas thou sawest the eight small under feathers sticking to her wings, this is the interpretation:

    20 That in him there shall arise eight kings, whose times shall be but small, and their years swift.

    21 And two of them shall perish, the middle time approaching: four shall be kept until their end begin to approach: but two shall be kept unto the end.

    * Verse 18 is taken from an alternate translation.

40. Thanksgiving Day - Notre Dame, Indiana

    See Appendix A

    Ezra's Eagle is not only about America. For that would

include George Washington and the rest of the presidents. The Eagle Kingdom described in Ezra's Eagle is about 3 sleeping "behind the scenes" power centers that rose up after 1900; with the first one starting before 1929.

41. Thanksgiving Day - Notre Dame, Indiana
See Appendix A
The last 2 feathers that were "short" in the past were John F. Kennedy and Richard Nixon. They were on the Eagle's left side.

42. Thanksgiving Day - Notre Dame, Indiana
The very word "secrecy" is repugnant in a free and open society; and we are as a people inherently and historically opposed to secret societies, to secret oaths and to secret proceedings. We decided long ago that the dangers of excessive and unwarranted concealment of pertinent facts far outweighed the dangers which are cited to justify it. Even today, there is little value in opposing the threat of a closed society by imitating its arbitrary restrictions. Even today, there is little value in insuring the survival of our nation if our traditions do not survive with it. And there is very grave danger that an announced need for increased security will be seized upon by those anxious to expand its meaning to the very limits of official censorship and concealment. That I do not intend to permit to the extent that it is in my control. And no official of my Administration, whether his rank is high or low, civilian or military, should interpret my words here tonight as an excuse to censor the news, to stifle dissent, to cover up our mistakes or to withhold from the press and the public the facts they deserve to know. - President John F. Kennedy, Address before the American Newspaper Publishers Association, April 27, 1961

https://www.jfklibrary.org/Research/Research-Aids/JFK-Speeches/American-Newspaper-Publishers-Association_19610427.aspx

43. January 2nd - Nephi, Utah
See Appendix A
Ezra's Eagle is recorded in the book of 2nd Esdras in the Apocrypha. 2nd Esdras was written by Ezra, a contemporary to Daniel, helper to King Nebuchadnezzar of Babylon when the Jews were taken away. The same Ezra that is in our modern-day Bible.

44. January 2nd - Nephi, Utah
2 Esdras 11:25-26
25 And I beheld, and, lo, the feathers that were under the wing thought to set up themselves and to have the rule.
26 And I beheld, and, lo, there was one set up, but shortly it appeared no more.

45. January 2nd - Nephi, Utah
2 Esdras 11:7-9,20-22
7 And I beheld, and, lo, the eagle rose upon her talons, and spake to her feathers, saying,
8 Watch not all at once: sleep every one in his own place, and watch by course:
9 But let the heads be preserved for the last.
[...}
20 Then I beheld, and, lo, in process of time the feathers that followed stood up upon the right side, that they might rule also; and some of them ruled, but within a while they appeared no more:
21 For some of them were set up, but ruled not.
22 After this I looked, and, behold, the twelve feathers appeared no more, nor the two little feathers:

46. January 2nd - Nephi, Utah
    Isaiah 10:13-14

47. January 2nd - Nephi, Utah
    Isaiah 10:16-19
    16 Therefore shall the Lord, the Lord of hosts, send among
    his fat ones leanness; and under his glory he shall kindlc a
    burning like the burning of a fire.
    17 And the light of Israel shall be for a fire, and his Holy One
    for a flame: and it shall burn and devour his thorns and his
    briers in one day;
    18 And shall consume the glory of his forest, and of his
    fruitful field, both a soul and body: and they shall be as when
    a standard bearer fainteth.
    19 And the rest of the trees of his forest shall be few, that a
    child may write them.

48. January 2nd - Nephi, Utah
    Revelation 13:16-17
    16 And he causeth all, both small and great, rich and poor,
    free and bond, to receive a mark in their right hand, or in
    their foreheads:
    17 And that no man might buy or sell, save he that had the
    mark, or the name of the beast, or the number of his name.

49. January 2nd - Nephi, Utah
    D&C 45:39

50. January 6th - New York City
    We rejoice that the Joint Declaration on the Doctrine of
    Justification, solemnly signed by the Lutheran World
    Federation and the Roman Catholic Church in 1999, has also
    been signed by the World Methodist Council in 2006 and,
    during this Commemoration Year of the Reformation, by the
    World Communion of Reformed Churches. On this very day

it is being welcomed and received by the Anglican
Communion at a solemn ceremony in Westminster Abbey.
On this basis our Christian communions can build an ever
closer bond of spiritual consensus and common witness in
the service of the Gospel.
http://en.radiovaticana.va/news/2017/10/31/catholics,_luth
erans_mark_500th_anniversary_of_reformation/1346149

51. January 12th - Berkeley, California
Ditch the hat and scarf – it's not fooling anyone. Face
recognition software can now see through your cunning
disguise – even you are wearing a mask.
Amarjot Singh at the University of Cambridge and his
colleagues trained a machine learning algorithm to locate 14
key facial points. These are the points the human brain pays
most attention to when we look at someone's face.
The researchers then hand-labelled 2000 photos of people
wearing hats, glasses, scarves and fake beards to indicate the
location of those same key points, even if they couldn't be
seen. The algorithm looked at a subset of these images to
learn how the disguised faces corresponded with the
undisguised faces.
The system accurately identified people wearing a scarf 77 per
cent of the time – a cap and scarf 69 per cent of the time and
a cap, scarf and glasses 55 per cent of the time. This isn't as
good as systems that recognize undisguised human faces, but
it is the best at seeing through disguises, says Singh.
The system only needs to be able to see a fraction of facial
key points – most of which are around the eyes and mouth –
to be able to guess where the other points are likely to be.
Based on that guess, it can identify the person if it has already
been shown a map of their key points.
"In effect, it is able to see through your mask," says Singh. -

by: Matt Reynolds
https://www.newscientist.com/article/2146703-even-a-mask-wont-hide-you-from-the-latest-face-recognition-tech/

52. January 20th - Notre Dame, Indiana
Wherefore, my beloved, as ye have always obeyed, not as in my presence only, but now much more in my absence, work out your own salvation with fear and trembling. - Philippians 2:12 (KJV)

53. January 20th - Notre Dame, Indiana
For behold, this life is the time for men to prepare to meet God; yea, behold the day of this life is the day for men to perform their labors. - Alma 34:32

54. February 14th - Notre Dame, Indiana
February 17th - Notre Dame, Indiana
May 26th - Notre Dame, Indiana
See Appendix B: The Baptism of Fire and of the Holy Ghost

55. February 14th - Notre Dame, Indiana
Titus 3:7 That being justified by his grace, we should be made heirs according to the hope of eternal life.
James 2:21 Was not Abraham our father justified by works, when he had offered Isaac his son upon the altar?

56. February 17th - Notre Dame, Indiana
2nd Verse of We'll Sing All Hail to Jesus' Name:
He passed the portals of the grave;
Salvation was his song;
He called upon the sin bound soul
To join the heav'nly throng.
Hymnal for The Church of Jesus Christ of Latter-day Saints
Hymn 182

57. February 17th - Notre Dame, Indiana
O God, the Eternal Father, we ask thee in the name of thy Son, Jesus Christ, to bless and sanctify this wine to the souls of all those who drink of it, that they may do it in remembrance of the blood of thy Son, which was shed for them; that they may witness unto thee, O God, the Eternal Father, that they do always remember him, that they may have his Spirit to be with them. Amen. - D&C 74:79

58. February 17th - Notre Dame, Indiana
And lo, he shall suffer temptations, and pain of body, hunger, thirst, and fatigue, even more than man can suffer, except it be unto death; for behold, blood cometh from every pore, so great shall be his anguish for the wickedness and the abominations of his people. - Mosiah 3:7

59. March 3rd - Warsaw, Poland
Twelve Shi'as cite various references from the Qur'an and reports, or Hadith, from Imam Mahdi and the Twelve Imams with regard to the reappearance of al-Mahdi who would, in accordance with Allah's command, bring justice and peace to the world by establishing Islam throughout the world.
 - Hadith

60. March 15th - Washington, D.C.
The assault left Paul, 54, with six cracked ribs and a case of pneumonia, and it briefly sidelined the Republican senator during a crucial debate over a tax overhaul in Washington. Boucher, 59, has pleaded not guilty to a misdemeanor assault charge in the case and could yet face more serious consequences.
The Washington Post, 6 Dec 2017 Intrigue grows over what sparked the attack on Rand Paul

61. March 28th - Springfield, Missouri
BREAKING! ATTEMPTED TRUMP ASSASSINATION
CAUGHT ON VIDEO?
Vehicle unexpectedly drives towards Trump motorcade from
the woods
Infowars.com - AUGUST 30, 2017
https://www.infowars.com/breaking-attempted-trump-
assassination-caught-on-video/

62. April 6th - Alexandria, Virginia
The Fourth World shall end soon, and the Fifth World will
begin. This the elders everywhere know. The Signs over many
years have been fulfilled, and so few are left.
This is the First Sign: We were told of the coming of the
white-skinned men, like Pahana, but not living like Pahana --
men who took the land that was not theirs and who struck
their enemies with thunder. (Guns)
This is the Second Sign: Our lands will see the coming of
spinning wheels filled with voices. (Covered wagons)
This is the Third Sign: A strange beast like a buffalo but with
great long horns, will overrun the land in large numbers.
(Longhorn cattle)
This is the Fourth Sign: The land will be crossed by snakes of
iron. (Railroad tracks)
This is the Fifth Sign: The land shall be criss-crossed by a
giant spider's web. (Power and telephone lines)
This is the Sixth Sign: The land shall be criss-crossed with
rivers of stone that make pictures in the sun. (Concrete roads
and their mirage-producing effects.)
This is the Seventh Sign: You will hear of the sea turning
black, and many living things dying because of it. (Oil spills)
This is the Eighth Sign: You will see many youth, who wear
their hair long like our people, come and join the tribal

nations, to learn our ways and wisdom. (Hippies)
And this is the Ninth and Last Sign: You will hear of a
dwelling-place in the heavens, above the earth, that shall fall
with a great crash. It will appear as a blue star. Very soon
after this, the ceremonies of the Hopi people will cease. -
White Feather, Bear Clan, Hopi Tribe
From
http://www.twohawks.com/hopi/hopififthworld.shtml

63. April 7th - Hanover, Germany
Mission of the World Communion of Reformed Churches
Drawing on the heritage of the Reformed confessions as a
gift for the renewal of the whole church, the World
Communion of Reformed Churches is committed to
communion and justice and, in partnership with other
ecumenical bodies and organizations, we participate in God's
mission in the world as we proclaim the saving grace and love
of our Triune God by mutually working for:
Christian unity and renewal in worship, theology and
spirituality
Justice
Eradication of poverty
Building right relations
Integrity of creation
Interfaith relations
Reconciliation, healing, peace and the transformation of both
churches and society.

64. May 26th - Houston, Texas
Isaiah 5:20

65. May 26th - Notre Dame, Indiana
Hymn Number 270, Hymns of The Church of Jesus Christ of
Latter-day Saints, 1985

Appendix A: Selections from "The Last Days Timeline" by James T. Prout

3: America's Rise to Full Influence in the World–Ezra's Eagle (1929-2017 Plus)

We were to the point of about 1900AD, toward the end of the Indian Wars, at the middle of 1st Nephi chapter 14. We will fill in the holes with Ezra's Eagle which picks up in the early 1900s… and takes us into **our near future to 2017**.

This material on Ezra's Eagle will be very new to most people. I first discovered it in the book *A Remnant Shall Return* by Michael Rush (See book review www.LastDaysTimeline.com/remnant-shall-return). Rush did a great job identifying the feathers of the Eagle in the Ezra's Eagle Prophecy; however the work you are now reading, has additional symbolic identifications and comes to a much different conclusion as to the outcome of the final feathers of the prophecy. This book is being first written just after the election on November 8, 2016. This is important timing because of what happens with Ezra's Eagle and President Elect Donald J. Trump. Let us begin.

The Apocrypha – What is It?

Ezra's Eagle is recorded in the book of 2nd Esdras in the Apocrypha. 2nd Esdras was written by Ezra, a contemporary to Daniel, helper to King Nebuchadnezzar of Babylon when the Jews were taken away. This was just a few years *after* Lehi's family and Ishmael's family left Jerusalem.

The Apocrypha was included in the original 1611 King James Version of the Bible and was removed from the Non-Catholic King James Bibles in 1885. The Apocrypha was included in the Bible for a long time, and just **recently** in the last 130 years taken out. (see https://en.wikipedia.org/wiki/Apocrypha)

Joseph Smith was engaged in the work of translating the King James Bible in the late 1830s and early 1840s. He got to the Apocrypha in his King James Bible and received the revelation as recorded in Section 91 of the Doctrine and Covenants:

(D&C 91:1-6)
"1 Verily, thus saith the Lord unto you concerning the Apocrypha—There are **many things contained therein that are true, and it is mostly translated correctly;**

2 There are many things contained therein that are **not true**, which are **interpolations by the hands of men.**

3 Verily, I say unto you, that it is not needful that the Apocrypha should be translated.

4 Therefore, whoso readeth it, let him understand, for the Spirit manifesteth truth;

5 **And whoso is enlightened by the Spirit shall obtain benefit therefrom;**

6 And whoso receiveth not by the Spirit, cannot be benefited. Therefore it is not needful that it should be translated. Amen."

Learning Points:
A.   The Apocrypha contains **many things that are true** along with many interpolations by man. Read it with the Holy Spirit in prayer to gain the **true material.** For it can be gained.

The Dark Eagle

Note: I am not going to propose that the entire Apocrypha is true. The Lord told us that is not the case. However, Ezra's Eagle takes place in only 2 chapters. These 2 chapters fall within a piece of the Apocrypha 2nd Esdras (4 Ezra) that has been argued for centuries about being incorporated into the actual cannon. 2nd Esdras (Chapters 3-14) was so important of a work, that the Christian Church translated it from Hebrew and Greek to Latin by Jerome in 382AD … and **Jerome didn't like the Apocrypha. Jerome was overruled** and 2nd Esdras became an appendix item of the official cannon in Latin. Many Christian Churches of today in Europe and other places, still have this one book of the Apocrypha "The Apocalypse of Ezra" included in their official cannon of scripture.

(See https://en.wikipedia.org/wiki/2_Esdras and also https://en.wikipedia.org/wiki/Vulgate)

Currently the Church of Jesus Christ of Latter-Day Saints uses the 1769 edition of the King James Bible without the Apocrypha. This is why many church members have never heard of Ezra's Eagle, because we don't have common access to the Apocrypha.

You can read the Apocrypha online for FREE here: http://www.kingjamesbibleonline.org/2-Esdras-Chapter-11/

Hugh Nibley wrote highly of the whole Apocrypha in his book *Since Cumorah.*

("A New Age of Discovery," CWHN 7:29)
"What are the Apocrypha?

They are a large body of writings, Jewish and Christian, existing alongside the Bible, each of which has at some time or other been accepted as true revealed scriptures by some Christian or Jewish group.

Where do they come from?

The actual manuscripts are as old as our Bible manuscripts and are sometimes written by the same hands, but their contents betray widely scattered sources, some of which are orthodox and some of which are not.

Then why bother about them?

Because writers of the Bible respect them and sometimes quote them, thus including excerpts of the Apocrypha in our Bible, while the fathers of the church in the first three centuries accept many of them as genuine and quote them as scripture."

So, as a source rating, the Apocrypha is right up there, just under scripture, because it was scripture for 1000s of years. However, the Lord did say that not all of it was correct. Read it with the Holy Spirit and pray for guidance.

The specific "part" we are going to read is 2nd Esdras. This book of 2nd Esdras written by the prophet Ezra in our Bible cannon was found written in Hebrew in the Dead Sea Scrolls. Thus it is older than the Bible's Greek or Latin translations. It's old. This one book *may be* higher than "interpolations of men" … because it may be part of the **absolutely true parts** that the Lord has affirmed.

I choose to believe these **2 chapters** whole heartedly… based on the researched evidence below…and upon seeking God the Father in prayer and asking if it be true. The Father confirmed that it was true to me. I encourage you as the reader to research this out, then seek Him and ask. He will tell you.

> **Important Interjection**: If you have a problem feeling the Spirit and getting answers to your prayers, simply read and follow D&C 9:7-9. Repent first and exhibit your faith by praying in the manner described. Research the subject in question. Pray and phrase your questions with "Yes/No" answers at first. Then wait and *feel* how you feel. It's that simple.

Ezra's Eagle Empire Rises in 1929 to Develop into The 4th Beast of Daniel

Ezra's vision of the Eagle was recorded in 2nd Esdras Chapters 11 and 12. Let us go through it verse by verse.

Author's Analysis:
Many scholars believe that this Ezra's Eagle Prophecy is speaking of Rome as the Eagle, because Rome used the Eagle as its national symbol. I have read material saying that Hitler's Nazi Germany is the Eagle, because the Nazis used the symbol of the Eagle. However, America also uses the Eagle as its national symbol. It's clear that everyone that knows of this prophecy is trying to match up the Eagle, but careful consideration must be paid to **the full prophecy** of Ezra's Eagle in both chapters 11 and 12. Not just "looking for a convenient Eagle", as the scholars have done.

This is the same situation the scholars were doing with the 4 beast kingdoms of Daniel Chapter 7. (See Appendix 1: concerning the beasts of Daniel Chapter 7)

(2nd Esdras 11:1-6)
"1 Then saw I a dream, and, behold, there **came up from the sea an eagle**, which had twelve feathered wings, and **three heads**.

2 And I saw, and, behold, she **spread her wings over all the earth**, and all the winds of the air blew on her, and were gathered together.

3 And I beheld, and out of her feathers there grew **other contrary feathers**; and they became **little feathers and small**.

4 But her **heads were at rest**: the **head in the midst was greater** than the other, yet rested it with the residue.

5 Moreover I beheld, and, lo, **the eagle flew with her feathers**, and **reigned upon earth, and over them that dwelt therein.**

6 And I saw that **all things under heaven were subject unto her, and no man spake against her, no, not one creature upon earth.**"

Learning Points:

A. The dream shows Ezra an Eagle coming out of the sea or water. One definition of "water" in the scriptures, means "many peoples". (See Rev 17:15 water=people. Many of the Beasts in Daniel and Revelations rose out of the water.) So, this Eagle kingdom is "rising out of the people", is one way of defining this verse.

B. The eagle has lots of feathers on 2 wings. Later on in the vision we see that the wing count is 2 (not 12). Also that there are 12 **long** feathers.

C. The eagle has some **short** (small) feathers. We shall see later a total of 8 short feathers. For a total of 20 feathers.

D. This eagle has 3 heads. The middle head is larger than the other 2.

E. This eagle apparently is "at rest" or sleeping. Even while it is soaring and exerting great influence over all the nations of the earth. The 3 heads are all sleeping.

    a. (**Author's Analysis**): My opinion is that the 3 heads sleeping means that the people working in the "background", not in the open. When they wake up, they will be working in the "open". As we shall see.

        (2nd Esdras 11:7-10)

"7 And I beheld, and, lo, the eagle **rose upon her talons**, and spake to her feathers, saying,

8 Watch **not all at once**: sleep every one in his own place, and **watch by course**:

9 But let the **heads be preserved for the last**.

10 And I beheld, and, lo, **the voice went not out of her heads, but from the midst of her body.**"

Learning Points:

A. The eagle comes down from the flight and sits upon her talons to continue sleeping. This seems to be quite a lazy eagle. It sleeps while flying and sleeps while sitting.

B. The voice to the feathers is not from the Heads, but from the Body.

    a. (**Author's Analysis**): My opinion is that the body is "the people" of this kingdom or nation.

C. The voice tells the feathers to "be alert and watch" in a consecutive fashion. Not all at once.

D. The heads are preserved for the end times of this Eagle Kingdom. (we shall see the explanation of this in Chapter 12 of 2nd Esdras)

God's Interpretation

    Let us match up God's own Interpretation from Esdras Chapter 12

        (2nd Esdras 12:13-16)

"13 Behold, **the days will come**, that there **shall rise up a kingdom** upon earth, and it shall be **feared above all the kingdoms** that were before it.

14 In the same shall **twelve kings** reign, **one after another**:

15 Wherefof the **second** shall begin to reign, and shall have **more time than any of the twelve**.

16 And this do the twelve wings [feathers] signify, which thou sawest."

Learning Points:

A. There will be a "last-days" kingdom that shall be feared (or respected) above all kingdoms before it. (The "last-days" part shall be demonstrated shortly.)

B. There shall be 12 kings/feathers/Presidents/rulers, that come in order. Not all at once.

C. The **second** feather/king/President will rule twice as long as all the other feathers/Presidents. This, second feather, and some other feathers in the middle, are used in identification of the kingdom itself. So we in the latter-days could see it.

Long and Short Feathers

Continuing with the last days timeline narrative in 2nd Esdras Chap 11:

    (2nd Esdras 11:11-12)

"11 And I numbered her **contrary feathers**, and, behold, there were **eight** of them.

12 And I looked, and, behold, on the **right side** there arose **one feather**, and reigned over all the earth;"

Learning Points:

A. There were 8 total **short** feathers.

B. On the **left** wing of the eagle (Ezra's right) the 1st feather/President rose up and reigned with great influence.

Author's Analysis:

This **right / left** thing had me pondering for 2 weeks. Either the few good feathers are on the Eagle's **left**, which is opposite to God keeping his good sheep on the **right**, and the goats on the **left**. Or, … Ezra is simply looking at the Eagle and recording this vision on **his** right and left.

Either way though, it doesn't matter; just realize that the majority (14) of these initial 20 feathers are all following the 3 sleeping Eagle heads. The only feathers that give the Eagle heads problems, they will **eliminate**. Thus, the few good feathers are all short and attacked by the 3 Eagle Heads… as we shall discover.

For the purpose of the scripture below, we will **assume** that the Eagle's **left** is Ezra's **right** and vice versa.

God's Interpretation

Let us discover what God's Interpretation about these 8 short feathers are from 2nd Esdras Chap 12:

(2nd Esdras 12:19-21)

"19 And whereas thou sawest the **eight small** under feathers sticking to her wings, this is the interpretation:

20 That in him there shall arise **eight kings**, whose **times shall be but small, and their years swift.**

21 And **two** of them shall perish, **the middle time approaching**: **four** shall be kept until their **end begin to approach**: but **two** shall be kept unto **the end.**"

Learning Points:

A. There were 8 total **short** feathers/kings/Presidents that will have short terms of office.

B. Two short feathers of the 8 total will be "used up" during the **middle** of the time of the feathers/Presidents. Meaning, look for 2 short feathers during the middle of all the **Presidents**/rulers.

C. Four more short feathers will be toward the end. Then the last two short feathers are at **The End** of all the feathers/presidents/rulers.

The Extra Long 2nd Feather

(2nd Esdras 11:13-17)

"13 And so it was, that when it reigned, **the end of it came, and the place thereof appeared no more:** so the next following stood up. and reigned, and had **a great time**;

14 And it happened, that when it reigned, the end of it came also, **like as the first**, so that it appeared no more.

15 Then came there **a voice** unto it, and said,

16 Hear thou that hast borne rule over the earth so long: this I say unto thee, **before thou beginnest to appear no more,**

17 **There shall none after thee attain unto thy time, neither unto the half thereof.**"

Learning Points:

A. The first feather/President had an end come and it faded off the scene of history.

    a. (**Author's Analysis**): Just like when the term limits of a President come and they go off the world stage.

B. The second feather/President starts to rule and it rules for a "great" or long time. It rules twice as long as any following feather/President.

C. Notice the "voice" may be from God, or the "voice" may come from the body/people of the Eagle. The text doesn't say. The "voice" tells the 2nd feather that none of the other feathers that come after it shall be even ½ as long as the 2nd feather.

    a. (**Author's Analysis**): Franklin Roosevelt died just months into his 4th term of office. He was elected for 4 terms and died in office in April 1945. Republicans in congress passed the 22nd Amendment to the Constitution limiting Presidents to 2 Terms in 1947; and was ratified by the States in 1951. There has not been any President elected to more than 2 terms after the 22nd Amendment was passed. Thus, "none after thee" has been fulfilled. So, to get our bearings on the Timeline, if the 2nd feather/President is Franklin Roosevelt, we have our year on the Last-Days Timeline set to about 1945. (See https://constitutioncenter.org/interactive-constitution/amendments/amendment-xxii)

The Feathers/Kings/Presidents Continued Their Rule … Consecutively

(2nd Esdras 11:18-19)

"18 Then arose the third, and reigned as the other before, and appeared no more also.

19 So went it with all the residue one after another, as that every one reigned, and then appeared no more."

Learning Points:

A. The third feather/President stands up to rule and does like normal and exits office at the end of their time. Then all the rest of the feathers/Presidents do likewise.
    a. Remember, there are **long** and **short** feathers/Presidents in this initial 14 feather mix. (more on this in Chapter 12 of 2nd Esdras)

(2nd Esdras 11:20-21)

"20 Then I beheld, and, lo, **in process of time** the feathers that followed stood up upon the **right side**, that they might rule also; and some of them ruled, but within a while **they appeared no more**:

21 For some of them were set up, but ruled not."

Learning Points:

A. "In process of time" means "after a while" or "a length of time goes by".
B. All the rest of the feathers/Presidents on the Eagle's **left** (Ezra's **right**) side ruled for a time and then were out of office.
C. Some feathers/Presidents were set up, "but ruled not." I do not know what this part means. If you have information on this part, please contact me and if it makes sense, we'll add it to the book.
    a. (**Author's Analysis**): My hunch is that a feather/President would be elected but would not take office at the Inauguration Day. This is just a hunch, *but* at this point we have not seen this concept happen.

No More Feather's on the Eagle's LEFT Wing

(2nd Esdras 11:22)

"22 After this I looked, and, behold, the **twelve feathers** appeared no more, **nor the two little feathers**:"

Learning Points:

A. Up to this point in Ezra's Eagle Prophecy, we now have 12 **long** feathers/Presidents + 2 **short** feathers/Presidents = 14 Presidents. These

14 feathers/Presidents are on the Eagle's left wing. These are all the feathers up to this point in the history of this Eagle Kingdom.

Remember, we have 20 total feathers/Presidents from the start of this Prophecy. Later (in Chap 12 of 2nd Esdras) we see that the Eagle's **left** Wing holds the 14 bad feathers (12+2).

Author's Analysis:

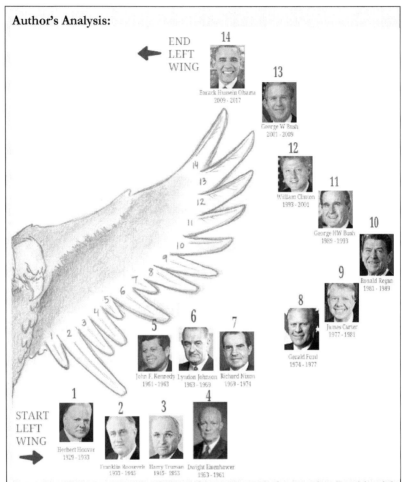

For Ezra or anyone else, to have guessed the precise Presidential sequence of the last 14 Presidents in last-days United States of America, the probability odds would be miniscule. In Rush's work, he calculated the odds at a number with 35 zeros. I don't think it's quite that that bad, but it's certainly small.

The statistics calculation: Taking a possible long feather or a possible short feather is a ½ or 0.5 possibility. Then calculating that over a 14 President sequence.

The probability = 0.5^{14} = .000061

That probability statistic has a near zero chance of occurring in real life.

You can calculate the even smaller probability of that 14 President sequence:

- Happening within an "Eagle" Kingdom.

- Occurring within the last days of the world.
- Being recorded by Ezra as a slave in Babylon 2600 years ago.
- Having the 2nd feather being twice as long as the other normal long feathers.

I see the foreknowledge of God is at work here. Ezra recorded the vision from God. God saw the future of the last-days Eagle Kingdom of the United States of America.

The Great Seal of the United States has been used since 1782. It is an Eagle.	Not only is America's official seal an Eagle, but the Presidential Seal itself is an Eagle, as well.

(See https://en.wikipedia.org/wiki/Great_Seal_of_the_United_States)

These 14 Presidents are the end of the "bad" feathers on the Eagle's **left** (Ezra's **right**) wing. The next section is where America elects a good ruler that will take "rule unto himself" away from the 3 "evil" Eagle Heads. *Then* the whole vision tumbles...into dark problems. Before the ultimate LIGHT breaks forth.

Before we go there … Let us stick to the **timeline of this study** and cover Daniel's 4 Beasts up to the present, about 2017.

NOTE: 1928 was the last time America had a **firm** Republican controlled House, Senate and President. Karl Rove says here that the 1920s and 1930s was the last time "a populist candidate" was in control. (See www.LastDaysTimeline.com/karl-rove)

We know that the beginning of the George W. Bush administration, January 2001 had slight Republican control of the House and Senate. In June of that year one Republican switched parties to become a Democrat and the control was lost. The Calvin Coolidge Whitehouse in 1928 was the last time that *firm* control was had by the Republican Party. The very next year, 1929 is the beginning of the Ezra's Eagle vision with Herbert Hoover as the 1st long feather.

Why Herbert Hoover? To understand this topic, we must understand the modern Prophet Ezra Taft Benson. Ezra Taft Benson served for 8 years as Secretary of Agriculture to President Eisenhower. This is a cabinet level position that is in-line for the Presidency under the chain of succession.

Elder Benson as an Apostle, served for a while in **both posts at the same time**. He had more first hand knowledge than anyone else in church leadership about the inner-workings of government.

In the April 1972 General Conference of the Church, then Apostle Benson gave a talk from the pulpit called *Civic Standards for the Faithful Saints*.

> (Civic Standards for the Faithful Saints, Apr 1972 General Conference, Ezra Taft Benson)
> "... Moroni could have pointed out many factors that led to the destruction of the people, but notice how he singled out the secret combinations, just as the Church today could point out many threats to peace, prosperity, and the spread of God's work, but it has singled out the greatest threat as the godless conspiracy. There is no conspiracy theory in the Book of Mormon —it is a conspiracy fact.
>
> (Space with nothing there in the text dictation of the speech...)
>
> Then Moroni speaks to us in this day and says, "Wherefore, the Lord commandeth you, when ye shall see these things come among you that ye shall awake to a sense of your awful situation, because of this secret combination which shall be among you" (Ether 8:14.)"

Video: https://www.lds.org/general-conference/1972/04/civic-standards-for-the-faithful-saints?lang=eng
Text: https://www.lds.org/ensign/1972/07/civic-standards-for-the-faithful-saints.p9?lang=eng

The text transcript of the conference talk on the Church website leaves out a small "blurb" at the 12min 30sec mark of video, where Elder Benson recommends that the whole church read the book *None Dare Call it Conspiracy* by Gary Allen written in 1972. The book contains:

- A forward essay written by a congressman.
- The Secretary of Agriculture (Elder Benson) wrote a snippet on the back cover.
- A former assistant to FBI Director J. Edgar Hoover wrote a snippet on the back cover.
- A Government Investigator on the Reece Committee wrote a snippet on the back cover.
- A Former Chief of Security for the Atom Bomb Project wrote a snippet on the back cover.

I have read the book *None Dare Call it Conspiracy* based upon the recommendation from Elder Benson and it says the <u>Counsel on Foreign</u>

Relations (C.F.R) was founded in 1921. (See Appendix 1: Secret Combinations)

President Herbert Hoover was elected as US President in November 1929 and was an early member of the C.F.R.

(See – This URL lists President Herbert Hoover (31st President of the United States) on the list of early CFR membership: https://en.wikipedia.org/wiki/Members_of_the_Council_on_Foreign_Rel ations)

This would mean that Hoover was the first US President to start the control of the C.F.R. on the Whitehouse. Over the next 14 Presidents all of them have been C.F.R. members directly, or have loaded their cabinets and staff with CFR members.

(Get the None Dare Call It Conspiracy book here – www.LastDaysTimeline.com/none-dare-call-it-conspiracy)

This means, in my opinion, that the **current** 2017 C.F.R. organizational lead members and their corresponding international groups would represent *a part* of the 3 sleeping Eagle Heads that are about to awake and take an **active role** in governance of the United States of America.

(None Dare Call It Conspiracy – by Gary Allen, page 87)
"Today [1972] the C.F.R. remains active in working toward its final goal of a government over all the world – a government which their INSIDERS and their allies will control. The goal of the C.F.R. is simply to abolish the United States with its Constitutional guarantees of liberty."

This idea of "global government" and "internationalism" becomes very important as the 3 Eagle Heads wake up and take power in the world, as shown in the 2nd half of Ezra's Eagle.

Think of it: November 8, 2016 is the first time since 1928 that the American people have elected and given the Republican Party (usually the more Constitutionally conservative party between the 2 main political parties) the total reins of government: the Presidency, the House, the Senate, the important outstanding Supreme Court nominations, the bulk of the new state governorships, and the local county and city officials as well.

That has *got* to make those 3 sleeping Eagle Heads very upset. They like to stay behind the scenes and pull the strings of the feathers/Presidents. But, they are about to take a more active role and "waking up" after eliminating the next 4 short feathers.

Newt Gingrich said in March 2016, during an interview with Fox News concerning the Republican Leadership …

"And now they're faced with a very real prospect of Donald Trump becoming the leader of the party, and it absolutely drives them crazy." ... "Because he's **an outsider**, he's not them, he's not part of the club. He's uncontrollable. Uh, you know, he hasn't been through the **initiation rites**; he didn't belong to **the secret society**."

Many members of the LDS Church are familiar with the topic of secret combinations since it is taught in the Book of Mormon. Study it for yourself. If you are not familiar or are new to the subject, these are your best resources on the subject. (See Appendix 1: Secret Combinations) (See also Book Reviews in Appendix 3)

1. The Book of Mormon – by God
2. None Dare Call it Conspiracy – by Gary Allen
3. The Naked Communist – by W. Cleon Skousen
4. The Naked Capitalist – by W. Cleon Skousen
5. Strategic Relocation – by Joel Skousen
6. Foundations of Betrayal – by Phil Kent
7. Other People's Money – by Brandeis – Written in 1914. A detailed expose' on the power of the Money Trust. The data in the book comes from **before** the Money Trust was codified into law in December 1913. Available in audiobook for FREE Download at www.LastDaysTimeline.com/other-peoples-money

We have covered the feathers/Presidents right up to current with President Barack Obama. The future is in front of us.

THE FUTURE BEYOND 2017 – STILL WITHIN JOHN'S 6TH SEAL

SECTION 3: America Morphs into The Gentile 4th Beast Kingdom - Grows Rich - Oppresses the Saints with STATE Religion of The Whore Church. (2017 – future)

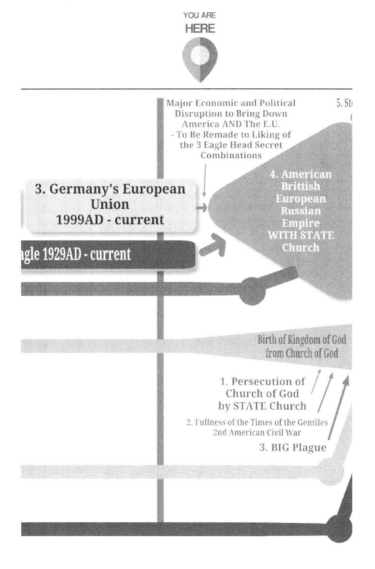

4: America's Last 6 Short Feathers and the "Awakening" of the 3 Eagle Head Secret Combinations

This is in the future to 2017. In this book I will try to paint it in very clear concise terms. I want the truth, and believe that the reader wants the same. We will continue to review all the relevant information that I have found on the subject and give ratings to the information as to its reliability.

Up until now, we have been dealing with the past. Now the heat is turned up a notch and some clarity is coming into view.

Note: that this prophecy of Ezra's Eagle couldn't have been fully known until about this time in history (2017) ….when the last long feather President Barack Hussein Obama ends office.

Onto the 2nd half of Ezra's Eagle (2nd Esdras chapter 11 and 12)

(2nd Esdras 11:23)
"23 And there was **no more** upon the eagle's body, but **three heads that rested**, and **six little wings [feathers].**"

Learning Points:
A. All the feathers/Presidents on the Eagle's **left** (Ezra's **right**) "bad side" have been used up.
    a. (**Author's Analysis**): These would represent 14 Presidents from Herbert Hoover through Barack Obama. All 14 of these Presidents have dismantled our Constitution heavily and have generally not been the people's friend. They have generally been agents or "**front men**" for the 3 conspiring Eagle Heads. Much damage has been done. (See FREE video www.LastDaysTimeline.com/oligarchies-republics-democracies about Oligarchies VS Republics VS Democracies. Oligarchies always put one of their own members out in front.)
B. At this moment in the history of the Eagle Kingdom, only 6 short feathers/Presidents remain plus the 3 Eagle Heads which were to wait until the end-times of the Eagle Kingdom to reign.
    a. (**Author's Analysis**): The six short feathers/Presidents that remain in our future from 2016, going forward, start with Donald John Trump. He is the 1st feather on the Eagle's right wing.
C. The 3 Eagle Heads are still sleeping

(2nd Esdras 11:24)
"24 Then saw I also that **two little feathers divided themselves from the six**, and remained under the head, that was upon the **right side**: for the four (feathers) continued in their place" (on Eagle's Right side).

Learning Points:

A. CRITICAL PART WITH SPECIAL ATTENTION: Ezra saw 2 of the last 6 short feathers on the "good side" (Eagle's **right**=Ezra's **left**) move over to the "bad side".

    a. Later on, we will see in God's interpretation that these last 2 little feathers that moved from the "good side" to the "bad side" will reappear at the end of the whole saga … **after** the 3 bad Eagle Heads take over.

God's Interpretation

Let us match up God's Interpretation from Esdras Chapter 12

        (2nd Esdras 12:29-30)

"29 And whereas thou sawest **two feathers** under the wings **passing over** [to] the head that is on the right side;

30 It signifieth that these are they, **whom the Highest hath kept unto their end**: this is the **small kingdom and full of trouble**, as thou sawest."

Learning Points:

A. These 2 "moving" feathers from Ezra's **left** to Ezra's **right** (vice versa for the Eagle) would be 2 feathers/Presidents that God has kept back for **The End** of the Feathers/Presidents of this Eagle Nation.

B. And when these 2 short feathers rule at the end, the kingdom is **smaller** than it had once been. And it's full of problems and trouble. So, if modern America is the Eagle, then these last 2 feathers/Presidents are presiding over a smaller America. I won't speculate as to how America is smaller at this point in the future.

C. Note: these 2 last short feathers come *after* the 3 Eagle Heads. However, when these last 2 official feathers/Presidents are in office, they serve under the "bad" side and *with* the last remaining Eagle Head.

    When these last 2 feathers/Presidents serve, the whole kingdom is full of trouble and has great problems. The whole Eagle kingdom goes down…and is "restored again" (as shown in later verses).

"They Thought to Set Up Themselves, And to Have the Rule"

Continuing with the Timeline Narrative of 2nd Esdras Chapter 11:

(2nd Esdras 11:25-27)

"25 And I beheld, & lo, the [short] feathers that were under the [Eagle's Right] wing, **thought to set up themselves, and to have the rule.** 26 And I beheld, & lo, there was **one set up, but shortly it appeared no more**.

27 And the **second was sooner away then the first**."

Learning Points MIXED with **Author's Analysis:**

A. **MISSION CRITICAL TO 2017 ALERT:** The defining characteristic of feathers/Presidents under the Eagle's "good" **right** wing is that they "take rule unto themselves." At first I thought that was a bad thing, as it seemed against the Constitution…. However, when the standard rule-of-the-day is what the 3 conspiring Eagle Heads are dictating, then this is a *very good thing*. We haven't had a feather/President stand up from the Eagle's Right Wing **ever** in this Eagle's history since 1929. We haven't had a President elected from a populist movement in America since before 1929. All the previous 14 feathers/Presidents have come from *The Establishment*. The 2600 year old prophecy of Ezra's Eagle is lining up with **real life** right now, in 2016.

   a. This 2600 year old Prophecy by Ezra just said that the 15th feather/President who we **now know** is President Elect Donald J. Trump **would be a "short feather**," and that he would be set up, but *shortly* appear no more. In other words "be taken out".

   b. The last 2 feathers that were "short" in the past were John F. Kennedy and Richard Nixon. They were on the Eagle's **left** side. (We will discover more about these 2 short feathers in God's interpretation of the dream.)

      i. John F. Kennedy – President Kennedy (1961-1963) was elected to 1 term and was cut down while in office by assassins. **So, a short feather may be created by assassination**. There is much controversy as to who, what, and how President John F. Kennedy was murdered. (See Jessie Ventura, former Governor of Minnesota, give evidence on our website www.LastDaysTimeline.com/kennedy). The facts remain that the man who was placed on the Warren Commission to investigate the murder of the President and who *invented* the "Magic Bullet Theory" to explain away that there was only **one** Gunman but *lots of holes*…was none other than Gerald Ford. The man that was *replaced* into the Vice President's chair, just before Richard Nixon resigned. Ford became the first non-elected President in US history… with a Rockefeller as an *appointed* Vice President. (See book "The Making of America" by W. Cleon Skousen on www.LastDaysTimeline.com/making-of-america)

      ii. Richard M. Nixon – President Nixon (1969-1974) was elected to 2 terms and resigned from office over the *Watergate Scandal*. So, a short feather may be created by resigning office.

B. The 2nd short feather from the Eagle's **right** side would then come to power through the authorized Line of Succession only to be "cut down" even quicker. This next eliminated, or short feather/President would be current Vice President Mike Pence.

NOTE: From the observation of the last 2 short feathers Kennedy and Nixon, it is possible that a short feather could get all the way to the 2nd term of office before being "taken out". So, we are looking at a maximum 7 year timeframe of December 2016, to a possible 2023, for Donald J Trump to be a short feather.

However remember, "shortly it appeared no more." I have no deeper information on this subject, until it happens.

You can read the Apocrypha for yourself at

http://www.kingjamesbibleonline.org/2-Esdras-Chapter-11/

Appendix B: The Baptism of Fire and of the Holy Ghost by Simon Driscoll

What is the Baptism of Fire?

This is a personal sacred event where we are filled with the Holy Ghost, literally immersed in it, figuratively immersed in spiritual fire. It is the spiritual heavenly acceptance of our baptismal covenant. After our Baptism of Water, during our confirmation as members of the Church, we are commanded to Receive the Holy Ghost. Basically, we are commanded to seek out the Baptism of Fire. Most of the time it does not happen at that time or even the same day. Usually it takes years before someone is prepared for it, but it does not have to take that long.

> Mosiah 5: 2
>
> And they all cried with one voice, saying: Yea, we believe all the words which thou hast spoken unto us; and also, we know of their surety and truth, because of the Spirit of the Lord Omnipotent, which has wrought a mighty change in us, or in our hearts, that we have no more disposition to do evil, but to do good continually.
>
> Alma 5:14
>
> And now behold, I ask of you, my brethren of the church, have ye spiritually been born of God? Have ye received his image in your countenances? Have ye experienced this mighty change in your hearts?

By this we see that this mighty change is being spiritually born of God, the results of a complete baptism (water and fire).

Didn't I Get That Already?

It is my judgment that there are many members of this Church who have been baptized for the remission of their sins, and who have had hands laid upon their heads for the gift of the Holy Ghost, but who have never received that gift—that is, the manifestations of it.

Why? Because they have never put themselves in order to receive these manifestations. They have never humbled themselves. They have never taken the steps that would prepare them for the companionship of the Holy Ghost. Therefore, they go through life without that knowledge; they are lacking in understanding.

– Joseph Fielding Smith Ensign, June 1972

Far too many members of the Church think that if they do all the ordinances required, they will be saved in the Kingdom of God. Yet they walk through life on borrowed light, trusting in the inspiration and revelation of their leaders, feeling no need to seek for anything greater. The time is quickly coming, if not now upon us, when borrowed light won't get us through the day. Without the Baptism of Fire, without the constant companionship of the Holy Ghost, we are in serious danger of losing what little testimony we have.

We must order our lives, prepare ourselves for inspiration and personal revelation, asking God to carry us to the next step in our spiritual progression. In *The Dark Eagle*, Gideon prepares himself for this step, seeking to be justified and obtains a forgiveness of his sins. He then takes the next step, which is the sanctification of our lives.

What qualifies us for the Baptism of Fire?

Romans 6:23

23 For the wages of sin is death; but the gift of God is eternal life through Jesus Christ our Lord.

We first must make the baptismal covenant, be buried in the water, and receive a forgiveness of our sins. This satisfies the demands of justice for our past misdeeds and we are justified before the judgment bar of God through the atonement of the Savior. Yet this is not enough. We must purge from our hearts any desire to do evil and be filled with a desire to do good continually.

Man, being carnal, can never set aside these desires on his own. That is why we must ask God for the gift of being spiritually reborn.

"You cannot get the gift of the Holy Ghost by praying for it, by paying your tithing, by keeping the Word of Wisdom—not even by being baptized in water for the remission of sins. You must complete that baptism with the baptism of the Spirit. The Prophet said on one occasion that you might as well baptize a bag of sand as not confirm a man and give him the gift of the Holy Ghost, by the laying on of hands. You cannot get it any other way."

– Address by Elder Joseph Fielding Smith before Seminary Teachers

To be more specific, we have to be prepared to have all desire to do evil removed from us. What I mean is, we have to be willing to let go of evil desires and allow our hearts and minds to be filled with the desire to do good continually.

Alma 19:33-34

33 And it came to pass that when Ammon arose he also administered unto them, and also did all the servants of Lamoni; and they did all declare unto the people the selfsame thing—that their hearts had been changed; that they had no more desire to do evil.

34 And behold, many did declare unto the people that they had seen angels and had conversed with them; and thus they had told them things of God, and of his righteousness.

How do we receive it?

The Baptism of Fire, in my experience, comes as an answer to prayer or need. Enos prayed and received the Baptism of Fire. Lamoni and Limhi prayed for it and received it. The Nephites and Lamanites who went to slay Nephi and Lehi witnessed those two prophets surrounded by light, while they were surrounded by darkness, and heard the voice of God. When they wondered what they had to do to get rid of the cloud of darkness, the reply came:

> Helaman 5:41-43
>
> 41 And Aminadab said unto them: You must repent, and cry unto the voice, even until ye shall have faith in Christ, who was taught unto you by Alma, and Amulek, and Zeezrom; and when ye shall do this, the cloud of darkness shall be removed from overshadowing you.
>
> 42 And it came to pass that they all did begin to cry unto the voice of him who had shaken the earth; yea, they did cry even until the cloud of darkness was dispersed.
>
> 43 And it came to pass that when they cast their eyes about, and saw that the cloud of darkness was dispersed from overshadowing them, behold, they saw that they were encircled about, yea every soul, by a pillar of fire.

Look carefully at what they had to do and how quickly the response came. Contrast this with what happened to the same prison when it was destroyed in Alma 14.

As with the example in Helman 5, there are always angels present, though we are often not prepared to see them. God will not give us more revelation or spiritual progression than we can handle. On the other hand, He will give us as much personal revelation and spiritual progress as we are ready to receive.

How Do I Know If I've Had the Baptism of Fire?

The simple answer is to ask God. Mike Stroud teaches that angels always accompany the Baptism of Fire, though you may not see them. If you have prayed for an answer to a question, or for a testimony, and received that answer so strongly that it felt like your entire body was filled with the knowledge of the answer, that is likely a Baptism of Fire event. To be sure, pray to God and ask Him specifically if you have received it, and if the answer is yes, ask Him when. If not, ask Him what you are still lacking in order to receive it.

The other way to know is to look at what comes next in the path of spiritual progress. Nephi gives a great description of this.

> 2 Nephi 31:13
> Wherefore, my beloved brethren, I know that if ye shall follow the Son, with full purpose of heart, acting no hypocrisy and no deception before God, but with real intent, repenting of your sins, witnessing unto the Father that ye are willing to take upon you the name of Christ, by baptism—yea, by following your Lord and your Savior down into the water, according to his word, behold, then shall ye receive the Holy Ghost; yea, then cometh the baptism of fire and of the Holy Ghost; and then can ye speak with the tongue of angels, and shout praises unto the Holy One of Israel.

> 2 Nephi 32:1-3
> 1 And now, behold, my beloved brethren, I suppose that ye ponder somewhat in your hearts concerning that which ye should do after ye have entered in by the way. But, behold, why do ye ponder these things in your hearts?
> 2 Do ye not remember that I said unto you that after ye had received the Holy Ghost ye could speak with the tongue of angels? And now, how could ye speak with the tongue of angels save it were by the Holy Ghost?
> 3 Angels speak by the power of the Holy Ghost; wherefore, they speak the words of Christ. Wherefore, I said unto you, feast upon the words of Christ; for behold, the words of Christ will tell you all things what ye should do.

As we can see from Nephi's words, there is much more to do after we have received the Baptism of Fire. There is further progression to make, more personal revelation to seek and receive. The Baptism of Fire is but the next step after our baptism of water.

Does the Baptism of Fire Only Happen Once?

Like stretching a muscle, it is a new experience the first time it happens. Yet we should experience this over and over, seek it, look for opportunities to be filled with the Holy Ghost until it is an everyday experience. Even then we must work to maintain that.

If all members of the Church were led by the constant companionship of the Holy Ghost, Zion would soon be established among us and God would fight our battles. We could enter into the Rest of the Lord and welcome angels to walk among us. It is my fervent prayer and hope that every baptized Christian who reads this will seek the Baptism of Fire for themselves, not just once, but multiple times, until we are constantly immersed in the Holy Ghost, truly having the Holy Ghost to be our constant companion.

- Simon Driscoll

About the Authors

Simon Driscoll

Simon Driscoll grew up in the shadow of the Rocky Mountains. He is a graduate of Brigham Young University. He has been writing for the last three decades and minored in English in college, focused on creative writing. Writing has always been his first passion. His understanding of the Scriptures and Prophecy comes from a lifelong study of the written word. These two passions are combined in this series.

You can connect with Simon in the following ways:
Email: simon@grendelmen.com
Website: http://www.grendelmen.com/
Twitter: @AuthorSDriscoll
Facebook: https://www.facebook.com/Driscoll.Books/

James T. Prout
Author: The "Last Days" Timeline

James T. Prout is the author the books: ***The "Last Days" Timeline*** and ***Ezra's Eagle***. James is an expert on the specific last-days events and is the founder of www.LastDaysTimeline.com

Find out how you can prepare your family for the next event in the sequence. Prophecy is simply the future, shown to Prophets of God in advance. Why not help your family by knowing the signs-of-the-times before they happen?

James has spent 20 years studying the scriptures, and other authors. He pulls out the nuggets of truth and cuts through the clutter that has been recorded surrounding prophecy of the end-times leading to the 2nd coming of Jesus Christ. Let him help you discover the next domino to fall; so you can prepare your family for the next event in the sequence.

See the Presentation: "What the Scriptures Say about Donald Trump – How Long Will He Last?"

Other Works by Simon Driscoll

The Dragons' Bane Chronicles
(YA Fantasy Adventure)

The Dragons' Bane

Two people with broken hearts enter the Forgotten Forest, a place people go to forget their troubles, and themselves. Each of them has a story of their own, but Zanima, the dragon who rules the forest is looking for a champion to wield a very dangerous sword against her greatest foe. Can these three help each other, before they all lose everything?

Orphan **Dani**

Dani is a young orphan girl, living on the streets of a medium-sized border town. Her only friend in the world is a dragon. At fourteen years of age, she should be starting her apprenticeship, but all her schooling has come from a dragon. The same day he promises she can someday become a dragon herself, a Mage finally comes looking for her. But is he there to help her, or control her?

Traveler Dani

Dani's journey to become a dragon has finally begun, but it means leaving behind the only town she's ever known, just as she was finding a place for herself within the community. Bixby, the Mage who helped her is still looking for her, but he isn't the only one. One year ago, she was an orphan girl with no past. Now she must hide from those who fear her future if she is to complete her quest to find the crystals of Kaldonia and learn their secrets.

Joining her on this journey is a young man named Mervad, who is also hopeful of becoming a dragon himself. But as Dani begins to develop feelings for Mervad, she learns she may have to choose between being with Mervad and becoming a dragon. Will she find the crystals, fall in love, or be caught by those who are hunting her?

Princess Dani

Dani's year long journey to reach the cave is finally over, but her reunion with Miazan, the green dragon, is interrupted by Gwrana, an orange dragon sent by the Dragon King himself. Just when all seems lost, Dani is rescued by Prince Eyroc, to whom she was betrothed at the age of two. Now Dani is trapped in the gilded cage of Bimtor Castle, with the title of princess, and so many secrets to keep. Can she escape the castle and be reunited with Miazan? Or will her new fiancé condemn her as a Thrall?

Dani's Choice

Dani's quest began when she had nothing to live for, and no one to love her. Now she has an entire kingdom looking to her as their future queen, and a young Prince who loves her. She could delay becoming a dragon for several decades and have a human life, as Queen of Nebo, or she could leave the castle, leave Eyroc, and become a dragon now. The choice is hers to make, and it seems an easy decision at first. But when Dani meets her grandparents, their knowledge of her true past and the future they had planned for her comes into full focus.

Apprentice Eyroc - Coming Soon

Eyroc has lost his title as Prince, his home in the castle, and the love of his life in a single day. Now he must embark on a new journey as a Mage's Apprentice.